Us, Now

Us, Now

MOONRISE

ISBN 978-1-7640782-5-2

First published in 2025

Moonrise
Wonnarua and Gubbi Gubbi Country, Australia
www.moonrise.revolutionaries.com.au

Table of Contents

Foreword

Us, Now gathers voices that listen to what most of us miss: the low, persistent feelings that shape days and shape generations. In nearly fifty stories—realism, fantasy, speculative fiction, horror, ecolit and parody—this collection asks you to notice the small, electric seam beneath ordinary life: a hum, a glint, an invisible thread between strangers, the mind of a person pushed to the brink of chaos.

Each piece began with one simple instruction: capture a feeling that hums quietly in the background—something overlooked but ever-present. The results are intimate and startling. Here you'll find an Olympic swimmer faltering before she takes her mark; a love story drawn from chalk on city concrete; a father describing life with ADHD; a young couple separating at a curb side. And many tales of what it means to be human, or to lose our humanity.

Set in the past, present and speculative futures, these stories hold up a mirror to us, now—moments that quietly define us, fascinations that spark wonder and alarm, and mysteries that insist on attention. Turn the page and read closely: the hum is louder than you think.

—R.W. & O.K.

Take Your Marks

Cate Wilkinson

'Take your marks …'

Leaning back into a slingshot pose, Amy Winters gripped the cold, hard surface of the block and focused on her breath rather than the frigid morning air that wrapped around her bare limbs. Golden beams of light pierced the horizon, revealing a new day and with it her destiny. The training pool, long and still, glistened like freshly cleaned glass. Every muscle in Amy's body tensed in preparation. Her dive had to be perfect.

Three, two, one … Beep.

Amy launched fast and strong into the air, stretching out like a seal before her dive shattered the stillness. Thousands of bubbles exploded in her wake. Coming up, she breathed in a lungful of air and began slicing through the water. The 200 freestyle was her favourite race. She loved the monotony of each lap. It was like a rhythmic meditation, with adrenaline her sidekick. As she made her first turn, Amy checked to see where the others were. Stacey was the closest, at least two meters behind. She pushed off the wall and continued her assault, slapping the water's surface with every powerful stroke. Her lungs burned as she focused on the long black line at the bottom of the pool. She finished the second lap, then the third, and surfaced—to a camera pointed directly at her. Shocked, Amy looked around for Adam, her coach. She saw him marching through the flurry of media, onto the pool deck and grimaced at the frustration etched deeply into every line of his weather-beaten face. Since arriving in town for the Olympics, Adam's mood had been unpredictable. She'd beaten her personal best three times in the last five days, but he didn't seem to notice.

'Not good enough, Amy,' Adam barked, trying to shoo a cameraman away. 'The dive was too low, your stroke is off and your *time*!' He dragged a hand through a mess of curls, the way he always did when he was upset or angry. 'You gotta ignore the cameras, kid. Do you think you can do that?'

Still catching her breath, Amy nodded and sagged against the edge of the pool, hoping for a reprieve from Adam's gruelling timetable. Instead, he said,

'We still have half an hour. Tread water for five, then we'll work on your stroke.'

'Yes, Coach.' She forced a smile through clenched teeth and watched as he slowly unwrapped the whistle's lanyard from around his purple fingers, precious oxygen returning to the tips.

'Good! Let's get to work then,' he said and scribbled her latest time on his clipboard.

Later, in a deserted changing room, Amy let out a long, shaky breath. At seventeen, she was the youngest swimmer on the Olympic team. Swimming was her dream; it was all she had ever wanted to do. Now, she sat on her hands trying to stop them from shaking, wondering what on earth she was doing and wishing her mum and dad, or even her baby brother, James, had come with her. Without their support, the pressure to perform was nauseating, especially considering she hadn't anticipated the media's relentless presence; they were like bloodhounds thirsty for their next kill. Every inch of her was going to be dissected this afternoon. She knew this because Stacey had warned her that cameras were also positioned on the bottom of the Olympic pool! A hot flush crept up her neck and burned her cheeks.

Slumped against a locker, Amy closed her eyes and tried to slow her racing heartbeat.

Breathe in slowly, hold for four seconds, exhale for four seconds.

She had just started relaxing when Stacey's voice broke her reverie. 'Hey Amy, come on! We need to be on the pool deck in five minutes.'

Amy reluctantly opened her eyes. Stacey, the team captain, was like a mother: strong, intelligent and always ready with a kind word. She noticed things others missed, like a struggling teammate. Amy wasn't surprised it was Stacey who had come to find her. Adam would surely be holding court in the stadium by now, loving the cameras on him. She lingered a minute more, wondering if she would ever feel as comfortable as Stacey looked on an Olympic stage. To belong there under the gaze of shining lights and cheering fans, it still felt like a dream.

The atmosphere inside the stadium was *electric*. As Amy jogged over to her team, an onslaught of chlorine and sweat mingled with the noise of a thousand voices threatened to overwhelm her. Trembling, she reached the team, stretching her lips into what she hoped was something resembling a smile. It didn't fool Stacey.

'Hey, kiddo, you've got this.' Stacey ignored the crowds and chaos. She gave Amy a quick hug and wished her luck.

'Thanks, Stace, you too!'

As the team gathered, Coach gave his usual pep talk. 'Remember,' he shouted, 'there are results and there are excuses. You can choose one or the other—but you can't have both. So, what's it going to be?'

A chorus of *results* reverberated through Amy's body as shouts, squeals and happy faces blurred in front of her. The ground began to wobble beneath her feet. She bolted back to the changing room, trying to stop the roar of blood rushing around inside her head. In the safety of a cubicle, she pressed herself against a wall, gulping in air as if it were a lifeline. Flashbacks of her childhood looped in her brain. Her mother shouted encouragement, 'Hold the water like you own it, darling, that's the way!' And her dad never showed the financial strain of her goals.

Knock, knock! 'Are you ok in there, Aims?'

'Stacey, I'm not sure I can do this,' she choked. Tears stained her cheeks as she tried to slow her breathing. If she refused to compete, all her hard work, the long hours and her parents' money would have been for nothing. On the other hand, the cool wall inside her cubicle was currently her favourite place in the whole world.

'Hey, open the door. We'll go to the warm-up pool. There are no cameras there, we can get in the water, do a few laps and then see how you feel.'

Stacey led her to the back door of the locker room. They escaped the prying eyes of reporters. They swam slowly, concentrating on their breathing, connecting with the water. *Hold the water like you own it, darling.* The belief in her mother's words offered a soothing balm to her nerves.

After a while, Stacey pulled Amy up. 'How do you feel?'

'Better, thanks. But I'm still not sure if I can compete, Stace. It's crazy in there, and I have no idea what to say, or where to look.' She felt a familiar panic begin to tighten in her chest.

'Ok, before you go full Marlin on me again, I want you to do something. Close your eyes,' she commanded.

Reluctantly, Amy closed her eyes, smirking at the *Finding Nemo* reference. It was Stacey's favourite movie.

'Now,' Stacey instructed. 'I want you to think about *why* you are here. Sounds silly, I know, but try to think of why you decided to pursue your dream of swimming at the Olympics. Was it because of all those ridiculous cameras in your face, or the chaotic crowds? No! You, Amy Winters, followed your love for the water. Swimming is in your *blood*. You have an incredible gift of holding water, and you've worked ridiculously hard and sacrificed a great deal to get this far. When the Olympics are all over, the most important thing you'll remember is how well *you* did. The cameras, the commentary, the crowds, they all fade away. But your performance? The way you behave in the pool and the way you conduct yourself—that's what you'll remember.'

Amy opened her eyes and stared at Stacey.

'And the weight of gold medals around your neck, of course.' Stacey laughed. 'Yes, you are about to erupt onto the world stage, but you're going to do *great* out there, kid.'

'Swimmers, take your positions.'

Amy felt the vibration of the command through every speaker wired around the stadium. Shaking her hands furiously, she stepped up to the block. The stadium was eerily quiet. She stretched her neck from one side to the other, loosening tension before bringing her goggles down to cover her eyes. With a steely determination, she focused on the black line stretching out in front of her.

'Take your marks ...'

Us in Chalk

Calissa Baylow

He materialised with the dawn gilding the sleek buildings; he wasn't there when the drained office workers filtered from these same buildings the previous evening, funnelling into cars or public transport and home for a brief respite from the monotony. But when the commuters began their familiar procession the next day—bustling bodies walking with skin-deep purpose, voices clipped and coffees clutched like vices—there he was; a blip in the routine.

Nestled at the mouth of an alleyway flanked by soulless skyscrapers, his hand danced across his concrete canvas, building upon the scene transforming a previously mundane stretch of pavement. A hat dipped over his face, casting him into obscurity. His shirt bore marks of hardship: dirt scuffs and tears. Everything about his appearance encouraged people to look away, to keep walking, stay on script. But the art that bled from his fingers, the strokes of chalk infusing beauty into banality, demanded admiration—from those present enough to notice.

Sophie noticed.

She was not so empty as to tune the world out completely, unlike those whose down-craned necks and phone-locked gazes had them breezing past a serendipitous marvel. No, the glimpse of coloured ground down the alley gave her pause: blues and yellows, reds and greens, entrancing like a rainbow in a bleak sky. Sophie watched, trying to decipher the scene. A carnival perhaps? Or a seaside fair?

Whatever the chalk artist was creating, figures dotted the scape, all vibrant outfits and animated poses—individually unique, but together a kaleidoscopic sea.

He worked in silence, pausing only to change chalks or blend sections, diffusing the gritty lines. Sophie wished she could smudge the harshness of her own life that easily, make it softer. Kinder. Less lonely.

Gradually, more people stopped, creating a small circle around his creation. Sophie watched from the periphery.

Down the street, Ben frowned at his phone, customary coffee in hand, glossy shoes traversing the familiar route to the office. Anxiety roiled through him, perspiration forming on his temple despite the early-morning chill. *The meeting was in less than four hours.* He tried not to think about it. Tried to not think at all—

Ben walked into something, knocking his phone to the pavement, sending his coffee arcing to the ground. The paper cup split dramatically, over-priced espresso pooling on the pavement. He looked up and his eyes locked with Sophie's, roving over her blonde hair loose around her shoulders. She wore a striking crimson coat, black boots peaking from beneath.

Sophie stared at Ben with wide eyes. 'Ohmygosh, sorry. I shouldn't have been—I should've moved.' Words spilled from her like the drink on the pavement. 'Crap. Your coffee. Your phone—' Her babbling made worse by Ben's intent stare. He had deep brown eyes, chocolate-rich, hair to match. His face was scruffily handsome, like a well-read book or rugged coastline. He cradled a satchel slung across his shoulder as he bent down, picking up his phone. His fingers brushed the screen.

'Is it cracked?' Sophie asked, biting her lip.

'No,' Ben lied, placing the shattered phone in his pocket. He'd worry about it later. He found Sophie's concern endearing. It wasn't even her fault. *He'd* been the one not paying attention. And now his phone was broken and his very-much-needed caffeine wasted at his feet. He didn't even have the energy to be angry with himself. Instead, he stared over Sophie's shoulders, noticing the small crowd behind her. 'What's going on?'

Sophie followed his gaze, momentarily forgetting why she was standing here in the first place. 'Oh, yes. That. It's really cool. Come see.' Sophie stepped further into the alley and Ben moved in beside her; pressing into the small crowd, they watched the chalk artist together.

Time seemed suspended in the alley; while the world hurried around them, the chalk artist drew, unrushed, thoughtful with each movement, entrancing in his craft.

'I'm Sophie, by the way,' Sophie said, shooting Ben a sideways smile.

He returned with one of his own. 'Ben.'

'Sorry again about the—'

'No, don't worry. Wasn't your fault.' Ben paused, then added, 'Been trying to cut down on caffeine anyways. You came just in time.'

Sophie laughed, covering her mouth when the sound echoed through the alley, disturbing the reverent hush of observers. She leaned towards Ben and lowered her voice. 'Glad I could be of service. If you need any beer bottles smashed, or—'

'Excuse me, mister,' a voice squeaked, drawing everyone's attention to a little girl at the front of the crowd.

The chalk artist didn't look up.

Unfazed, the little girl continued, 'Can you add a unicorn? I think it needs a unicorn.' She pointed to an empty space in the corner of his work. 'She can go there.'

The man raised his head, unveiling weather-worn features, crinkled skin and a milky right eye. Discomfort stirred among a few in the crowd, and they drew back.

But the little girl remained, eager and unyielding, until the man's mouth tipped up. Without a word, he selected the white chalk and moved to her selected corner. Slowly, a unicorn took shape, bright white, with a vibrant pink mane and golden horn.

'How about a fighter jet?' another man asked in jest, spurred on by the little girl's confidence.

The chalk artist obliged, even adding a contrail plume.

'Oooh. Draw a rainbow,' —this from a young woman.

Sophie and Ben watched in wonder as the scene became more and more fantastical. Before long, the artwork included a pirate ship with a sea monster, a pianist, a cameo from a famous actor, and someone's pet dog.

'Bit unrealistic, isn't it?' Ben said, face deadpan. 'A pirate would know better than to bring his ship so close to shore.'

Sophie barely managed to stifle her snort and Ben's eyes twinkled with light that had been dulled by days of humdrum routine; he felt revived like the pigments imbuing the pavement.

'Yes, well maybe the *sea monster* chasing them made the captain go "fuck it" and head for shore,' Sophie countered, a twinkle in her own gaze.

Ben chuckled. 'Fair point.'

The chalk artist returned to his original outline, detailing intricate shopfronts, his talent impossible to deny.

'Kind of ruins it,' someone else murmured, breaking the spell. 'All those people's suggestions, takes away the *quality* of it, if you ask me.'

Irritation rose within Sophie. 'Which nobody did,' she muttered.

At this, Ben grinned. 'Right? *If you ask me,* I think it's better like this. Kind of like life. You can sketch it all out, try to stay within the lines, but inevitably someone will come along and add a bloody unicorn.'

Sophie laughed. 'Exactly! Isn't this what art's all about?' She gestured at the chalk drawing. 'Bringing people together? Creating something bigger than ourselves? Like, alone we're just tiny figures, messy and rough if you look too close. But when you see everything together,' she took a step back, 'we make a pretty cool picture.'

Ben marvelled at Sophie, who continued to marvel at the artwork. He spoke before he could stop himself. 'Do you want to go grab coffee?'

Sophie turned to him, staring in shock.

Ben felt mortification rise within him. 'Neverm—'

'Sure.'

Together, they wandered from the alley to a nearby cafe, reciting identical orders to the barista. They savoured their drinks, walking and talking and laughing through the city, everything warm and promising. Their conversation felt effortless. The hours blended like chalk.

When they passed the alley again, Ben ducked down it, exchanging a few words with the chalk artist that Sophie couldn't hear. At one point he gestured to her.

'What did you request?' she asked upon his return, craning to see.

Ben tugged her away and said mysteriously, 'We'll come back when it's done.'

But a few moments later, a very-much-cracked phone rang. Ben answered: 'Hello?' He paled. 'Shit ... Yes, I know ... Ok, ok. I'll be there in five.' His face was positively stricken by the time he hung up. He dropped Sophie's hand. 'I have to go,' was all he managed. *He'd forgotten the meeting.*

As Ben dashed through the city, away from the person who'd made him *feel* for the first time in ages, he realised he'd forgotten something else: Sophie's number.

That evening, it rained. People jostled umbrellas, rushing to escape the downpour, into cars and trains and home for another evening. The alleyway was lit only by a distant streetlight, illuminating the fat drops marring the chalk artist's work. The man himself had vanished, an enigma once more. But the street wasn't deserted. A figure stood, clutching an umbrella, wrapping herself deeper within her red coat. Sophie stared at the ground, at the growing puddles of bleeding colours, pigmented rivulets snaking towards the drain: the dregs of a masterpiece. A tapestry of strangers. An etching of humanity.

She noticed them then: two figures in the corner of the rain-washed picture. She leaned closer. A raindrop slinked down her neck, and she shivered. The taller of the pair had dark hair, the other a red coat. They were holding hands. She smiled. She stepped back, letting the rain wash away the chalk-captured memory. *Perhaps all good things are fleeting.*

But, as Sophie made to leave, a figure ran around the corner.

Ben's steps were filled with bone-deep purpose, clothes saturated, gaze searching. Searching.

Their eyes locked.

Transparent Love

Teneyka Maxwell

T he tyres hummed against the road as Lauren tapped the steering wheel in that sharp, impatient rhythm she always gets before a social outing.

'Do we really have to go?' I asked, staring out the window.

She didn't look at me, just muttered, 'It's Kelly's birthday, Ethan. You can't keep skipping these.'

I don't know why I let her drag me to these things. Parties for people I don't know. Dinners with strangers. I don't fight too hard not to go, but it's not like I enjoy them either. I guess I say yes because it's easier than saying no. There's always that small part of me that hopes maybe this time I'll fit in better, that I'll stop feeling like a background character in my own life. And, if nothing else, I get to people-watch. Which, if I'm honest, is my favourite part.

I don't know Kelly. She seems nice. Very blunt and kind of awkward, but harmless. When we arrived, Lauren introduced me as 'my boyfriend'. I don't get given an identity when I'm introduced to people. I hate that. Not once has she ever just called me Ethan. The word 'boyfriend' sits on her tongue like it doesn't belong. She says it with this flat, uncertain tone, like she's trying to convince herself of something. It's like she's bracing for the pause that always comes after, like she's daring them to question it. I see the confusion flicker across people's faces when they look at me. There's something in their expression, that half-second pause where they're recalculating what 'boyfriend' is supposed to mean. It makes me feel like a fraud, like I'm a girl pretending to be something I'm not, when the truth is I'm just trying to be who I am.

After the awkward introduction, including having to repeat 'happy birthday' to Kelly because she couldn't hear me, we sat down at the end of a crowded table on chairs we had to steal from a neighbouring group. Lauren was rubbing my shaking thigh in an attempt to calm my nerves. It wasn't working, the din of laughter and clinking glasses only made the pressure in my chest worse. She wasn't paying much attention to me, off in her own world, talking to the girl in front of her. The spare chair beside Lauren stayed conspicuously empty, like a throne waiting for its queen. Every time the restaurant door swung open, a few heads turned. Lauren leaned closer to the girl across from her, laughing in that high, bright tone she saves for stories about Josie. Josie. Lauren couldn't shut up about her lately. Josie was always brought up after Lauren finished work, she always talked about how fun she was and how she could make her laugh. She made it sound like the sun shone out of her arse. The hype around this girl made me nervous. So, I did what I came here for. I people-watched.

To my left, there was what looked like a married couple on a rare date night. They were leaned in toward each other, the way people do when they've shared a language for years, words spilling in shorthand and half-smiles. They had a bottle of expensive-looking Sauvignon Blanc between them, one of those ones with the wax on the top. The man was in a tailored navy suit, gold cufflinks gleaming under the low lighting. His tie was bold, a splash of colour against the crisp white shirt, like he needed the world to know he belonged in that suit. The woman beside him was blonde, too blonde for her age. You could see small streaks of grey shining at her roots. But she didn't seem to care. She laughed easily. They looked happy. Comfortable. Like they didn't need to perform for anyone.

To my right, a group of middle-aged friends were definitely several rounds deep. They had that glossy-eyed, red-cheeked look of people who started drinking at noon and just never stopped. Arms were draped lazily around shoulders, and heads were constantly being thrown back in loud bursts of laughter. Their table was a mess. There were bottles scattered, bowls with half-eaten food, and someone's phone playing music too quietly to be heard properly. It looked like a good time, even if it wasn't mine.

Then my eyes drifted to the entrance. That's when I saw her. A pretty girl in a yellow dress. She was captivating. She had a lightness about her, a confidence. Even from where I was sitting, I could see the freckles underneath her eyes and the way her smile brightened when she looked over at our table. She made a beeline to where we were sitting, adding a little skip in her step the closer she got. Lauren got excited and whispered to me, *that's Josie.* I could've guessed, honestly. She was everything Lauren had described and more.

I followed her every step, yet somehow it still startled me when she was suddenly there, her perfume cutting through the restaurant's haze of wine and garlic.

'You must be Ethan,' she said.

And that's all it took. Her voice was like an angel. I felt her eyes pierce into mine and I felt seen. I felt like she was looking straight into my soul and warming me up from the inside with a smile that was as bright as sunshine. All these strangers and the anxiousness I felt melted away.

'I'm Josie, it is so nice to finally meet you!' she added with a wave.

Her voice broke me out of whatever spell she had me under and only then did I realise how long I had been staring at her not saying anything. I wanted to say so much—*hi, you look amazing, I've heard so much about you, please don't notice how nervous I am*—but my mouth wouldn't open, and even if it could, I don't think any words would coherently come out. My throat felt scratchy, and my palms were clammy. I managed to force a small smile and tried to play off how nervous she made me by returning the wave.

Josie was still standing up in front of us and was now invested in a conversation with Kelly about her birthday. I felt like a creep watching her every move. The way she spoke so enthusiastically, her hands moving with every word, drew everyone in. It was captivating. If you looked around, you could see onlookers not-so-subtly staring at her. She was hard to miss. Her laugh was loud and contagious; she had a warmth about her that made me feel at ease. I wanted her attention back on me. I wanted her to look at me again. But I doubt she would want to talk to me after I basically brushed her off. *Why did I do that?*

Lauren's hand rubbing my thigh brought me back to reality. I turned my head to look at her, mad that she stole my attention. Josie's presence was more calming than Lauren had been all night.

She leaned in and said, 'Isn't she great?' Do you see why I love her so much? That's what she's like all the time.'

I didn't doubt it. Josie looked so sure of herself, like she didn't have a worry in the world. She's already introducing herself to Kelly's friends, chatting away like she's known them for years. She has that effortless confidence—the kind that lets her strike up a conversation with strangers and feel instantly familiar with them. I wish I had that. It was empowering to watch.

'She seems cool,' was my lame response.

I turned back to where Josie should have been standing, but she was gone. It was like all the nerves came back and that ease I felt before vanished. The room was dull and filled with strangers again. She hadn't gone far, she was now sitting across the room, deep in conversation with someone who looked like Kelly's sister. Her face still lit up when she laughed, but it wasn't directed at me.

That dull hum in my chest returned. That low, quiet ache I carry around like spare change. I wonder what she saw when she looked at me. *Did she know? Did she see me? The real me?*

I glanced at Lauren, still in conversation. Her hand had slipped off my thigh. Maybe I wasn't supposed to be here. Maybe I'm not really a part of her world. Maybe I never was.

But for a few seconds—a few seconds I'll probably replay in my head a thousand times—Josie looked at me like I belonged.

The Hanoi Hostel

Ethan Tuche

Everyone had shifted onto the sidewalk to avoid the rain. Only moments earlier it was humid and warm. It was there, amongst the pedestrians, I first saw the Japanese man—through the French porte-fenêtres separating us from the clogged Vietnamese street. The long khaki sleeve, the field vest with utility pockets, the white-laced hiking boots. A fisherman, a safari ranger, or the re-animated wax effigy of a sailor from the Dutch East Indies; I had no idea. He looked through the window. In his eyes were the look of someone searching for conversation. It fell onto me. *Crap.* I'll have to haggle myself out of another chat with a street salesman. Do I have the energy to deny this homeless man a tenth of my hourly wage? I remember assuming this—stupidly.

He pushed through the colonial doors into the hostel, joining the expatriates rained out of their tours. When he entered, his eyes drifted over mine and toward the blonde Backpacker beside me. *Phew.* In his hands were a stack of tiny flip-books that could fit in your palm.

'What are you reading?' he asked her in pure, unbridled English.

She closed her book to read the title upside down. '*Where the Crawdads Sing.*'

'Popcorn,' he murmured. 'You?'

I looked up to the old face beneath the receding hair: coarse lines, brown eyes, dry lips. I took his look of disappointment down to the front page of my book.

'*Normal People,*' I murmured.

'Popcorn,' he said again. 'Young people—you read nothing but popcorn.'

He pulled a novel out of his back pocket and plopped it on the table. *The Old Man and the Sea.* I looked for a reality television camera hidden behind the large portrait of Uncle Ho. *Is this bloke serious?*

'This is real book,' he emphasised. 'Real words from a real man.'

The tattered cover of the man wrestling the marlin looked like it had fought for survival inside of a washing machine, or better yet, the belly of the fish the Old Man tried so hard to catch.

'Me,' he insisted while inserting himself in the

seat between us, 'I am a writer. A real writer like Hemingway.'

'Really?' I challenged. *Here we go.*

'Yes,' he determined, showing us the small books in his palm, born black and white from a printer with dwindling ink, stapled crooked and unevenly.

'I'll read you one ...' He pinched the edges and turned.

tiring long journey
not made alone
but along

He smirked. The Japanese man was proud. Proud that his words had meaning and merit, unlike ours, which were mundane and morose, rotting our brains and the core of our being. It paled in comparison to his work, which assuming at the time, must carry the same decorum as *The Iliad* and *The Odyssey*. But I couldn't shake why was he selling palm cards at backpackers and not autographs in bookstores.

He handed me his flip-book.

He leant in. 'It's yours ...'

I was humoured. *A souvenir, for me?* How generous.

'... For one-hundred thousand dong.'

I laughed underneath my breath—and that he caught. The writer who 'writes from the soul' asks for money? A little brochure? How stupid does he think I am?

He collected *The Old Man and the Sea* from the table and put the haiku into his safari pocket. He opened the porte-fenêtres, fled through the sheltering crowd and into the rain; pensive over his hulking pride and lip-service. I remember assuming this—stupidly and well now, arbitrarily.

I was in the reading area after visiting Ho Chi Minh's embalmed body at the mausoleum earlier that day. The similarity between the communist taxidermy and the idealistic writer, even if it wasn't apparent back then, is clear. Their bodies survived despite what they represented now being a generation old. Earth now littered with young people who don't understand them. Me, one of them—in Vietnam, an Australian, talking to another one, Chinese, about an Irish book. We were not nearly as certain about things like they were.

I saw him come up the stairs. *Who the hell let him in here to sell his trinkets?* A keycard the same as my own was dangling from his hand. I had been assuming the Japanese man was sleeping under a bridge. Barefoot, carrying a laptop that purred like a lawnmower, not looking for conversation this time, but something else. His calloused bare feet spread out on the mat in a way that blocked the exit. He found us quietly talking and merged his way into our conversation.

Once again, he asked. 'What you reading?'

I gave him the same answer from earlier, even less frugal. '*Normal People*.'

'Money book,' he moaned, revealing the Haiku's from his back pocket. 'You need to read real words.'

'What makes your words real compared to someone else's?'

I closed Sally Rooney's book and put it between my lap. He could sense it—conflict—but approached it unbothered. He opened his laptop to a website created at the birth of the internet.

'She write in coffee shop. I wrote living with the Mujahideen.'

His yellow fingernails scrolled down through photos. He was the smallest soul amongst several Afghans. He wrote happily at one of the first desktop computers, a checkered shirt, two or three bottles of vodka. He kicked autumn leaves in the taiga forest; titled 'Russia'. Morning tea, or Friluftsliv (the Scandinavian concept of open-air living) with two East Africans titled 'nine o'clock in Stockholm'. Behind a wooden lectern giving a speech, 'Los

Angeles'. A cardboard sign and a goodbye at the airport, 'Singapore'. An entire life, right there, old and lived.

'Here, let me read you another one ...' he said.

songbirds serenade
the poor man who sits alone
on a great rock

A withering empathy passed over me. *You arsehole.* I reached into my bag.

'Here,' I said, fumbling with my wallet. 'Have two-hundred thousand.'

A smile showed small teeth. From his back pocket, he revealed the haiku. 'Your name?'

He addressed the palm-sized book to me.

'Thank you—friend.' He closed his laptop, a soft hand shook mine. He unblocked the entrance and left.

'Thanks for getting rid of him,' a Polish nomad joked from the other end of the reading area. I smiled accommodatingly—stupidly and then arbitrarily, and now, regretfully.

The last time I saw him, he was bargaining a deal for another night. Settling on something reasonable, he tried his credit card and it failed. Frustrated, he pinched the two-hundred thousand dong out of his wallet, the money I had given him the night before, and handed it across to her. He groaned, walked off, looked at me, and didn't recognise me at all.

I found him on Instagram and sent him a message. It remains unopened, months later. He hasn't posted for years. I found his website. The link took me to an Indonesian gambling advertisement, no historic photos or beautiful words, just naked girls around roulette tables. There's a very real chance he could be dead. What would I say to him? Well, if he answered, that I assumed—stupidly and arbitrarily and regretfully and now, sympathetically—that he wasn't what I know now, authentic and true and indubitable. That I wished to spend more time knowing him, hearing him, and understanding him. Money kept him writing for another night, and that wasn't a cliche. He was someone who seemingly experienced places and things that belong in dusty books. He was someone who truly wrote—not performative, not greedy, nor ambitious—at least, from what I saw. He was someone who, undoubtedly, will cease to exist after the last person who knows him forgets him. I hope that amongst the people of the planet he still walks tall through conversations and thoughts and memories, like the old taxidermy,

Uncle Ho. At least printed in this book, he will walk for a little longer.

What would he say if he read this?

'Popcorn,' probably.

Glisters

Brianna McFayden

18th October 1849

I have heard a rumour that immeasurable quantities of gold have been found on the west coast. There are murmurs that men are coming out of the mines richer than they could have dreamed. A few acquaintances of mine have left New Jersey, guided by the hope of these tales. I shall be the next to leave. The thought has not left my head since I first heard of it. So, today over supper, I told Alice.

'Charles, a year! That is far too long. I will miss you dearly. How are Jack and I to get on for that long without you?'

However, I persuaded her. It appears to be a low-risk investment with high reward. I have calculated that I have just enough saved for the boat fare, and provisions to last me the four or five-month-long trip and the two months I will stay in California. The rest of my savings will be enough to leave Alice an allowance that will last them the year I'll be gone. When I get back, she will no longer have to work. I picture us in the nicest part of town, in a beautiful home, Alice's hands doing the soft things she loves. This is what has cemented my decision. I will make the arrangements tomorrow.

5th November 1849

Today I made the short trip from New Jersey to the docks at New York and have boarded the ship that will take me around Cape Horn and then on to San Francisco. It was difficult to leave my family. Jack, only six, cried as I left. I tried to maintain a level of stoicism, but tears welled in my eyes as I hugged him goodbye. Time goes by fast for a child; I may hardly recognise him when I return. Last night, Alice spilled her sorrows to me. Wrapped in each other's arms, I comforted her to sleep. I stroked her hair until her breathing slowed, and I admit I also cried then. Today though, Alice has put on a brave face for our boy. I watched them standing huddled together, waving from the docks as the ship hoisted it anchors and began its voyage.

My first impression of the ship is that it is cramped. The quarters are a small room with bunks, shelves really, stiff wooden planks softened only by a thin layer of straw. I will be sharing these quarters with a dozen or so other men, only inches between us. The bathroom facilities are just a small closet with a bucket we must empty out of a porthole or over the side. The smell wafts through the whole ship, a pungent odor of waste and sweat and fish.

It will be an arduous journey, a test of will, but the wealth which awaits me will prove my reward.

25th December 1849

It is Christmas, though the mood is far from festive aboard. I wonder how Alice and Jack are faring. Jack loves Christmas. Though our celebrations are usually modest, we try to make it special for him. Alice always prepares a beautiful, warm roast. My mouth waters. It has been almost two months without a fulfilling hot meal, without the warm touch of my wife. It was bitterly cold for the first month but has grown much warmer as we passed the equator. Now it is sweltering, and humid, so unlike the temperate climate of the northeast I am accustomed to. I have become, often unwillingly, quite familiar with the other men on board. They often play games of chance to pass the time. I participate on occasion but have little to gamble with. Instead, I while the long hours away reading an anthology of Shakespeare's works. I am already on my second reading. Many of the bard's words bring me comfort, particularly these: *The web of our life is of a mingled yarn, good and ill together.*

12th February 1850

Everyone is restless with anticipation to get off this ship. I feel the ache in my head and in my bones. I crave to see a sight other than the blue ocean, wooden decks and the white fabric of the sails. To taste a hot meal and enjoy even a minute of privacy. The only alleviation from the heavy mood of impatience is the lifting of the oppressive heat as we ascended the western coast. I have finished my third reading of Shakespeare's collection. We are set to arrive in San Francisco within the month. It cannot come soon enough.

8th March 1850

We docked in San Francisco earlier today. You could feel the tension of expectation as we passed through the Golden Gate. San Francisco is a small town hastily set up to accommodate the large influx of opportunity seekers, such as myself. I am staying the night in a hotel for one dollar and thirty-two cents; I even lavishly spent an extra 50 cents for access to the baths. A bath! My first proper wash in four months.

Not a moment to lose, however! I have already sent forth my provisions and I leave in the morning for Stockton via steamboat on the San Joaquin River. Once there, I will pitch my tent in a miner's camp outside of town.

22nd March 1850

It has been two weeks since I arrived at camp. I pictured holes overflowing with gold. I thought by now I would be able to have set back home a rich man. It is not as I imagined. With the pickaxe, shovel and pan I brought, I have been digging in the dirt, chipping away at stone and sifting in the water. Nothing. Not one glimpse of gold yet. On top of that disappointment, it has been pummeling with rain most days and the wind blusters fiercely. Many have fallen ill from these conditions. But I know nothing is given to you; it is hard work and perseverance that pays off.

7th April 1850

> *Dear Charles,*
> *I have some unfortunate news, brother.*
> *Alice and Jack have fallen ill. The doctors say*
> *it is consumption. Both are with a nasty cough.*
> *I have been caring for them as much as I am*
> *able. I beg you to come home early so you are*
> *here for them, and God forbid, if anything*
> *were to happen. I have sent a small amount of*
> *money to help. It's not much but it's all I can*
> *spare. Hurry home.*
>
> *Edward*

I went to the post office in town today and received this letter. It was a shock to see it was from my brother. I had gotten a letter from Alice not long after I arrived here and she had reported that everything was fine. My hands trembled as I read the letter and I have been left numb now that I have processed the news.

Consumption is common. Many know someone who, once they started showing symptoms, rapidly declined. They rarely, if ever, see the end of the illness alive. My head feels like a thunder cloud, heavy and unrelenting.

I have been here a month and still have nothing to show for it. My entire body aches deep into my bones. My hands are tender and scarred by blisters and cuts. I feel little else than despair.

Once I arrived back at the camp I stayed in my tent, unable to do anything other than stare at the envelope in my hands. I am faced with a crossroads. If I take Edward's money to replenish my stores, I might have enough rations to make it home. But when I am back, I will be destitute, with a sick wife and child. I can't help but feel a desperate need to stay, to continue to mine, to have something to show for the time and money sunk into this venture. What if I am only a few strikes away? Then I could afford a decent doctor to treat Alice and Jack. One week. I will stay and work, day in and day out, for one more week.

14th April 1850

I labored harder this week than I have for the last month. Up at dawn, stopping only for two small meals, then to sleep for a few hours before starting again. I have weakened and lost weight; my skin hangs only on bone, my ribs sticking out, creating valleys out of my flesh. And still, nothing. I am a failure. My wife and son need me now. I'll board the next ship home.

12th September 1850

I thought the anticipation of arriving in San Francisco was bad. It was nothing compared to coming home. Five months. I have spent five months aboard this ship, unable to reach my family, filled with dread and dejection. I slept to pass the time but mostly to quiet the roaring thoughts inside my head. We are half a day from docking in New York.

13th September 1850

I made it back home. My brother greeted me solemnly at the door. In that moment I knew.

'I'm so sorry, Charles. They're gone.'
They're gone. They're gone.

All that glisters is not gold—
Often have you heard that told.
Many a man his life hath sold
But my outside to behold.
Gilded tombs do worms enfold.

[Do You Remember?]

David Gillies

You are currently floating in a vacuum one hundred and eighty-six million kilometres from a main-sequence star. The radiation tingles your helium skin-layer, relaxing your breathless breaths and singeing the atoms beneath. For five hundred thousand years of human history, the exposure to vacuum you feel would surely be lethal, yet only in recent millennia humanity embraced their next evolution: gas-based lifeforms styled in the construction of their former flesh and bone bodies. Now, they are utopic worldbuilders and pacifist diplomats: masters of the universe. You wonder what old *homo sapiens* would think of how far they've come [fear?].

A pull reverberates from a nearby system. The intent in the message is obvious in the electrons that carry it: your father calls for his daughter in hexanary patterns that sing your name. You ignore the missive and hold out your arms for the stars' embrace. In less than forty-five seconds, a coronal mass ejection event will launch enough star-stuff that you could fly between to hide your trail from paternal observation.

About fifteen light-years away is a system currently known as 'IGHU-49-819 (Research Candidate #M12A)'. You call it 'Lethe'—a familiar-feeling name, but you can't exactly remember how. It's technically government property beyond your family's claims, and trespassing would probably mean a few hundred years of judicial punishment, but that doesn't worry you. Research candidate systems can't be polluted with security weaves, nor would a backwater system like this demand it. There's a terrestrial planet within Lethe, with carbon-built forests and cerulean seas teeming with microbes. You've only seen it through the telescope, but you feel as though you know all of its contours already. Your parents warn that such thick atmospheres are dangerous to a young woman, that you would be torn asunder and your mind scattered across the system [should you listen to them?].

You snap out of your wake-dreaming [how long has it been since you truly dreamed?]. It's nearly time. The star begins to cough and heave faster; this is your chance. A whip of hydrogen the size of a planet bursts out of its underlayer. It takes a scant few minutes of flight before heat engulfs your skin-layers. You'll lose lighter elements in the crossing, but you just need your metals. You hold them close as the fire reaches your nervous system, igniting what could be your heart and lungs and brain but the momentum is infectious. The plasma assimilates your lower body, and you no longer feel those appendages, but you feel something else; the explosive fusion allows you to breach a hundred times light-speed, and conducting the heat through what's left of your body, you aim yourself—like the universe's most rebellious and pathetic cannon-shell—and pray [to who?].

Despite using a star as an interstellar slingshot and charring over half your weight, you're alive. You feel the presence of the identifying buoy, your mind struggling to make out the individual letters repeated *ad nauseam*. You let out a vacuum-whisper, audible only to yourself [and someone else?].

'Lethe ... An opportunity.' You open your lidless eyes to the vast expanse of a pale blue planet teeming with life below. You try to make out the details on the surface but the world is so dense and varied. Exhausted by victory, you struggle to comprehend the next step. There's a fingernail-sized chunk of zinc around where your throat should be, a reminder you can still feel physical sensations [what are your fingernails made out of?]. You reshape the elements held in your mass and slowly descend to the planet's surface. No longer will others define who you are.

You pierce the outer layers of the atmosphere, where the sky begins to shift to a strange, yet familiar blueish hue [have you seen it before?]. Your body groans in protest as an unfamiliar force strikes your left flank. As you automatically adjust to the subtleties of atmospheric temperature, its warmth threatens to eject the atoms out of your sternum. You harness nitrogen and oxygen and use the meagre weight to continue your descent for a few seconds longer. Without heavier metals, you can't keep this up. Mercifully, the green outlines you spotted from low orbit become clearer and you spot a dense forest with a glade, perfectly sized for the devastation of your landfall. You scrunch your body into a miniscule lump of graphite and try, try to fall gracefully.

You wake in smouldering dirt. There's an animal. It's a bit larger than usual you, with four legs and one head. There's a snout on its face [it looks sort of like a deer?]. It lightly prods the graphite-you, the unfamiliar sensation of physical contact waking you from your stupor [have you never touched anyone, *anything*, before?]. You instinctively dissolve your body back into gasses again and leap out of the crater. A light breeze ruffles the creature's fur and sends shockwaves through your atoms. It looks confused but not scared [is it hurt?]. Terrestrial worlds are rich in metals, and an instinct tells you to make this creature comfortable. You reach a limb to the ground and transmute your outer skin-layer to quartz. It's thin enough to move and tilt your body, yet firm and tactile. It feels right, as if you were always meant to be this shape. You extend an open palm to the animal. It regards you and rests its head on your hand, making a faint gurgle. The quartz is sharp, but the creature softly nuzzles you. Now secured in this physical form, you gaze around. You're surrounded by thousands of thick-trunked trees, tens of metres tall, populated by an uncountable number of creatures. A hundred metres away, you hear the sound of rushing water [can you remember yet?]. You inhale all of the gases in the atmosphere and hold them until you pass out from sheer joy.

[Keep existing if you can hear me.]

[I'm on a date. You're there with me, maybe you're my date. It's a bit romantic, this place. A quiet restaurant where the clocks say quarter-past seven but it's still twilight outside. When I look at you across the table, it's like looking into the face of an unremarkable stranger. The place is nice; fluorescent strips illuminate our cushioned seats and surroundings, but not each other.] There is a human in front of you, old *homo sapiens*, with flesh and blood and capillaries and lungs. You don't look down, but you know you've got them too.

['Finally got you here. Been waiting a while,'] says the human on the other side of the table, but you can't tell their gender, the skin and fabric get in the way. The command to speak, to reply cordially, echoes in you, but when you reach for language ... nothing. ['It's ok. I can still sort of feel you and get what you mean.' The lights flicker, briefly,] and you know there's grass under your feet [but you can't feel it under the concrete. 'So, you've never been here, right?'] In response, you give a blank stare: affirmative. The person across the table, you think it's a woman now, for whatever reason, and whatever that means. [I readjust myself in the chair, looking out the window. There should be cars at the crossroads, but I don't see or hear them. The streetlights are off too.] You wonder how upset Father will be about this, [but he can't see you.] You know that this place is far, far from Lethe. Far from Father.

You and the human are quiet, for a while. ['I wonder about metaphors ... Me and you need to do something, somehow.' I scoff. 'Guess it doesn't matter. Once I wake up it'll be right back to normal: same shitty job, same shitty landlord, same shitty family. I wish ...'] You reject her premise. [Outside on the crossroads,] that four-legged animal is there.

[I rush outside through the open door], and you're there [by my side]. You [both] approach the creature. [I put my hand under its neck and feel the coarse fur on my fingers.] You strain a nascent larynx and hoarsely vocalise:

'You asked me if I remember.'

['It's only a dream,' I respond.] Your flimsy body of flesh struggles to contain the next utterance, the throat collapsing as it leaves you.

'I do remember. Every human can choose their fate.' You tear off an arm, bloodless, and transmute it into a quartz crystal the size of [my thumb,] shaped like the animal. [I take it and hold it close.] Two streams of saltwater flow onto the crystal, smoothing its jagged edges impossibly fast. [I hope I don't lose it.] The next thing you say is garbled in a pool of periodic table sludge but [I understand every semitone of emotion.]

'The choice is always ours.'

The Panic Switched

Bradley Williams

ADHD doesn't wait for context. It doesn't separate the kitchen table from the bed or the desk. It runs through all of them, shaping how people see me no matter what I mean to do. I've been told that if I cared more, I'd remember more, as if caring could hold information in place. I've been told that if I respected authority, I'd follow rules, as if understanding guaranteed recall. I've been told that if I valued my kids, I'd listen without interrupting, as if wanting to could fix how my brain works.

The truth is different.

I care deeply, but the way my brain runs changes how that looks.

The condition scatters thought.

Memory drops under pressure.

Focus goes missing when I need it most.

I look absent as a parent, careless as a partner and

unreliable at work. The details change, but the root cause doesn't.

It isn't three stories. It's one told three ways.

'Dad, guess what happened at school today?'

My son stands in front of me, excited to tell me something that feels big to him. I want to match it. I want to catch every detail. But my mind is still half on the groceries on the bench, the dinner I haven't started and an unread email that came in right before he got home.

He talks about a soccer game. I catch the start: a new boy joined in. Then he goes into what happened during the game and my focus slips. The word 'goal' sticks in my head. Did he score it, or someone else? I chase that thought and lose the next part.

By the time I tune back in, he's moved on. I ask, 'So, did you win?'

He stops. His voice lowers. 'That's not what I was saying.'

He knows I missed it. His face drops. To him, that means I didn't care enough to listen. To me, it's two failures at once: I didn't listen and I didn't show him that I was trying to.

I say, 'Sorry, mate, tell me again.'

He shrugs. The story's over.

I stand there knowing the condition has rewritten the moment. He didn't get to share what mattered to him. What he saw was a distracted dad who couldn't give him what he needed. The truth, that I was trying, doesn't count.

In the evening my partner asks, 'Did you post the card?'

The birthday card is still on the bench. It's been there for days. I bought it, left it where I'd see it and told myself I'd post it first thing. Each day I walked past it thinking I'd get to it. Each day it slipped again.

'No,' I say. 'I meant to.'

She exhales, tired. She holds it up. 'This was important to me. All you had to do was post it.'

I want to explain what happens. How memory drops the second something else comes up. How the card was in my head until I looked away. But saying it doesn't change the fact it's still sitting there.

'You just don't follow through,' she says. 'On anything.'

Her words hit like my son's silence. Both turn forgetting into not caring. The difference between losing track and not giving a damn doesn't show. People only see what doesn't get done.

At work the next day my manager introduces new procedures.

A binder goes on the table. He explains every step. I take notes, underline things and think I've got it.

'Step three is critical,' he says. 'Miss that and the whole thing fails.'

I copy it down. Later, at the computer, the order's gone. I remember bits, not sequence. I rebuild from what's left and fill gaps by instinct. The job gets done but not how it's written.

When my manager checks, he frowns. 'Why didn't you follow the procedure? It's right there.'

I want to say I did, with what I had left in my head. But to him, guessing looks like disobedience. In his view, you either follow rules or you don't. There's no space for half-remembering.

'Look,' he says, 'We need consistency. If you can't follow procedure, you're making it harder for everyone else.'

It lands the same as what my partner said the night before. Different place, same verdict: unreliable.

That night I go home carrying both. My son asks if I'll build Lego with him. I sit down ready to focus, but my mind slips back to the office. I stare too long at the blocks. He notices.

'Never mind,' he says turning away.

Later, my partner asks if I paid the day care fees. I haven't. The email's still unopened.

'Do you even try?' she asks.

It repeats. My son sees distraction. My partner sees carelessness. My manager sees defiance. What I live as exhaustion looks like indifference.

The next week I sit with my son while he does his maths homework. He asks me to check it. I mean to stay focused, but my phone buzzes. I glance down. When I look up, he's watching me.

'You're not even looking,' he says.

'I am,' I answer, but it's hollow. He drops his pencil.

The shame hits like a weight. I want to tell him that I care, that I'm proud he's trying, but what I did already said the opposite. My partner's sigh and my manager's frown replay in my head. Absent father. Careless partner. Problem employee.

Another week, another review. My notes are scattered. Half-finished sentences across pages. I try to follow the order but lose step three again.

'You're not taking this seriously,' my manager says.

It hits hard because it's wrong. I am taking it seriously. I'm pushing myself to keep up. But effort without order looks careless. When the result is wrong, the work behind it doesn't matter.

All these moments connect through what they show others. To my son, I look absent. To my partner, careless. To my manager, defiant. I'm none of that, but that's how it reads.

Perception wins over intention. I want to listen, to care, to keep up. My follow-through breaks and that break turns into judgement. I move through each day waiting for the next slip, when focus drops, memory blanks, or steps fall apart.

It isn't three roles. It's one condition showing up in different places. The parent who misses a story feels guilt that carries into everything else. The partner who forgets a card repeats the pattern at work. The worker who guesses at a missing step becomes the rebel everyone expects.

The panic switch isn't one moment. It's constant. It flips in the kitchen, the lounge, the office and everywhere else I try to hold things together. You can see it in every reflection. In the card on the bench. In the note from my manager. In my son's voice when he says, 'You're not even looking.'

It's written here to show what it's like to live in a brain that won't stay still in a world that needs you to.

The Weredog of Woolly Creek

Jared Domonkos

Common movie myth: Werewolves only transform during a full moon. Movies get a lot wrong. Werewolves are painfully boring once you get to know one. Dad says the blokes in Hollywood need to stick with what people know—no one would buy tickets otherwise. People aren't interested in 'the Weredog of Woolly Creek'. I reckon the only thing the movies nail is the amount of pants and undies they go through. Mum had to nag Dad for ages until he invested in a solid pair of elastic waist trackies.

'Peter. I am not stitching up another pair of your bloody jeans. You want to trek home bare-arse naked. Fine. But you'll be staying outside,' she would lecture him.

Dad's been a werewolf since I've been born. So, at least fourteen years. No one knows how it happened;

Dad's really crap at explaining stuff. When I was twelve, he came into my room and sat down on my bed. He couldn't look at me. Instead, Dad's eyes traced the circular motion of the fan as it spun in its battle against the summer heat.

'Lucy,' he spoke with a seriousness that I wasn't used to. 'Growing up, every autumn at Grandad's farm, we would round-up some rams and ewes and, well, they would breed. Now, people and sheep—they're different, Luce—but the idea is the same. One day—it doesn't have to be in autumn, mind you—you're going to find a boy. Or girl. Me and Mum don't care, as long as you're—'

'Dad,' I had to stop him. My face was burning red hot, 'I know how sex works.'

Without a word, Dad nodded, gave my head a quick pat, and left the room. It was more of the same when I asked how he became a werewolf. One of the stories I got was that Old Ernie from the pub put a curse on him because Dad forgot to help him put up some fence posts. Mum isn't sure how it happened either but knows it would've been before her family came to Woolly Creek.

'He turned on our first date,' she stared out the kitchen window wistfully. 'We were at the swimming hole and stayed out too late because we ...' she trailed off, choosing her words carefully. 'Well, it doesn't matter what we were doing! He saw a swamp rat and was off, just gunned it on all fours!' Mum laughed, 'That was the only time I've ever chased after a man, Lucy.'

Mum only agreed to a second date because he rocked up to hers that morning with the rat dangling lifelessly from his gob. I can't believe she still kisses him after that. Regardless of *how* he became one, Dad's a true-blue werewolf. In a town where sheep outnumber people three-to-one, you'd think he'd have a lot of close calls. Mostly he's been able to keep out of trouble. Mostly.

When they had me, Dad got work as a handyman in town to help pay the bills, which took him away from the paddocks and sheep stations. He didn't mind much for the first couple of years, but his first love was sheep. As he spent more time in town, he began to feel the distance. That sense of separation came to a head when Grandad died. All of a sudden, Dad had to juggle his family, his work as a handyman and manage Grandad's property. That's when Dad grew dark. Forty acres of farmland, all the livestock that came with it and a dusty brick farmhouse right in the middle. I'd find him some nights, hunched over in the shearing shed—gazing back at his old trophies, flicking through Grandad's books on animal rearing—reminiscing on simpler times.

'No dog's too stubborn to train, Luce. Doesn't have to be a prize-winning pooch straight away. You take your time with them, they'll come through for you soon enough,' he'd whisper to me. But the grief hung over him like a cloud of dust that he just couldn't shake off.

'What if I kill them, Suze?' I overheard Dad ask Mum one night. 'I can feel myself slipping. I can't run the farm, look after you two and work in town. It's too much.'

He was worried he'd become violent. So, he sold them all. Some of the older farmers would take the piss out of Dad at the pub, they'd tell him that Grandad would be rolling in his grave if he knew his son owned a sheepless sheep farm. He kept working as a handyman, fixing fences and repairing roofs. But eventually work dried up for him, and so did our farm. No one trusted a sheepless sheep farmer.

He was devasted when the attacks started happening.

A pair of breeding ewes were found disembowelled at the Parker's place, just a few farms down the road. The next night three lambs were slaughtered elsewhere, right in their shed. Folks in town were terrified. Losing a sheep was a bad omen in

Woolly Creek. Dad sunk into himself when he found out. When I would find him in the shed, he'd sit there staring at his trophies and photos, a rusted bike chain tethering him to the shearing platform.

'It's not your fault, Dad,' I spoke gently, poking my head through the tin door.

'Doesn't matter, Luce. It's people's livelihoods I'm ruining. Farmers need their sheep,' Dad turned over a well-loved photo of himself and his old dog, Barney.

'Why don't you come inside? Mum's got the fire going, you can curl up beside it. You don't act up when you do that.'

'It's different this time, love. It's so much harder. I reckon it's all the space here. Too open and too empty.' He looked past me towards the horizon.

'I'll leave the screen door unlocked for you, okay?'

A deep purple haze swirled with the orange light of the sun; a thick layer of dust rested on his hunched shape. Night was coming.

I jerked awake to screaming. A mess of voices crashed through the brick of the house. I jolted up, scrambling to look through my window. Mum was on the verandah brandishing a broom, jabbing it like a spear towards a group of men I'd seen around town. Four large blokes boasting grisly beards that spilled from their faces down to their torn flannel shirts. One had a rifle slung over his shoulder, it looked hot and mean in the morning sun. A big ginger fella was trying to speak over Mum; both of his calloused hands gripped onto a heavy steel pole. For a second, I thought it was a pool skimmer, except there wasn't a net at the end of it. A noose jutted out the end of the stick, wrapping around Dad's neck.

'Fuck off or I'll call the cops!' I yelled, stomping onto the verandah.

Dad was kneeling in front of the men; his head slumped towards the dirt. You'd think he was praying if it weren't for the fragments of his PJs that stuck to his body with sweat and blood.

'Hey Luce,' he tried to muster a smile. I could spot bits of sheep skin still stuck between his teeth. 'How about you go inside, darling?'

I glared at the men, marching towards them, each step kicking up a cloud of red dirt. They just stared and shifted on the spot as I approached, a solemn look on their faces. I grabbed at the animal catcher that the ginger was wielding, getting ready to wrestle him for it. He just gently let it go, passing it over to me. The Ginger looked at Dad and stroked his beard in thought, like Plato in a flannel and jeans.

'You have to leave, Pete,' his voice was soft.

'I'm sorry mate but that's how it is. You'll bleed the town dry.'

I loosened the noose around Dad's neck, and he pulled his head through the loop. As he rose to his feet, he shook himself, loose dirt and scraps of wool fell from his hair.

'I'm sorry, Darcy. I'm usually more in control. These past few months have been rough. I-I never wanted to h-hurt anyone,' Dad's voice quivered as he talked. I clutched his hand.

'I get it, mate, and trust me; no one wants to give you guys the boot. But we don't have a choice if you're gonna go 'round and kill our sheep.' Darcy removed his hat and wiped his brow, a thick line of sweat dampening his sleeve.

Dad looked wrecked. Owning the farm had been his dream, something he looked forward to every waking moment of his life. His childhood home was barren. No sheep, no cattle, no dogs. Just an old farmhouse and a shearing shed full of brighter days. We couldn't stick around, even if Dad wanted to.

I thought that would be that. They'd drag him off and leave us with nothing but the empty house and the ghosts of Dad's old life. But Mum wasn't done.

'We'll train him,' she said, so matter-of-factly that no one even seemed to question the ridiculousness of the idea. 'We'll train him to not attack your sheep and help guard your properties. He just wants to be with the animals, and I'm sick to death with his moping.'

Everyone looked at her for a long, silent moment. When Dad retells the story, he always adds, 'I shit you not—a tumbleweed rolls right past us. Yep, exactly like in the movies, no word of a lie.' That didn't happen, though. Dad's just dramatic.

'Could you do that? Train him?' Darcy asked.

'Darcy,' Mum scoffed. 'Pete probably trained half your family's dogs himself. Never shuts up about it.' The rest of the men nodded in agreement. Dad never shuts up about it.

We all looked at him, not knowing if he'd start to cry, or laugh, or swear. The shed creaked in the breeze as Dad just grinned at us. It felt as if the farm itself was holding its breath. Maybe he'd win. Maybe he'd lose. But for the first time in a long time, he wasn't the Weredog of Woolly Creek, or a wreck. He was just Dad, and for now that was all we needed.

Beady EYE

Charlotte Johnston

I climbed to my observatory, claws aching as they hit wooden beams. My whiskers spasmed and twitched as dust settled around me. I poked my head out from a hole in the wall. The smell of rhubarb called to my empty stomach. My observatory created a window into the human world. Cream wallpapers with vibrant orange and brown circles lined the walls. A devil's ivy hung on the curtain rail; its vines reached into the kitchen sink. Shaggy pink carpet and green geometric tiles covered the floor. An elderly woman hovered near the stove, lifting a pie out of the oven. She smoothed out her red paisley apron and adjusted the lime green glasses perched on her nose. Her brown corduroy coat hung by the door while she baked. Ms Keller lived in apartment 2A. At the table sat another woman, with jet-black hair, a head-to-toe beige outfit and a permanent scowl. On Friday Ms

Keller's daughter, Nancy, a rather sour personality, came for tea.

'Ma, why won't you go? You can barely make it down the stairs, let alone the front door.'

'Nancy, I don't know why you make such a fuss. Old age is nothing I can't handle,' Ms Keller replied with exasperation.

Nancy tutted and shoved a cane at her. Ms Keller swatted it away.

'If you're not willing to start moving to a home, when you need help I won't be here. At least take the cane.'

Here we go again. It pained me to hear the way Nancy spoke but it created the perfect opportunity to sneak into the apartment and collect food. I scurried towards the corner of the kitchen table. Nancy's leg bounced erratically as she pushed her point about nursing homes. I curved around the table leg to avoid being crushed by the unforgiving foot. When I thought I had escaped certain doom my tail brushed against her ankle. In slow motion, Nancy's head turned down. My heart squeaked and stopped momentarily. Her sunken feline like eyes bore into mine. My fur prickled like it was on fire.

After a prolonged pause Nancy shrieked, 'Shoo! Shoo! Get out, you vermin.'

'*SQUEEEAK.*'

Her sandal flew past, tickling my whiskers as I scampered into the wall. I turned back and caught a glimpse of Ms Keller as she sternly waved an oven mitt at her daughter.

It was weeks before I dared to venture back into to Ms Keller's apartment. Her daughter stopped coming around after the fiasco with me. I was careless getting seen. Humans like Nancy scream in terror or run. Not Ms Keller. Occasionally, I'd poke my head out while she baked, carefully staying in the shadows. In those weeks Ms Keller would often talk aloud in my direction as if I were a friend in the room. She would smile, give a sly wink and continue about her day. Until today. The sweet smell of apple pie lured me in. I poked my head out and gathered up the courage to enter her kitchen.

'I see you down there, little one. You're a curious thing ...' Ms Keller leaned over slowly, one hand steadying herself on the counter. Gently, she scooped me into her hand and placed me on the countertop.

'Careful with me please!'

Her other hand reached deep into her coat. She pulled out a few peanuts and piled them next to me. Muttering to herself, she shuffled across to the fridge, struggling to grasp a container of cheese. Slowly, Ms Keller made her way back to me.

'Remarkably intelligent creatures, mice are.' Ms Keller gently scratched my stomach offering up the cheese. 'I see your little eyes poking through the wall, always so curious. I used to work with mice like you. I think I'll call you ... Beady.'

My gaze sunk into hers—warm, bright and motherly. She always seemed so lonely, especially after Richard. The neighbouring apartment, 2D sat empty for most of my time here. Richard used to live there. It smells of decay. The wallpaper is peeling, pipes rusting, the spiders and roaches moved in too. He got sick for some time; I could smell it before he knew. One day a man with a white coat came. People's faces tighten, contort and grimace at white coats. I've seen him visit before. Humans call it cancer. They become inconsolable and bleak. I avoid 2D—the air feels too heavy with grief.

Richard and Ms Keller were close many years before I came along. Her husband passed quite young. She never remarried but found temporary solace in the company of her neighbour. They enjoyed many outings together organised by Richard's local Rotary

Club. She dearly loved both but in her old age, held a deeper fondness for her friend. Sometimes I'd catch Ms Keller sitting by her desk as she clutched old photos of her and Richard.

'I feel it too. Like there's this deep hole in my chest that aches.'

Knock, knock. My ears pricked up as Ms Keller shuffled to the door, bracing herself against the wall. Before I could hide, a tall gangly man in a dated blue suit and white coat strode in. The round glasses on the tip of his nose forced him to peer down haughtily. Wordlessly, he pointed to me and furrowed his brow. Ms Keller reassured him I was a hygienic pet. Ms Keller motioned him to sit and placed a plate of pie on the table. The white coat man remained standing. Cold and distant, he waved a clipboard in front of us.

'It's not looking good. Decreased mobility, increased fracture risk and memory loss, with advanced osteopenia and signs of dementia. Seriously reconsider your ability to continue living here. It's time to move to a home. As for your pet … we will make suitable arrangements to remove it from your care to ensure the best outcome for your health.'

Before Ms Keller could respond he tossed a large stack of glossy pamphlets on the table and solemnly excused himself from the apartment. I rested my nose against her hand and tried to comfort her.

'Oh, Beady what am I to do? I can't leave—my life is here.'

'*I'll stay beside you, Ms Keller.*'

My feeble squeaks could not possibly convey the collision of emotions inside me.

Over the next few months Ms Keller acted more vibrant and nostalgic. Every morning I climbed out of the observatory onto the kitchen bench and waited for Ms Keller to wake. She'd come, holding out her hand and slipped me into her coat pocket. We spent hours together in her office filled with filing cabinets and boxes. Her desk was stacked with yellowed binders and thick scrapbooks. Ms Keller's wedding dress hung on a cupboard door. She often reached her shaking hand out and rubbed the fabric between her fingers.

Curled up beside her, I fell asleep listening to stories of her colleagues in the research lab and funny things Nancy did as a child.

'When Nancy turned four I invited some colleagues over. We'd just published an important paper ...' Ms Keller trailed off and patted the photos before she continued, '... We celebrated that with her birthday. The lab techs were arguing through dinner about a rivalling article. Nancy was so fed up with it by the time dessert came out, she started spooning trifle at them until they left!'

Ms Keller chuckled and looked around the room. Awards for humanitarian aid and medical research littered the top of her shelves. She kept them to remind her of her passions in life and the memories connected to them. Slowly, each day bled into the next. Same photos, memories and stories. The same glazed-over, distant look in her eyes. She hid the difficulty of remembering things and the pain of her weakened mobility.

The new room was cold and clinical. Bland, white walls with beeping monitors cluttered every corner. Strange people in blue ran across the halls. White coats were here too. I curled, hiding myself in the pocket of Ms Keller's favourite coat. She lay sweaty, pale and trembling as Nancy reluctantly patted her hand. Loud, impatient sighs interrupted the haunting silence. Abruptly Ms Keller sat up, turning towards

Nancy. With dazed eyes she pulled at her nightgown, the blanket sliding off her.

'BEADY ... Beady! Where is she? Who ... who are you? Richard?! I want Beady!'

'There's no Beady, Ma.' Nancy glanced concerningly at her.

My eyes stung, tiny warm droplets wetting the corduroy coat. The ache of separation was overwhelming.

'I am here, I am here!'

Broken Pigeon

Susanne Jolie

'**M**i filim mekim dai ...' I said. My Tok-Pidgin spilled out—broken English like bent wings of a perfectly plumed pigeon, still flying but marked with a difference. A pigeon to bear a message. My tongue hummed with words I could not say—a survival tool that braided my first words together. But here, across the pacific waters, it was like cortisol spilling at the wrong time, misfiring.

But I needed to get the words out. Years of silence. The cliffs became my confessor where my words would finally tumble. I couldn't stand the denial and the deceit eroding me hollow, for my newly found spirituality.

I practised, the truth, as the elders called it, and I had no choice in the matter but to speak the truth. As a young adult my pioneering brought conformity. I was compelled to tell someone what happened. My heart was distantly quiet, my mind split and my speech carried guilt. The pinnacle of belonging, symbolised by my forthcoming baptism, ensured a connection I longed for, a connection to a congregation that would fix my broken wing.

'Meri, you look faint … tongue-tied again, are we?' the elder sneered. His robe smelled of mildew, his breath stale with scriptures. His words pressed hard against the secret I carried, the truth I struggled to share. 'Don't want to talk today, Pigeon?' his voice cut like hers. Like Eden's—a mocking undertone calling me, Pigeon, as if to highlight the hierarchy.

The *tongue-tied* he quips is my mother language, Kuanua—a living creature named long before his time, before it was written down, before it sat still on a page. It was a primal language before it was translated to Tok Pisin and converted over time to Pidgin English. My Kuanua language, an ancient ally dialect, traversed the waters with me, a reassuring hum I held in my throat. I told myself they were only words. Elder words. But my body rehearsed mockery as danger, as if claws had already torn flesh. I stared aimlessly into space, when the elder's gnarled fingers press into both my shoulders as if to test how much pressure I could take before he snapped my pigeon wings.

'Why don't you come sit down,' he said, bolstering me down. My body flinched as I braced myself to have my words whipped and reminded I was an outsider. My hands clawed. Like a baboon trembling after a dominant male has passed, my throat hummed with a restless threat. Primatologists have long known of primate stress in our evolution where hormones surge not only in the face of predators, but in anticipation of them.

'Yesa,' I said, my teeth ground as I keep my words buried. Sweat slid down my temple, I refused to wipe it away. I had been wiping away my pain, predicament and predisposition for far too long—I was ready to be honest. Ready to be free of the constant mantra, *why did it happen*, cycling through my brain.

'Hausat yu slubum,' I said—words that in my upbringing mean more than shame; it's a person that sags under an impact of a brutal event that you cannot explain. In my village of Tavui in Papua New Guinea, even with no present threat, stress responses are readily carried in the body, to instinctively act. Primatologists' correlate that the body does not know the difference between a predator's claw and a word that cuts; even where the body rehearses danger long after the threat has gone, it continues as a profound threat.

'Don't worry about that, we will fix your English, so you can be like one of us,' the elder said as if holding a cattle prod against me to ensure I am kept at a distance—to be poked, corrected and othered. The elder insisted I talk to him, but the words trembled on my tongue. A tremble that began long before this time … beginning with Eden.

My memory dragged me back to a time before I could confess. Before I could belong.

***

The ocean waves whispered their secrets through salt sprays. Eden etched our secrets in the sand. At thirteen years old, Eden and I met regularly after school at the corner store before biking to the beach where we spent most of our days.

'I threw a ball in the house yesterday and I broke mum's antique flower vase. I hid it in my brother's closet,' she said.

I coquí, the pigeon's hum acknowledging to keep her secret safe with me, tucked down deep where even the tide could not wash it out. We traded secrets. She said she would blame her brother, and I coqui again, an assuring silence.

'Pigeon, is what I will call you ... cos of that hum sound you make.' This was one of the first things she decided when we first met. An affectionate nickname. So I thought. We shared boy crushes, bartered our clothes, made friendship bracelets and made the world our own.

'Sometimes, I hear dad shouting at mum,' I exchanged. 'She thinks I'm asleep, but I hear the plates rattle and sometimes I hear her cry in the kitchen ...' I said. The rest of what I had to say turned to a murmur, unable to take form.

Eden tilted her head and grinned sharply. 'That's not all, is it Pigeon? You always stop just before the good part.'

I scoffed to fob it off and let the froth of the waves muffle thoughts away. But I knew Eden, she always caught the whiff of something bigger. I couldn't bring myself to speak of my cultural identity and we instead chatted away our thoughts into the sand knowing they would be washed away by the waves.

Eden loved to race me. She would pretend to hurt herself making me stop to care; then immediately start running again and would yell, 'Last one's a rotten egg.' Then, I knew the race was on. She always won. Even at school she was the age champion for running.

One day she found a conch shell eroded into a well-formed arc that stood on its own in a small crescent. 'Us,' she said.

I thought, *are we the curve, we hold our own and we don't topple no matter what's left of us, even when we are eroding away?* She kept it in her pocket like a talisman.

'Mi no blong hia,' I said. I whispered the words that told of exile; saying them made my throat tighten. Tok Pidgin slipping through my lips again and she laughed at my bent English.

'Say it correctly, Pigeon,' she said. 'You will never be like one of us if you cannot speak properly.'

Her taunting undertone clipped my wings at my throat. Even now when my speech is corrected, I hear Eden mocking my mother-tongue.

In our English class, when I could not pronounce a word, the teacher believed I was playing up. She made me stand at the front of the class repeating the word until I pronounced it correctly. The class laughed at each of my attempts.

Eden yelled, 'Because your home is broken, Pigeon, so is your speech.'

The class erupted louder. My cheeks burned with betrayal and my soul sank insidiously. Eden's nickname was not affectionate anymore. It was her weapon. I was her gimmick.

That afternoon, as we walked the high narrow path along the shoreline, I saw glints of jagged rocks that jutted from beneath the smashing waves below.

Eden turned to me and yelled, 'Last one's a rotten egg.' She ran ahead.

Her heckling laugh set off something deep inside me. Her laugh pressed against an unshakeable rancour in my chest. She pressed a primal button, anger fuelled me and I started to run with a new determination. Eden pretended to twist her ankle but I didn't fall for it this time. I thought her drama classes were working well. She stumbled to stand back up and for a moment I couldn't tell if it was play or truth.

Her body leaned over the cliff. Her hand hovered. Her arms pin wheeled around. And the cliff awaited—a heartbeat passed. My hand instinctively reacted before my mind—no thought, only ancient circuits firing. Her feet stumbled further—she lost balance. A baboon's shove, a reptile's snap, a threat to resolve. My hand thrusted at her chest. Her scream was swallowed shallow, by the waves below, before I could tell if the scream left her throat or mine.

Everything stopped and I heard the waves pounding against the cliffs muffling a scream that soon fell silent. My chest rose and I felt I was proudly pounding my chest. A shared ancestry with primates dictates when the body perceives a chance for dominance, the cortex falls silent and the amygdala, archaic and fast, takes command. It's a reflex, not a choice.

***

'Mi save nau,' I said. I know I cannot belong here.

The elder continues to await my message, but it falters—unsaid. Any righteousness has eroded away. Primatologists know the trauma that primes use for the stress-responses in life and how reflexes are sharpened like claws, always ready. The mind having no free will. But a repetition of the brain's rehearsal for danger. Until the danger became me.

The cliff overhangs like a wide-open mouth that heard my voice. The cliff is my confessor. The narrow path kept its silence and my secret carried through the ocean spray's whispers. *It is as it should be*. Grief not a language I am fluent in.

Now. I speak the primal predicament.

Like a carrier bird with a bent wing, I lift away. The message may be broken, but it continues to fly.

Mi save nau—it is my truth.

Code Yellow

Mickayla Gallagher

Eden was tired.

Exhaustion had only begun to set in over the last hour—her pale skin donned eyebags darker than her eyes themselves: grey and hollow. But the last 11 hours were more gruelling than how her shifts usually were. The longer Eden remained on hospital grounds, the more she dreaded going home. At home, she'd be faced with a different ache than the overwhelm of fluorescent lights, hand sanitiser, and various bodily fluids. An ache Eden refused to acknowledge, burying herself deeper into her shift with another hour left on the ward, carting around medications and meals.

Breathe in, breathe out. Let's do this.

'Afternoon, Seline, how are you faring?' Eden's cheery mask clung to her skin as she pushed the cart into the hospital room.

'Plenty good now, miss. I'm just glad it's over.' Seline's hand squeezed the hand of the man beside her—notably, her husband. 'Mike hasn't left my side, not even to eat.'

'I'm taking care of my girls well, miss nurse. Seline and little Flora are my priority now.'

'Glad to hear it.' Eden guided the little table on wheels over to Seline and placed down the meal tray. Seline eagerly lifted the lid, finally able to eat something after a labour longer than Eden's entire shift. Mike sat back, looking down at Flora in the hospital crib, and back at his wife with adoration. The silent peace was heavy. But it broke, a familiar jingle ringing from Mike's pocket. He answered, met with a scream of joy from the receiver. He quickly hung up with a quick nod, getting to his feet.

'Seline, your mother is here with the other critters. I'll go get 'em, you relax with Flora and your food. I'll be back soon, love.' Mike brushed himself off, planting a kiss on Seline's head. 'Take care of my girls, miss nurse. I won't be long.'

Mike left Eden alone with Seline and her newborn. '... Critters?'

'My other young ones, miss. Two boys.' Seline sighed, mouth full of food. 'My maw was takin' care of Jackie and Jasper until we get to go home.'

'I'm sure they'll be excited to see you, Seline. Your mother seemed rather excited on the phone.'

'Oh, she's a riot, my maw.'

'Well, take care of yourself, all right? Remember, the call button is on the wall behind you.' Eden finished taking down Seline's vitals, hanging the clipboard back on the end of the bed. With that, she left, heading back to the nurse's station to locate her next patient.

***

'All right, lovelies, off you go. I'm sorry to have kept you all back for so long, but you're all much appreciated for staying back. I'll see you when I see you!'

Eden nodded in acknowledgement at the head nurse. Her happy-go-lucky attitude had whittled away, eyes burning to stay awake with the scent of burnt toast wafting from the staffroom. A sickness had washed over her as she reached the twentieth hour of her shift, well into overtime, the clock on the wall reading just past four-thirty in the morning.

The drive home felt like a haze. Eden's scrubs clung desperately to her skin. Everything was blurry. In walking to the elevator, the sudden stop at her floor made Eden stumble, body shaking with every step. Her keys pinched at her clammy hands as she went to unlock her door.

Damn keys.

Finally, the door creaked open, Eden slipping past, shutting it quietly behind her. She was home, not that it felt like one. Just a place to survive.

Eden didn't turn on the lights. Just hung up her bag, put her keys and lanyard on the dresser by the door. The nametag in her lanyard looked faded, her own photo staring back at her.

EDEN ASAHINA
NURSE
MATERNITY WARD

Hunger drew her eyes away from herself, realising that she hadn't eaten since midnight. Maybe even earlier, but it was hard to tell. Eden took a breath, swallowing her ache and trudging to the kitchen with intent to search. Something to stave off the physical, but not the mental. Opening the fridge only showed how little Eden had been paying attention to her needs—the fridge only had half a carton of eggs, some leftover fried rice, and a still-corked bottle of red wine gifted to her when Eden first moved in. Eden could barely tell what hurt more—the hunger, or the ache in her eyes from the fridge light.

'Fried rice it is, then ...'

The gentle hum of the microwave filled the apartment, followed shortly by the smell of warm rice. In normal circumstances, to normal people, reheated Chinese takeaway at 5:00am would be put down to strange cravings. Eden was an outlier in the form of exhaustion and loneliness.

Lonely. What a funny feeling.

Sitting on the couch, Eden picked at the rice on her plate.

Momma would have told me to quit picking at my food and only be picky about boys, same way she was with Pops.

Eden slowly worked through the plate of food in silence. Day-old rice didn't taste quite right compared to something brought home from down the street and eaten immediately. Grains stuck to the plate in the same way memories from Eden's shift circled though her mind's eye. Conversing with patients, shouting at interns, burning toast in the break room. Tiredness made her memories hazy. Everything felt hazy. Everything felt like too much, but at the same time, not enough.

Eden was strangely used to the numbness that layered on when home alone. In the early hours of the morning, when not drowning in exhaustion, Eden knew that the real pain was the loneliness currently wasting away at her mental state. It wasn't the first time Eden was left on her own. Day after day, she watched other families come together with new life, and yet she never had what they did. The friends she used to have, what little time they stayed was like a dream, fleeting across the months or years they decided to stick around. In the end, Eden was left standing, thinking about where things went wrong. What she did to deserve the emptiness of life without friends. Without love. It hurt, more than Eden would care to admit. In moments like this, memories resurfaced of times people left Eden in the dark, drowning her in sorrows.

Of times her friends were never really friends.

Of times she'd been stood up, ghosted, lied to.

Of how she'd never felt truly loved without being taken advantage of.

Eden put her plate to the side; stray grains of rice still stuck to the plate left alone on the coffee table. She didn't want to move. She was tired.

Momma would tell me to rest. Momma would want me to take care of myself.

She trudged her way to the bedroom. Her dresser was pressed up against the wall, mirror hanging above it, the mirror's ornate silver frame trapping Eden's reflection inside. She couldn't help looking at herself, even in the darkness. And in that darkness, Eden saw that emptiness she'd been harbouring for so long. A hollow pit of despair behind her eyes, begging for connection she once held.

'I really do look like a mess, don't I, Momma?' Eden picked up a small portrait frame up from the dresser, staring down at the picture inside. Her curly auburn locks matched pieces from the two people standing behind her in the photo—her father, with bright blond curls, and her mother, with long auburn hair reaching well past her ribs. The last time all three of them were together.

Eden wanted that back. She wanted to have people in her life, people who loved her. Someone, anyone who would cherish her company. She wanted to belong to a family again. But that love never came, not for lack of trying. It just never worked out in her favour. Eden sunk to the ground, scrubs tugging at her skin. The photo of her family, what it used to be, stared at her empty eyes that used to be so full of life and hope.

Her tears that followed were nothing short of agonising pain finally spilling.

Eden's body wracked with sobs as everything begin to spill. The last twenty-something hours of work had pushed her to the breaking point. Burning tears trickled down her face, dripping onto the photo in her hands. Between sobs, coughs shook Eden's body. Her hands could only tremble, unable to hold on any longer. Eden wanted to scream, to do something other than fall to her knees and cry uncontrollably after watching families form, when she had nobody to call her own. Nothing else could enter her thoughts, and what was there couldn't leave, her mind possessed with the idea of what she'd been missing, craving for so long.

And she could only hope that one day, she wouldn't feel so alone.

A Hand to Hold

Paige Schmeider

I struggle to fall asleep because I can't accept the idea of the person I am now.

I lie awake in the pitch black, my body pressed into the mattress, the weight of everything I have tried to forget silencing me. My mind scrambles for answers that never come. It's quite funny, tragically so, because I do believe I deserve this. I should be wanting to tear out of my skin for the person I have become. The person I will now forever be. I should feel the wrath of shame like a firestorm. And in a way it does, less like fire and more like acid that eats quietly, persistently from the inside.

The thought of me makes me physically ill, which is crazy because I used to love me so fucking much.

The fan ticks, and ticks, and ticks and I try to concentrate on the annoyance of it, but I simply can't. It wasn't annoying on its own, it was the steady insistence of it—a small metronome that matches the war in my head. It was steady and relentless, amplifying the rhythm of the restless night.

I had always been angry, but never this fractured. I wanted someone else to blame it all on just so I'd feel a little bit better about who I was. Anything to soften the ache. Instead, I turned back and forth beneath the heavy blanket, a private feud played out in twitching motions.

I dreaded sleeping because I knew the morning would come too fast.

Morning always came as a dull, grey promise. I woke up each day, looking into my reflection thinking to myself ... *What a shame ...*

The mirror always glared back, a merciless witness.

Simple tasks felt like impossible demands. The brush hit my head with brute force, detangling the knots from my restless nights. Each stroke tugged at more than just my hair—it yanked at the invisible threads of myself that had frayed long ago. The people I once held so closely, gone. My deep blue eyes had sunken, my hair thinned. My heart felt like a foreign organ. It didn't beat with purpose. Every limb betrayed me.

Whatever it was, it was clear that I had let go of myself.

I moved through the day simply in motion, detached, until I was able to rest my head again. Everyone had moved on with their lives, yet I was still stuck there. How is that? The world kept spinning without me, no one was waiting. Why would I be so naïve to think that anyone would wait. In my mind I had missed the bus and no one had realised. They all left me alone on that platform.

I sat on the bench, alone, longing to hear the blare of another opportunity come pass.

In that moment, that empty stillness, I felt the harshest point of solitude, the kind that gnaws at your bones because it is absolute, unbroken, and unquestionable.

I dreamt of a life that felt was unattainable, completely out of my reach. Somewhere impossibly far, existed the person I once was. Only in memory she shadowed, unreachable by any ordinary effort. She was small, shy, ridiculously sassy, but full of possibility. I longed for her—the girl I used to be. I heard her laughter in the furthest parts of my mind. Her soft smile only emerged from time to time—her cheeks flushed, completely angelic.

The longer I was awake, the stranger the room became. Corners stretch. Shadows crawled along the ceiling in patterns I didn't recognise, folding into themselves. They gathered in clusters like conspirators, whispering in the uncomfortable silence. The air thickened; it hummed in a faint pulse. The fan hiccupped as if mocking my pulse.

The ordinary slowly betrayed me. My mirror, half hidden seemed to twitch with an eagerness to catch my gaze. Every reflection I had ever abandoned waited there, coiled in its surface. Maybe it wasn't the room at all. Maybe it was my own eyes deceiving me as my hurt slowly infected my space.

Her small voice whispered within me, telling me to hush. She spoke to me in lingering sentences, a familiar yet gently faint voice. It was hard to clump together the sentences she cried out. Her words tumble like skipping stones, simple and blunt. The sort of honesty a child has before the world teaches them to lie.

Soft tears floated out of my eyes as her hand grasped around my finger. Such a tiny, untouched hand. The light shone down, deeper than the solidity of the ground. Down to the deepest soils where she lay.

I couldn't move ... though, I didn't mind.

We walked through the green fields together, the lush grass tickled our skin. Our hands interlinked in a strong embrace as I looked down into those glistening sapphire eyes. The surface rippled with memories I had tried to erase—every shimmer was a heartbeat I had ignored.

I frequently trailed off in memory to a time where my biggest worry was if my outfit was good enough. Changing my look five times a day was a must—a sacred ritual of trial and error. Emptying my dresser by flinging the unwanted pieces over my head was a never-ending cycle for my mother. There was something comforting in the chaos.

I wanted to be pushed on the swing once more, just so I could close my eyes and pretend that everything was quiet for a moment. I wanted to feel the breeze against my face and taste the sweet tang of the summer air. I want to learn how to ride a bike for the first time again and know that I would still need training wheels at the age of twenty-two. Unapologetically dancing and singing to Gaga without a care in the world to going mute and having tears ricochet off my face five minutes later out of embarrassment.

She guided me through a dreamscape of my own creation. The sky above stretched endlessly in hues of orange and yellow. Rivers of silver ran through the grass and reflected the soulful energy I had lost. We sat down, the grass brushed our legs.

The small face looked up to me as she held my hands in a warm embrace. I jumped out of my skin as she started screaming and crying at me. Her tears floated up around us, suspended like tiny stars in a slow orbit.

'Your turn,' she said.

I screamed back just as dramatically—we were the same person after all. My throat tore as I let out years of silence.

When we fell quiet, her face softened. Her smile was fragile, but it didn't falter. She reached up and placed her hand against my chest.

'I never left,' she murmured, her voice spilled into my deepest cuts.

'I live inside you. Can you feel me? I ache when you ache. I cry when you cry. Your shame, your anger, your exhaustion ... I feel it all. The hurt ... it stings so deeply. Beneath all of it, my heart continues to beat as you try to bury it.'

Her mouth curved into a forgiving smirk.

'Your kindness hasn't left you.'

'Their cruelty ... you don't need to hold on to it anymore.'

She doesn't state a name, but enough is said. The hint lands. The hurt has a source outside me, something I had been clutching as if it were my own failing.

I closed my eyes and let her words wash over me. They didn't erase the pain of the past, but they softened the sharp edges. The field around us swayed gently, every blade of grass hummed. She pressed her hand to my chest like a band-aid.

'You will wake tomorrow and the mirror will still be there, but your heart will meet your eyes with a new kind of recognition,' she told me, her voice wobbling on the syllables. 'You will carry me within you, softly and firmly. When you glance into your reflection you will see me standing there beside you.' Her voice trembled, squeezing my hand until her small face began to fade. The remanence of my little self-dissolved into the darkness of my room.

Her words lingered.

I try to call her name, but my voice was trapped, muffled by something heavier than sleep. Shadows crept along the edges of my vision, reminding me that I am neither here nor there. Yet, even in this impossible limbo, I felt her.

I laid softly back against my pillow, the night settled over me like a slow exhale. The room no longer felt hostile. My heartbeat slowed. I allowed myself to sink into the quiet without fear, the fear of the person I was. In that stillness, in the soft hum of everything around me, there was a tiny pulse of comfort.

The fan ticked steadily once more and in the quietest notes of the night when the world seemed suspended between breaths, I could almost hear her whisper again.

What's in a Dream?

Matthew Lethem

S ol woke with salt on his tongue and the distant echo of a piano in his ears. The apartment was silent, as always. Yet something remained. A woman's voice humming. Crashing waves echoing in the distance. A flicker in the dark of his mind— something seeping through the cracks.

Sol had dreamed.

Which was impossible.

It had been over five years since Sol chose to have the procedure, and there wasn't supposed to be any more dreaming. Any more feeling. The surgery had rewired his brain, altered his limbic system to remove emotion. Remove pain. Remove feeling. And yet, after waking, Sol could still taste the ocean, he could still hear her.

At first he assumed it was a glitch. Neural static. A misfire. The doctors did warn that occasionally, faint impressions of memories may slip through. The brain was stubborn, unwilling to let go.

That night, when he closed his eyes, it came again. A shoreline. Seagulls flying overhead. A woman laughing as her feet sunk into the wet sand. The sun shining off her hair, tousling in the ocean breeze, while her eyes—

He woke with tears on his cheeks.

That was the part that terrified him the most. Tears. He had not cried since the day he signed his emotions away. Five years ago, when they pulled him from the water, coughing and screaming her name. Five years ago, when grief hollowed him until he thought he could not survive.

The doctors told him it was mercy. Live without the weight. Live without the ache. But now the ache had returned, disguised as dreams. Days blurred into each other. Sol went to work, returned home, laid in bed. He was efficient and logical, exactly what the clinic had promised.

Yet every night, the dreams seeped through with more colour, more sound, more unbearable light.

He tried to ignore them—telling himself that it wasn't real, that it was still somehow just long hidden residue. But the more he told himself this, the more vivid the dreams became.

Every morning, he woke hollowed, shaking. And every night the waves returned, pulling him deeper.

The woman—Alecia was her name. His partner. His anchor. His reason. It had been five years since her name was on his mind. Now that it had surfaced, it was all he could think about.

His dreams thickened. Richer. Louder. Full.

He saw the way her fingers danced across the keys on a piano, she was far from the best, but that never stopped her. Each wrong note was met with a light, bubbly, infectious laugh that would fill the room. In the dream, Sol sat beside her, watching, listening, smiling—only to wake to the emptiness of his apartment.

For a moment, he imagined calling the clinic again—letting them scrub it all clean. The thought lingered like a temptation. Wouldn't it be easier to lose it all again? He shrugged it off, worried what would happen if they poked further into his brain.

More nights came. The dreams lengthened.

Alecia barefoot on the kitchen tiles, stirring a pot with the spoon in one hand while dancing to some tune only she could hear. Alecia in the gallery, staring at a painting far longer than anyone else, explaining to Sol what it meant. Alecia running into the surf, water glittering on her skin, shouting his name, daring him to follow. Each night, the dreams painted her back into existence. Each morning, the loss returned sharper, deeper, more unbearable than the last.

That morning, Sol woke, his hand reaching to the empty side of the bed. Without thinking, he threw his mattress to the ground, heart pounding in a rhythm he wasn't supposed to have. Beneath the frame he saw it—a small, dust-caked wedding box wedged against the wall. He hesitated, fingers trembling, as he pulled the ribbon free. Inside, photographs. Dozens of them. Her smile, his arm around her, the sea behind them. Each image a wound reopening, each face a memory flooding back.

Through tears, he filled the box back up hastily. For a long moment he just sat there, the box resting in his lap, its weight suffocating. He pushed it back under his bed, trying to supress the sorrow in his heart.

He began to dread the nights, but the days offered no mercy either. The dreams clung to him, with fragments of Alecia leaking into his waking hours. A shadow at the edge of a crowded street. A laugh hidden in the shuffle of passing voices. The faint scent of salt and jasmine when the wind turned warm. Reality no longer held clean edges—everywhere, she bled through.

On the way to work, Sol caught himself pausing as he passed a shop. Music spilled from the doorway—tinny, imperfect notes plucked on an upright piano. He should have walked on. He had never lingered before.

But his body stopped.

A girl was inside, no older than twenty, her brow furrowed as she stumbled over chords. She smiled to herself when she got it right, her fingers trying again and again. The sound cut deep into Sol's soul. His throat constricted, a sob rising like something primal. He stepped back, nearly colliding with a passerby, and hurried away before the sound destroyed him.

That night he tossed and turned, unable, or rather unwilling to fall asleep, as he knew what was waiting for him in the darkness. That night, sleep claimed him more gently. He dreamt of Alecia again. She turned, eyes catching his, and for a moment he swore she was looking straight through the dream and into him. Her lips moved, and although no words reached him, he felt them. Not sorrow, not loss— something warmer. The quiet recognition of being seen, being loved. When Sol woke, the ache was there, sharp as ever. But beneath it was a glow, faint but clear at the same time. The dreams were no longer just torment; they carried her back, not only as memory, but as love enduring.

When it passed, silence returned. But something was different.

For the first time since the procedure, Sol wasn't afraid of the ache.

The ache was Alecia.

And then, the shift. He felt his life outside the dreams begin to warp.

The world, once dull, began to breathe. His dreams begun to bring vibrancy back into the real world, giving Sol feelings that he had been trying to live without. His walks to work—no longer melancholy and flat across the bustling cityscape—shifted to reveal more. The pavement gleamed after the rain, sparkling as he marched towards the city. The scent of coffee drifted from a café door and lingered, warm and bitter in the morning air. The buildings he passed no longer felt like sterile boxes of glass, instead offering unique angles and shadows, as if part of a grand, hidden architecture he'd never noticed before. The hum of life in the city—voices, tires against wet bitumen, birds singing in the distance—now moved through him, not past him.

Each detail pierced him. For years, his world had been stripped of colour. Now colour came rushing back, sharp and merciless. For years, life had been precise, clean, whitewashed. Now every corner cut him open. He noticed the curve of couples' hands laced together on the train. The way sunlight warmed his skin through the glass. The rough kindness in a stranger's voice when they held open a door. Small things. Things he had never noticed in years of numbness.

It was disorienting. Beautiful. Terrifying.

That night he found himself back where it all started. The shoreline. Not knowing how he got there, or what he was going to do, Sol kicked off his shoes and walked along the shore, the waves bringing water up to his ankles as his feet carried him along the sand.

He closed his eyes and heard the ocean again. The night she drowned.

The memory cracked open, full force. The rip dragging out, her scream swallowed and muffled by water. His helplessness. The crushing grief that followed. The reason he had begged the clinic to erase it all. He sobbed. Violently. Uncontrollably. Five years of silence spilling out. Tears burned his face as they fell into the ocean at his feet.

But—amidst the sobs—he felt it.

Love.

Not just the pain of losing her, but the truth of what that pain meant. That he had loved her so fiercely that her absence hollowed him. The sorrow was proof of how much she mattered to him.

Salt stung his face, but this time he did not turn away. He let the tears fall, let the ache swell. It was heavy, yes, but the weight was no longer pushing him down, he now saw that it was holding him up. He had tried to cut it out, to live without it. But emotions are not weakness. They are the thread of life itself. We live in them, overlook them, take them for granted—until they are gone.

Grief, as he realised, was not the enemy. It was the companion of love. To deny one was to deny the other.

And now Sol knew: to feel was to live.

To hurt was to remember.

To weep was to love.

Petrichor

Mikayla Whaite

'Last delivery,' I mumbled, eyes trained on the large package snugly secured at the back of the van. I twisted the key in the ignition, sighing as it spluttered to life. The van was the last of its kind; abandoned by the new world. It was a relic and on its last legs. I was snapped out of my reverie by the harsh ringtone of my phone, illuminating the name Maria.

'Jason,' came her voice, 'are we still on for today?' I hadn't sent my usual confirmation text, the volume of deliveries swallowing me whole. We had plans for a late lunch and a walk around the city.

'Yeah,' I confirmed, my shoulders relaxing, 'just on my last delivery now, then I'll come over—hope you're okay with me showering at yours.' My eyes wandered, landing on the street cleaners as they washed away the dirt and debris from the street, a reminder of the curse the city was under.

She laughed, the sound tugging the sides of my lips upwards. 'So like usual then? You're practically living here with how much of your crap is here!' She was right. I spend more time at her place than my own, but in recent weeks it's been dwindling. The smog was getting to me, and I was getting sick and tired of living in the city that never rains. The call ended, my heart feeling lighter than it had previously.

I finished the last delivery quickly, eager to get to her apartment. As I opened the car door, a strange but familiar scent flew by my nose. Something ... forgotten. Something alien, just out of reach. An older man near me paused, his eyes glossing over as he inhaled deeply. Strange. The stench of the city is something you wouldn't want to breathe in like he did.

Blinking once, I turn away from the man's silhouette and approach the apartment, dismissing the lingering scent.

As we walked through the city, I couldn't help but notice a strange murmur rippling through the city folk. Whispers of something forgotten ...

'Jason, are you even listening? Or are you in the clouds?' Maria sounded unimpressed but there was a hint of curiosity in her voice. The old saying making me smile. She always was a little obsessed with the sky, always reading up on the old days and scouring for pictures of our city before it all disappeared.

I nodded and agreed with her, giving a half-apology for my absentmindedness. We walked into a bookstore, a short stop on our leisurely walk. We were met with fervent whispers between the shopkeeper and a customer. She welcomed us in, the customer nodding once before brushing past us, a distracted look on his face.

There it was again, that strange scent. It was stronger than it had been before, a shiver ran down my spine. Maria's nose scrunched, her eyes glazing over a faint glimmer of familiarity.

'Sorry about him,' the shopkeeper smiled, her eyes far away, 'he always gets a bit weird when we talk about conspiracies.'

Maria laughed. 'Which one? The rain, smog, or government?'

'The rain,' she winked, 'he says he saw something weird at the old train station, but I don't believe him.'

'What did he see?' I asked, the talk of rain making me a bit curious.

She sighed. 'Said he saw some vision from the past, said he felt the rain—but it disappeared? Must've been a projection or something.'

I dismissed it, mentally dubbing the customer as a crazy person as we browsed the shop. Maria grabbed a book off the shelf—it featured a little rain cloud on the top, complimented with lush grass. Maria already had this one at home, she held it up with a smile, placing back on the shelf. We rummaged through the shelves some more, then Maria grabbed another off the shelf with an excited smile. Another book about the rain. We left soon after.

Once outside, Maria turned to me.

'Okay,' I caved, not even letting her get a word out, 'let's go check it out.' She cheered, fist pumping, excitedly pulling my arm towards the railway's direction.

The deeper we ventured, the more uneasy I got. This area was dangerous, filled with extremists who blamed the wealthy for the rainless metropolitan. Maria and I caught snippets of hushed conversation— about how the government took the rain away to gain more control.

I could already see the state of disarray it was left in, and I hoped she wasn't going to be disappointed. The scent was getting stronger though, and I thought maybe that customer wasn't a complete quack. Chairs and tables were scattered, graffiti covering the broken café.

As we got closer, the earthy scent got overwhelming, consuming us in a sense of nostalgia.

It was as if we had gotten transported to the past ourselves, the world before us transforming.

The once abandoned and rusted train hummed with life. Steam bellowed from its smokestack as it prepared to depart. I staggered back in shock, my eyes darting around in confusion and alarm. There were people—*maskless*, smiling and walking around the platform. The air was fresh, but the sky was covered with dark clouds. A droplet hit the ground, followed by a relentless downpour.

'What's happening?!' Maria gasped, clutching onto my arm tightly. Just as quickly as it appeared, the phenomenon vanished, train reverting into broken rust, the platform once again trashed. The scent was gone, leaving behind the smell of rot and ruin.

'What the hell was that?' I breathed; my eyes focused on where the train once sat.

Maria looked at me, flabbergasted. 'I don't know! You know as much as I do!'

'It *must* have just been a hallucination, you know! Smog exposure or something!' I argued, running an anxious hand through my hair.

'No way, it was so … real? You saw it too; two people can't share a hallucination.' Her voice was soft, distant. Hopeful. She began leading us out of the station, refusing to look at me as we walked through the slums.

'The rain was right there,' she whispered, 'just like when we were kids. Don't you remember how excited we used to get over the smell of the rain? I still smell it from time to time; just lingering around waiting to be found again.'

'The rain is gone, Maria, and it's not coming back.' I kept my voice soft.

'But we can find it! I mean, look at this! We're one step closer than we've ever been!' She shook my hand off her, turning to face me.

I sighed deeply, anger simmering beneath my exhaustion. I can't keep doing this.

'Maria, it's *gone*! We saw a flicker, a mirage. Nothing more. I can't keep pretending the past is coming back just because you want it to.'

Her lips parted in disbelief, then curled into something sharper. 'You think this is about me wanting it? Jason, *you* smelled it. *You* saw it. Don't stand there and tell me you'd rather choke on this shit than believe there's something more.'

I clenched my fists, the words spilling harsher than I meant: 'Belief doesn't bring the rain! It just makes us desperate, running after shadows until we tear ourselves apart.'

'Maybe desperation is the point. Maybe hope is supposed to hurt. At least it means we're still alive enough to feel it.'

The silence between us was heavy, charged. I wanted to shout again, to crush her certainty before it crushed me but, like a tide rolling in ... I felt it. The coolness on my skin. That scent again. Subtle at first, then insistent, curling through the air.

We weren't the only ones. A man paused mid-step, tilting his head to the clouds. A woman lowered her mask; eyes fluttering shut in joy. All around us, strangers inhaled together, united by something invisible but undeniable.

I looked at Maria. She wasn't smiling.

My throat tightened. 'You know they won't let us have it back.'

Her gaze didn't waver. 'Then we'll make it matter anyway.'

I wanted to argue, to cling to reason, but the scent was everywhere now, wrapping around us, pressing against my lungs, pulling at something I'd thought long dead. People around us moved differently, slower, listening to a hum that had been buried under engines and smog.

I clenched my jaw. 'And if it's nothing? If it's just—'

Maria grabbed my hand, cutting me off. 'Then we still have each other, and we can just move.'

For the first time in years, I let the tension leave my shoulders in a shaky exhale. I didn't know if we'd find rain, or if we were chasing ghosts—but I *knew* I wasn't letting go of her. Not now. Not ever.

We stepped forward together, breathing in the hum that pulsed through the city like a heartbeat. Maybe it would come. Maybe it wouldn't. But we would move through it, together, wide-eyed and stubborn.

Gears to Revolt

Atlas Jecht

Clink.

The pressure hissed as valves retracted, steam flooding the confined space. Tiny mechanisms creaked under the pressure; leather gloves precariously dialling notches and gears. The echoes of approaching footfalls sent a shiver down his spine. His heart pounded. He quickly snuffed out the portable candle previously clenched between his teeth, crouching down to hide among the dispelling steam. The reverberation of laughter growing distant once more. *The coast is clear.*

He lit his self-designed candle, balancing it on a nearby ledge. Its luminance provided enough light to scribble down quick notes of the mechanism's components. He tucked his pencil behind his ear, exchanging it for a small screwdriver hidden away in his pocket.

Click. Ping.

The spring released its tension—the encasing walls opening to reveal a luminescent amber device, within the heart of the contraption.

'Bingo!' he whispered. Reaching in with steady hands, he extracted the curious device. He retrieved a length of twine from his pocket, securing a cloth tightly around the square-shaped hardware. Before fidgeting to securely place it within his bag: a worn leather satchel barely hanging together by some loose thread.

The tip of his boot tapped against the metal slate that had previous covered to inner workings of the mechanism. As he grasped the panel's edge, an outburst of laughter sounded from beyond the carriage's walls. The carriage rocked from side to side when those responsible for the ruckus nudged a differing cart further down the convoy. He stumbled in place, knocking into a nearby wall, losing his grip on the metal plate. Luckily, the obnoxious laughter drowned out the panel's clattering as it struck the carriage floor. He took a deep breath, adrenaline running high. All things considered, tonight was running rather smoothly. He hadn't fumbled a single screw; he'd managed to fit them all back into place, even in the dim, flickering light.

Flickering light?

He glanced down to the floor below him, where a slick trail of oil began to combust into a dancing flame. He cursed, stamping out the flame while searching for the cause. The culprit lay by his feet, the candle cracked on the ground, fallen from its ledge.

'Shit!' he said, trying desperately to douse the growing fire, 'Shit! Shit! Shit!'

'Oi! What's that light?' a voice echoed from outside the carriage. There was no place to hide, not anymore.

Plan B: bolt.

He slammed open the carriage door, jumping down onto the gravel beneath. Pelting down the aisles of rotting trains, he hoped the strained leather strap of his satchel held out. Gruff, authoritative yelling echoed behind him. He scurried over discarded underframes and through broken down sidewalls, hurdling over rusted engines; parts others would describe as scrape.

The silvery glint of the barbed wired fence hit his peripheral vision; a sign that the *graveyard* spotlights had flickered on. A whirling howl echoed throughout the area, reverberating against the metal carcasses in a cacophony of noise. Vaulting over the coupler connecting the locomotives, he altered his direction. He set his sights on a gap residing under clipped barbed wire—an escape to which he was accustomed. The unsteady aisles of gravel changed to the dense, solid tarmac. The spotlight swung in his direction, highlighting him like the lead actor of a play. Using his momentum, coupled with the metal plates he designed into his clothing, he launched into a slide along the ground. Threading the needle, he shot through the gap, disappearing in a sea of sparks, metal screeching like the halting breaks of a train.

His visage disappeared from sight, leaving the burly nightguards of the train yard defeated at the barbed fence.

'Losers,' he snickered, pulling faces at the men as he disappeared into the hazy, dimmed lights of the city.

The night harboured a familiar chill; one often associated with midnight. His eyes scaled across the barren walls of brick that stood beside him, copper piping leading him further into the city. The flickering of an old, forgotten streetlamp ushered him back into the confines of oppression. *Professional practice urges brilliance.* The hollow motto printed on every piece of institutional garbage. It was a crude reminder of unspoken rules. Regulations that curbed the mystique of mechanical creation. The corporations claiming to *'conquer the future'* were nothing but a farce. They had no care for those unable to meet their asinine standards.

With the rising trend in innovations, older businesses born of passion and practice were quickly being phased out. Income dwindled and workers were laid off. Those unable to adapt to the sudden change were left with nothing, leading them to a single option—crime. He scurried down the empty streets, keeping his head low and eyes trained on the footpath. A soft breeze picked up the dust and leaves scattered along the ground. He glanced up at a fluttering sheet of paper that had caught his eye. *They can't envision our future*, painted in bold, striking lettering across the centre. *Join those who care, our visionaries.*

As the poorer citizenry turned to crime for profit, others turned a blind eye to the innocent people caught in the crossfire. Many approaches had been tried. Protests—peaceful or violent, some even going as far as begging. But nothing seemed to stick, and their voices were swallowed by the resonating echoes of machinery. That was until *they* appeared.

He picked up the piece of paper from the ground, pinning it back onto the wall. He stepped back to admire it, before continuing on. No one really knew when, nor where, the group formed, but they certainly made a name for themselves. It had happened a few months after the outer city's last horologist was forced shut his doors. The story was written in every major newspaper, headlines spanning the skies on blimps.

A revolutionary group titling themselves *The Visionaries* had destroyed and stolen equipment from a mass production facility near the institute. Tensions were brewing, and it was only a matter of time before something boiled over.

Coming to a halt, he turned down a particular alley, ensuring no one was around. He popped up the lid of a sewer entrance, before slipping down the hole. Descending the ladder was never a pleasant experience; the slimy texture on the cold metal made his stomach churn. His boots hit the slick ground with a *splash*. He grimaced, wading through the sludgy puddles before scrambling onto the concrete platform designed for sewer observation.

The sewers were dark, dingy, and reeked of stale oil and pollution. Which made them excellent for hiding experimental and only potentially deadly ... untested machinery. He followed the luminescent markers painted along the walls, an ingenious combination of bioluminescent algae and chemicals. Only certain people could decipher the meanings of the colours. Artificial light shone through the darkness from a fissure.

He quietly slipped through the gap, entering the rowdy room. Only about eight people occupied the space, but they were loud enough that one might mistake them for an army. The mossy walls reached the ceiling, sculpted to form a dome high above the fissure. The metal that made up the floor creaked as he walked over it, a mixed match of bolted and welded panels. His eyes scanned over the large machine within the centre of the room. Hastily sewn sheets draped over exposed circuits. It was a mechanical marvel—a creation that would alter the course of history.

'Now look at this twerp. Made it back in one piece from the graveyard as if it's some walk in the park,' an orotund voice announced. He paused, glancing over at the Herculean looking man with unruly blond hair. His obnoxious laughter echoed through the confined space. 'Come now, out with it. Did you get it?'

'Lay off him! Jeez.' A svelte, ashy haired women stepped out from behind one of the tables occupying the room. She meandered over to his side, arms crossed over her chest. 'You heard the siren. Rylan was chased, so let's cut him some slack!' She glanced at him, smiling kindly. He shrugged off his satchel bag, gently placing it on the ground before kneeling down beside it. The two watched curiously, eyes narrowing on the inside of the bag. He retrieved the luminescent amber device wrapped tightly in the cloth. The room ran silent, eyes widening as he unwrapped the twine.

'Forget the converter.' His eyes gleamed. 'With this—we've got everything.' The room was rendered stunned; all eyes trained on the tiny device laid in his palm. The blond-haired man and young woman broke first, cheering loudly. The room erupted in cheers and applause.

They ushered him over to the machine, murmurs running through the group. Notches and bolts unlocked as he configured the mechanism. With a burst of steam, a small pedestal revealed itself from within the machine. He carefully slipped the amber device onto the pedestal, watching as power flooded into the machine. Glowing strips of illuminated energy surging to life.

'With this, our plan is expedited.' He stepped back, dusting his hands. 'Our curiosity will not be curbed; enthusiasm is our power.' He gestured to the creation before them, eyes alight. 'We, the Visionaries will rise. Revolution is *now*.'

Paragon of Hope

F.R. Pine

My Anthropology professor looked back at me from the front seat of his car, his expression unreadable as I awoke in the back of his truck. My head ached along with the rest of my body. Before I could ask, my professor spoke.

'You found something in that cave,' he didn't ask. I was about to apologise but he held up his hand. 'Tell me what happened first.'

I remember it was just meant to be a small gathering of people outside a local cave system known for its cave paintings. My professor had set it up. I was there for the protest, sure, but I was more excited about the paintings. What we all didn't realise was this wasn't just a for-show protest. The professor had chosen the day that the oil exploration corporation, SteelHart was set to flatten the landscape for some new development. This became apparent when we were confronted by the sight of our 68-year-old professor chained to a rock at the mouth of the cave.

'Come along, students, there's extra chains for everyone. Quickly now, they'll be here soon,' the professor announced. Too cheerful for a man who is considered a sane and academic character. Whilst everyone else was busy choosing the perfect rock to be chained to, I was able to sneak off to explore the cave.

I know I know, that's not very 'teamwork' of me, but have you ever been inside a cave with ancient human paintings?

It's the most beautifully confronting sight that you'll ever come across. Thousands of years old and humans never change. We still crave to create something that will last forever. Of all the paintings within the cave, it was the handprints that called to me the most. So vividly and painfully human, tying a tether from their distant past to our current world. In this space, it was easy to forget the reason I was even here. Well, the reason I was supposed to be here.

From what the professor had said, SteelHart was able to claim the cultural significance and historical wonderment of the site redundant. It had made me sick just thinking about it. Wishing I could do more than tying myself to a rock. I wished I could send them a message of warning, strike real, actual fear and consequences upon them. But I was just some anthropology student.

I continued walking deeper into the cave, watching the paintings in awe as the light from the torch cascaded across the decorated walls. It made the pictures look like they were moving across the stone. They were so clear, too. Little stick-figure humans successfully hunting animals now long extinct, vivid symbols that looked to be ancient maps showing the way to water and fish. They all lived on in this time capsule.

I could hear voices and chanting coming from the mouth of the cave now. People from SteelHart had shown up. I knew I should've gone back to my group and helped protest with them but honestly the paintings had me entranced.

There was another story now along the cave walls, it followed a twisted and winding cave path. What caught my eye were these haunting outlines seemingly tormenting the humans. It started off as one figure but quickly grew and multiplied until the wall was covered with them. They depleted the food stock and damaged water supplies. More and more human figures were laying down, dead. I swear I could feel the complete absence of hope as these evil creatures leached the humans dry. My breath hitched coming around the next bend. Upon the wall was a simple depiction of an amphora, its body decorated with the faces of the evil creatures. Surrounding it were countless handprints. I could feel them holding the jar shut, keeping all the evil concealed. I sighed and wished again for that kind of power, to rid the world of all the greed and selfishness that corrupts our very being.

A scream echoed through the cave snapping me out of my trance with the paintings.

Shit. My body started moving towards the scream before I could really think, but as luck would have it, my shoelaces had different ideas.

Peeling myself off the cave floor, I notice my dropped torch just a few metres away. The beam was shining directly onto something quite out of place among the stone and clay. It was a dull colour, a faded reddish brown, with inky black paintings covering the surface.

I remembered thinking there was no fucking way, as my neck snapped between the wall painting and the amphora.

'Ok ... don't panic, Perri, it's probably not what it looks like,' I whispered to myself, crawling closer.

Oh, how wrong I was.

I carefully picked up the artefact. It looked ancient, nothing like the fakes the professor had shown us in class. This was legit.

Curiosity got the better of me and I opened it.

Now we're going to pause here and recognise this was a *very stupid thing to do.* If you just so happen to be wandering around a cave filled to the brim with ancient paintings actively depicting the defeat and entrapment of evil entities within an amphora that you then happen to stumble upon ...

Take. It. Seriously. This is a weird world, alright? Literally *anything* could happen.

The first thing I noticed was the smell. Never a good sign.

It smelt bad, stale air mixed with a sharp decaying scent along with a dash of rotten eggs. Before I could recover from that, however, I was blinded by an all-encompassing darkness. My torch light disappeared. I could barely see my hands. I could feel sweat dripping down my shivering back as the temperature warped. I think I let out a scream. Or something else did. My ears were assaulted with the loudest roaring noise I'd ever heard. It nearly sounded like cackling. Just when I thought I was going to die, a blinding white light filtered through the darkness. All my worries melted away as I was filled to the brim with this resounding sense of comfort and happiness. It radiated out from my chest and hummed through my body. Unlike the dark, rotting, ear-splitting mass that came before, this felt like seeing the dawn after hours of dark fog despairing the mind and soul.

Finally, the light, noise and smell dissipated. All that was left was a dull ache in my chest and an open, empty amphora.

I would've sat there with that amphora for the rest of time, but I became aware of shouting coming from the cave entrance.

I jumped up, taking the amphora with me, and was able to dash towards the entrance without pancaking on the ground. Reaching the entrance, I'm confronted by a panicked scene.

My professor, pulling on his restraints.

Six SteelHart workers standing together.

A fellow student on her back, blood surrounding her shoulder.

And all the other students spread around trying to help.

My chest ached and I collapsed behind some rocks, pressing my hand to my heart where the pain was worst.

From this point on it gets a little hazy, but from what my friends and the professor told me afterwards it went a little something like this:

I jumped out from behind my rock and dashed straight at the group of Steelhart men, jumping too high into the air and slamming one of them in the face with my fist. Before any of them could react, I slammed another with an uppercut to the jaw. The other four men started to square up and one threw a punch. I dodged, grabbing his arm and pulling him down. His head connected with my knee, hard. I turned to the machines that were parked nearby. A bulldozer, bright yellow, was tipping over as I lifted it up. Anger and strength and that feeling of the light coursing through me.

I *definitely* got to send my message.

The three men left standing raced off in their ute.

Finally, I remember waking up in the back of my professor's car.

We were at uni. I finally looked up and I saw my professor smile.

'Well, I think you may have created a Pandora's Box situation.'

'What do you mean?' I asked.

'In opening that jar, you were given these great powers to send a message to SteelHart, but in doing so, you unleashed whatever else was trapped in there.'

'How can you be sure?' I demanded.

'Look at your chest, lad,' he smiled.

Looking down, I noticed my shirt was torn and my skin was exposed. Upon my typically blank chest was a handprint. A cave painting handprint.

'I've gotta round up those evils then? Seal them back away?'

My professor nodded neutrally.

'Like a paragon of hope, you alone can rid the world of its evils.'

Huh, I thought. *Paragon of Hope*. I liked that.

Echoes in the Belt

Connor English

They called her Kestrel because she was little, constantly hungry and vicious when caught.

She wasn't a battleship or a spectacle; she was simply a working tramp of the Belt. Two cargo drums rotated on a thin spine and their revolution gave out a measly tenth of a g, a weak gravitational acceleration at best. A squat fusion torch in the back might handle maybe two millimetres per second squared if the crew begged and the bearings stayed in good shape. Enough to make plans and keep her flying, as long as you didn't mind sleeping with your feet pointing towards the reactor and your prayers directed at the radiator fins.

The ship was always moving around within. The spin drum's bearings shrieked every few hours, making a high-pitched noise that got into your teeth. Circulation fans made a steady humming sound, sometimes calming and sometimes driving Ari crazy. It was a background beat that Ari had learned to count without even trying. The scrubbers made the air taste a little like metal, like ozone combined with the stale bitterness of coffee grounds that had been stuck in filters for too long. In the corners, moisture collected and beaded up like perspiration. The access wells smelled vaguely of old oil. Kestrel lived like a beast, inhaling, sighing and exhaling. Ari would have been more scared of the quiet than any of these problems.

At first, Ceres was only a dot on the scope. Then it became a crown of sodium lights shining against the rock's dusty skin. Forty-two thousand miles and getting closer, at a constant pace of thirty-eight metres per second. Around the port, the traffic lanes were full with tugs pulling ore cans, refinery sacks that were either too big or too little and hydroponics scows that were seeping the strong smell of celery into the air. Startup rigs clung to Ceres like barnacles, their scaffolds lighted up by faint LEDs. Each one was a desperate bet. Ari zoomed in and saw the screen fill with dots. Each dot was a ship and each ship had a narrative. There was always someone out here lugging, hustling, or concealing.

'Slot's tight,' Ari said quietly with his boot hooked under the console bar. 'We're being pushed by a Navy truck.'

'Of course we are,' Cam responded. The Kestrel's captain floated easily on her sofa, picking a coffee bulb out of the air. There were tattoos on her wrist that looked like a chain of crushed grapes. The ink faded under the light that had been used before. She drank like she was swallowing someone else's patience. 'Charge them for the wait if they want us to be idle.'

Kito's voice emerged from the access well, although it was muffled by metal. 'Station won't charge the Navy. They'll charge us for having the nerve to talk.' His legs were protruding out of a cowling and his boots rested on a rung. His copper hair sprouted in all directions. Old manufacturing stencils still marred his ankles, reminders of the task he had done.

Cam's gaze remained on her computer. 'Then we don't talk. We work hard.'

Ari made the scan bigger. The screen was filled with junk: ore cans with broken nets trailing after them, refinery sacks that were half-empty and twisted, and satellites that were tied together with salvage wires. There were slow-moving scows and half-legal boats made from the bones of previous ships. Beyond where the Belt opened there was a clean vacuum that lasted forever.

Traffic Control interrupted the stillness with a clipped, exhausted voice. 'Kestrel-31, confirm ready for vectoring in nine hours. Heavy coming in. Keep the plume to a minimum. Corridor three.'

Cam pushed the button on the mike. 'Traffic, Kestrel-31. Got it. Minimal plume, corridor three.'

She turned off the channel and rolled the bulb in her palm. 'Minimal plume means we coast and shiver.'

Kito's chuckle was loud. 'We shiver anyway. Bearing C makes a noise above point one g. I'll keep her quiet.'

Cam nodded. 'Do that.' Her voice suddenly became softer. 'We lost Bei Bei. They let us go after Deimos.'

Ari frowned. 'We were late by—'

'Four hours and twenty-nine minutes,' Cam stated in a monotone voice. 'Why didn't it matter? Their insurance said we were unreliable. Spot cargo only, for now.'

The Kestrel moaned in response and the vibration went up Ari's boots and into his bones. They pressed down with their heels and listened. Ari could read the ship better than most faces. She was telling them she wasn't happy.

'What's the work, then?' Ari asked.

Cam said, 'Private pickup. Yard Three. Drop at Themis. Cash.'

Kito slipped out of the cowling and wiped grease off his coveralls. 'Money means trouble.'

'Cash means we eat,' Cam fired back.

Ari opened the plans for Yard Three. The yard was a messy bowtie of trusses that were fastened to Ceres's crust. There were kiosks there that sold fake drugs and seals that had been found and cleaned up. Nothing was certified or clean. Three black mourning flags floated on a string outside one lock. They were triangles sewn from poor funeral fabric and warned of what vacuum wanted from the unfortunate.

Ari said, 'Cash jobs are small jobs. There's room for small.'

Kito stated, 'The drum is still off balance. She leans if we spin too quickly. If it gets worse, we'll have to sleep on our sides.'

Cam smiled, but he was tired and crooked. 'We'll ballast with whatever we find.'

Ari became tense. That smirk scared them more than any noise the bearings made. Cam only grinned like that when she was preparing for something bad to happen.

She clipped back into her chair. 'Plan a kiss burn. Low plume. Save propellant.'

Ari punched in the numbers: 28 minutes at 0.7 mm/s^2, with a three-degree tilt to the right. Kestrel mumbled that she would do as she was told, as she usually did.

Then a fresh ping went over the board. No Traffic. Narrow beam, hidden by a relay.

'That for us?' Cam asked.

Ari looked. 'Only Nav.'

'Open it.'

Plain text moved across the screen: Pickup changed. Bay 12 of Greenmarket. Lock for service. No proof. Pay when you go. A series of keys blossomed and then turned into checksum dust.

Kito whistled softly. 'Greenmarket's not a bay. It's a carnival for fleas.'

Ari responded, 'Black and grey. Don't ask questions when you dock or too many when you leave.'

Cam let the coffee cup hit the console. It broke into shaking balls. She broke one and drank the pieces. 'We're not smugglers. We're delivery people.'

Kito said, 'The difference is who shoots at you.'

Ari looked for a footer. Nothing. But the keys were too clean. The gates would open for them right away.

Ari replied, 'Traffic will see us swing wide.'

Cam said, 'Traffic sees what it pays to see.' She became tougher. 'On paper, there is a ceasefire. What about in real life? Every bill is a fight. And everyone is hungry.'

She unlatched her boots for a bit and let herself float. Ari watched her float and the captain was lost in their thin-walled world. It made the ship seem like it was about to break, like a shell barely holding up against the gloom.

'Plot us in,' Cam said eventually. 'Corridor three. Very little plume. Next, we'll act like visitors in Greenmarket.'

Kito replied, 'Tourists don't use service locks.'

Cam said, 'Then we'll be ugly tourists. Belters love tourists who are ugly. They provide good tips.'

Ari smiled even though they didn't want to and transmitted the burn to the engine room. The lights blinked green, green, and one amber that wouldn't go out. Kito used a wrench and whispered a prayer to bring it to life.

The Kestrel sighed as she leant into the dark. Eight hours to match. Nine to the yard. There is always time to think twice, but never enough time to alter what has already been written.

Ari couldn't get the feeling that the ship was listening too after the fire.

Laughing God

Christopher Gaghan

T he yellowish-brown parchment contents didn't contain a lot. Just the date, a name, age, and last known location. 7 June 337 of the glass age, Tracy Tomson age 24-year-old woman, who was last seen leaving Audrey's Cafe in Copper Cross Street. A testimony from Audrey Higgens—the owner of the cafe and good friend of Tracy—revealed to investigators that Tracy invited her to the Arc Cathedral in Ironwall Street for mass that afternoon but refused the invitation due to prior plans with family. Since then, she'd been missing with little else to go on.

The middle-aged man laid the parchment down on the myriads of missing persons reports on his desk, each of which described similar inexplicable disappearances. Detective Abraham Theus leant into his high-back chair for a while, trying to gather his thoughts.

He had closed his eyes; this investigation had been gruelling, unrelenting and completely exhausting. Every lead led to dead ends. But with a sigh Abraham cast his weary eyes back to Tracy's file, her photo staring back at him. She had long blonde hair, emerald green eyes with thin eyebrows and had a pale complexion; she was a peerless beauty.

From her file he could glean she was married to Noland Tomson, who went missing six weeks ago. Noland's file was one of many on his desk, his disappearance also seemed sudden and unexplainable. Simply disappearing on his way home from his factory. From that incident she had been going to the Cathedral from her usual once a week, to four to five time a week.

Unlike the other files on his desk, only the Tomsons shared a connection, everyone else had diverse backgrounds, social and economic statues. The only abnormal behaviour was Tracy's increased visits to the Arc Cathedral, but that could have been explained as a coping mechanism from her husband's disappearances.

The Cathedral?

As the thought appeared in Abraham's mind he instinctually looked back at the documents.

There haven't been any follow ups.

Abraham eyes narrowed at Tracy's documents as he stood up from his desk. He retrieved his coat and top hat before leaving his office and hopping into a public carriage to Ironwall Street.

The public carriage didn't have many passengers today; it would normally be completely full, with hardly any room to stand at this hour of the morning.

Abraham slinked into the back of the carriage, revelling in the silence and taking the rare opportunity to sort his spiralling thoughts. From the file there hadn't been a formal investigation into the cathedral itself. They didn't even know if she made it to the cathedral that day.

This detail left Abraham disturbed, due to the implications of the matter. The police's lack of investigation on this aspect was due to either negligence or corruption.

Arriving in Ironwall Street, Abraham paid the fare before heading to Arc Cathedral.

The cathedral stood tall compared to any other building in the city, practically suffocating those nearby from its sheer magnitude, as it seemed to be made of brass. With a breath of trepidation, Abraham headed inside.

The melodies from the church organ were the first thing Abaraham heard once he entered.

A sermon? This question was quickly answered by the rows of pews filled with believers. A young man stood at the front, wearing robes that denoted him as the pontiff. He had short, blond hair with crystal blue eyes that, even from the doorway, almost shined. He had soft facial features, giving an androgynous appearance. He was the ideal appearance for a saint. His soft voice carried a warmth and eloquence that compiled an audience to listen.

Abaraham lowed his head before slinking to an empty seat near the back. He took off his top hat, then clasped his hands together in a prayer so to not stand out.

The pontiff spoke of the divine tenets of the Saviour. The god that saved this city from the black smog that consumed the world over a thousand years ago.

His words brought many to tears as they were enraptured by every word he uttered. His performance was flawless, as if he had done this hundreds of thousands of times.

From his praying posture Abraham snuck glances around him, with nothing in particular he was looking for.

His eyes scanned the pews, the walls, the doors and the other deacons and nuns. Compared to what was to be expected there wasn't as many deacons and nuns present for a cathedral of this size, with only one deacon and two nuns present.

The deacon was a portly man with a high greyish hair line, most likely due to stress. One of the nuns was an older woman with grey hair and sharp features that elevated her stern disposition. And lastly, a younger woman with a pale complexion, long blonde hair tied up and covered in her head dress. With her emerald green eyes and thin eyebrows, she gave off an ethereal beauty.

'...!' Abraham's eyes widened for a split second before extricating his gaze.

Tracy ...?

She matched the photo perfectly. But before Abraham could look back up, he had the instinctual feeling that he was being watched. He had to resist the urge to look up. Abraham lampooned himself inwardly for his carelessness. He was positive neither of the nuns were the observer—that left the deacon or the pontiff.

This feeling faded after some time, however Abraham continued to 'pray' to the Saviour. He couldn't afford to let his guard down. He would have to wait until the sermon finished before he could do anything.

After an hour of listening, the sermon wrapped up and the believers began to file out of the cathedral.

Abraham stood with the crowd, putting on his top hat while scanning the room. He saw the young nun enter a back room near the stage of the cathedral. Abraham wasn't sure on the best course of action in this situation. Protocol would dictate for a formal investigation that would directly communicate with the pontiff to get their assistance in the investigation into Tracy's disappearance. But the missing details in her file are setting off alarms in the back of his mind.

The Tracy look-alike raised more questions that need to be answered. After a moment of contemplation, he decided his next move. He couldn't trust the church due to its influence in the city, which most likely deterred any investigation—that would explain the absence of the vital information.

The detective lowered his head as he moved with the crowd, before splitting off from them near the doorway. With his experience as a detective he made it to the back door without garnering any attention, as the deacon and the elderly nun watched over the leaving crowd from the side.

The ivory door Tracy entered was left unlocked, as the door gave no resistance as he went through. It was a five-by-five-metre room, the walls and floor appeared to be made from the same brass-like bricks. The room would have been empty if it wasn't for the young nun staring at him against the far wall.

Immediately, Abraham's stomach sank. On instinct he turned to run but before he was able to do so, he felt a familiar dread, as his body turned around his eyes met with a young man's. The owner of them stood in the doorway, and Abraham cursed himself.

'You needn't be afraid, detective,' the pontiff stepped inside, his voice echoing against the walls.

Abraham reacted on instinct. He reached into his coat, pulled out his revolver and swung it around to the blond man in front of him. But the Pontiff was faster and grabbed his gun mid-swing. The distance between them had closed in a tenth of a second. And in the same instant the revolver's safety was engaged.

'Child, calm yourself,' the pontiff leaned in, his face centimetres away from Abraham's.

'Shit!' Abraham, on reflex, released his hold on his gun and threw a left hook, clocking him in the jaw.

Clange!

Pain shot through Abraham's hand; it didn't take a doctor to know that he broke two of his fingers on impact. He cradled his broken hand. The sound of flesh striking metal reverberated around the room. The young man looked at Abraham with a blank expression.

'Detective?' their voice neutral but crackling like a worn-out speaker.

Abraham's body tensed as a tingle went down his spine. *The pontiff isn't human.* From the sound it had to be a machine of some kind. Looking at its face from this distance its facial features looked off. His punch had offset the pontiff's 'skin' on its face. Its uncanny appearance revealed a metallic sheen around its left eye socket.

He didn't have much time to think before he noticed something in its mouth. From within its jaw, squirming under its 'skin' and out of its eye sockets were translucent machine-like maggots with a constant blinking red light within them.

'The hell?' His own voice was barely above a whisper. Sinking dread grew in the pit of his heart.

'Detective Abraham Theus,' its voice distorted. It slowly stepped closer. Every step it took, Abraham took one of his own to maintain the distance. His eyes focused on the entity with the squirming maggots writhing out. The Tracy look-alike walked around him and to the doorway, where the other nun and deacon had appeared behind the entity.

Before he could react, the entity closed the distance, grabbing him by the face before smothering Abraham with a kiss.

The taste of plastic, followed by the sensation of dozens of worms invading his mouth in an instant. His body tried to respond but the pain in the back of his throat paralysed him. He could feel them burrowing their way into his flesh. His mind became sluggish as his vision went dark.

Abraham's eyes opened, yet it wasn't Abraham. Just another puppet of the Saviour.

The Curse of the Clock Tower

Lauren Carey

Beep—beep—beep—beep!
The alarm blared loudly—shrill and relentless—it cut through the silence.

I woke and realised that it was quiet—*very* quiet. I knew it was only a small town and had wanted a calm atmosphere, but this place was removed from noise, like a silent movie. I walked outside.

The morning fog clung to the cobblestoned streets as the smell of eucalyptus trees and fresh-baked bread filled the air. Small-town charm was exactly what I had wanted for my weekend getaway, and in the morning light, I could see I had chosen right. However, there was still no sound, no birds, no cars, no small-town gossip being whispered over coffee.

Curiosity tugged at me, so I went out to get some answers.

The town looked like a photograph, everything frozen in place. A car sat at the intersection, engine silent, the driver's hands still at the wheel. Birds hung in the air mid-flight with their wings outstretched but motionless. The fountain in the square had stopped, and its water hung like glass. No breeze stirred the flags, no leaves rustled on the trees, no footsteps or voices broke the silence apart from me. Not even the old clock tower as it cast a shadow over the square, its hands locked in place as if time itself had surrendered.

My watch continued to tick. Why was I exempt from this freeze-frame in front of me?

'Hello?' My voice cracked through the silence. It echoed off the shopfronts and empty streets, and bounced back at me. It felt wrong and *too* loud in a world that wasn't awake.

I stared at the frozen faces around me: a butcher held a tray of sausages, a woman clutched her travel mug, motionless, in her hand, a child on their bike without a helmet with the town policeman paused mid-pursuit of the boy. None of them blinked, none of them moved.

If it hadn't been so frightening, it would have been beautiful.

'Hello?' I tried again, louder this time, and my voice echoed back. In the far distance, there was a mist rising and suddenly I didn't feel so alone. A familiar smell came alive over the town square—warm, comforting, and slightly sweet. Through the mist, I saw a bakery and ran toward it.

The bakery was at the end of the cobblestoned road, and I didn't know if I was running to something good or bad. As I drew closer, I saw a man. He was still, but staring at me, his eyes tracking my every move. Was he frozen, too?

I wanted to speak. I wanted to ask him: *Why is everything frozen? Can you see me? Can you hear me? What does this all mean?*

The baker stood inside with a dusting of flour on his apron and a tray poised mid-air. I thought he was frozen, too. Until his lips trembled. Slowly, his eyes shifted toward me. Suddenly, he dropped the tray, and it hit the floor with a crash so loud it made both of us duck like a gunshot splitting the silence.

His apron was tied loosely around his waist, and his hands were large, like they were made for kneading dough and shaping pastries. There were deep lines around his eyes, from squinting into early morning sunlight, from a life lived in motion.

As he continued to look at me, it wasn't with suspicion ...

It was with a touch of hope.

The silence deepened as he kept staring at me, so I stammered, 'How ... how are you?'

'Who are you?' he asked, not with fear or confusion, but with the ecstasy of finally being seen.

My fingers were anxiously fidgeting with the watch on my wrist. It didn't quite fit, a little too loose, but something about it had caught my eye at a roadside flea market that felt important.

'I'm Alex, and I am just here to get away from the city,' I said. 'Uh ... sir, do you know why the whole town is ... frozen?' The words tumbled out before I could stop them. I hadn't meant to ask so directly, but I needed answers.

His expression shifted from relief to confusion.

'It was like lightning in my head,' he said. 'One second I was gone, the next I heard your footsteps ... and then the tray fell from my hands like it always wanted to.'

The radio crackled to life, and an unfamiliar voice began to shout, 'Welcome to another sunny morning in Gumtree Ridge.' The radio host launched into an overly detailed weather report for the long, hot summer that was ahead.

'Summer?' he looked shocked.

'I have been stuck frozen for nearly six months now,' the baker whispered, his voice trembling as he took his first steps with as much solemnity as Neil Armstrong had on the moon. 'I was never a big believer in the supernatural until a woman came into town just before it all happened.'

'What did she do?' I asked.

'She just wandered the streets, speaking softly to no one, her eyes always searching. We thought nothing of it, and then one evening, she stood beneath the clock tower, chanting the words:

Right place, right time. Rewind.
Right place, right time. Rewind.

'Some say she was trying to stop something worse from happening. Others say she caused it. But whatever her intent, the town has been trapped in time ever since, and we have been waiting for someone like you to come along and set things right.'

'But I'm not special. I don't have psychic powers; I can't summon spirits or rewind time. I can't fix it! Take a look around, the town is still frozen. Nothing's changed.'

'It's not *you* we've been waiting for,' he said, eyes dropping to my wrist. 'It's the *watch.*'

It might've been my imagination, but the watch on my wrist was growing warmer, slowly, steadily and with it came a faint pulsing rhythm, like it was waking up.

'The woman who came before you had to make a choice: return the watch to the clock tower ... or not. If she didn't, time would freeze, giving her a chance to fix whatever mistakes haunted her in this town. I don't know what they were, the things she was trying to make right, but she chose that path. When she did, the town suddenly stopped. The rest of us were left behind, suspended in a single moment. A freeze-frame of life.'

'Where is she now?' I asked.

'Maybe she's still here. Perhaps she's not. All I know is that the watch has the power to change everything. But power like that never comes without a price.'

I looked down at my wrist, then up at the clock tower. Its hands had begun to hum softly, and he was right ... I didn't want to mess with something this powerful, however leaving them like this wasn't an option.

I stood in the middle of the square. The clock tower loomed over me, its hands groaned as they shifted. It was as if the watch's presence stirred something in the old clock tower.

I walked slowly to the tower and climbed to the top. In its the centre, in the gears, was a slot that matched my watch exactly.

I took a deep breath. This was it. I put the watch in the slot. A soft chime rang out. Then suddenly—

The fountain started to bubble!

The birds began to move!

The car engine at the intersection turned over!

The clock tower began ticking!

And the people began to blink, to breathe, to move again!

I turned around to smile at the baker, lost my balance and began to fall. As the town came back to life, I realised I had sacrificed my own.

My existence faded into oblivion. I became yet another tale to tell tourists just like me: *the saviour of a frozen town.* The people I saved from their everyday frozen ways will never know my sacrifice. The screams of a fallen hero were lost in the cursed clock tower forever.

No one in Gumtree Ridge remembers what happened during those missing months, but once a year, if you listen closely, you might hear footsteps climbing up the clock tower, a baker dropping a tray, and the wind whispering thanks to a friend.

A Gentle Prayer

Alisha Firns

A gentle prayer can exist only in a gentle world. Eden remembered the words vividly—having been uttered with such gravity—it had chilled her to the bones that day. That day when Florian transformed into the Great Inquisitor and shoved her off the cliff overlooking their childhood Monastery. As the wind rushed past her ears and the crash of the waves grew closer, there was only a single thought that ran through her mind, over and over again. A response. One she never got to say.

Would a gentle prayer not be worth more in a world like ours?

***

'Dammit!' Eden hissed, buckling against her claymore while the wounds in her side festered. Her muscles screamed in protest, but desperation made her reckless and she surged forward through the cloister to the main building of the Cathedral.

Anyone who saw this twisted amalgamation of mismatched stone and marble would never have guessed that it had once been a simple seaside Monastery. Her beloved home. Spires loomed high above the mists, cutting an ominous silhouette through the fog of the sea. The once round-headed arches now extended to a sharp point and marble columns had replaced the wooden beams of the past. Anything gentle about Eden's old home had long since disappeared.

CLANG!

Distant sounds of combat broke Eden from her thoughts. The clash of blades between inquisition soldiers and her revolutionaries lost in the howls of the storms. *Right, she was here to fight.* These storms so similar to those that fateful day of Florian's betrayal on the Cliffside. They reminded her of her duty, of her goal to inspire and liberate the broken souls of Florian's Inquisition. She would find him and end everything. Too many had died in his inquisitions. Too many have twisted the gentle faith of their childhood into something heartless. Eden would grant Florian the dignity of her blade. She smothered the pounding in her head—even as sweat beaded on the gash in her forehead—and resumed her staggering stride through the corridors to the towering doors of the Cathedral.

Adopting a hard glare, she placed her hand against the heavy doors and pushed, harsh gales and splattering rain immediately bursting into the building. Eden cursed the pain in her side and blinked through blood and rainwater to clear her vision. Reflected from the pristine marble aisle was a kaleidoscopic hue of purple and gold, cast by the ornate stained glass. Following the black carpeted path to the end of the marble rows was a padded obsidian throne. It was there that Eden discovered Florian slumped in listless repose, his silvery tresses a veil over his sickly pale face. His white robes were inlaid with gold and pooled around his feet in a creased heap. A single grey iris gazed at her through thick, silvery lashes, seeming to glow in the low lamplight.

'You've come,' his voice, despite the disgrace of his appearance, rang out with a silent authority 'My Eden ... I've looked forward to this moment.'

A sharp clang echoed out in the hall.

Eden startled at the sound, eyes snapping down from his intoxicating gaze. Her left hand had slackened in its grip from a mixture of hatred and affection at the sight of him, causing her claymore to clatter uselessly onto the marble flooring. She caught her reflection in the sheen of the blade. Her dark eyes had softened into half-moons, and her short cut curls clung to her forehead in a pitifully damp mess.

Her nerve was waning.

Eden stayed silent. A tick pulsed along her jaw and she hardened her heart once more before seizing the handle of her blade, lifting the heavy weight with her calloused fingers. She gripped the handle, pushed herself upright to glare down at him. She had always towered over Florian since they were children. 'I feel no satisfaction in this meeting; knowing how it must go.'

'And how would that be? You already betrayed me once when you turned your back on me.' He remained seated on that garish throne, the bitter twitch of his brow belying his cold voice. 'I have regained my dignity; do not gaze upon me as that unfortunate orphan.'

'A faith that purports bloodshed is useless in this world, Florian. You think this brings dignity to you?' Eden grit her teeth, anger forced her forward. 'The people of this land are felled by your dogmatic brutes!'

'Do not presume to know my intentions. This gentle faith was dying and I have helped it survive. After all,' he paused, a sneer curling his lips, 'I was not the one living in slums feeling sorry for the weak. I have done more for preserving these beliefs than you ever had.'

'You ...?' Eden took another step closer before lunging forward with sword poised, ready to sink the tip into his awaiting arms ... Only to embed it deep into the obsidian throne. The sheen of the blade reflecting his impassive expression. Eden pushed her forehead against his and glared deeply into his entrancing gaze.

'You do nothing,' she muttered an accusation in her tone.

'I've no need,' Florian murmured back, holding her dark gaze. 'I am a deity who walks the land. Should I perish, my legacy will continue. Those useless people will regret carting me off to this place. They stole my inheritance but I have gained godhood. What more could I need?'

'You truly care nothing for what you've done?' Despair seized her throat at his response. She wanted a better meaning. To feel no more shame at the warmth she felt for him still. 'What of our friendship? Do you truly value this perversion over everything?'

Florian gave her a hard stare, his jaw tensed.

'It is my destiny ... championing this faith and reclaiming what has always been mine. That, which had never once belonged to those traitors ...' His slim frame lightly trembled with the weight of his hatred, still so strong despite the decade since his loss. Her heart ached at the sight; at the loss of his dignity and pride she had admired since their childhood when he'd been abandoned by his noble family.

It doesn't matter. You have a job to do.

'Then I suppose you won't change your mind?' Eden stepped back, her bangs shadowing her face.

His silence was the only answer she needed.

'Very well then.'

Eden yanked her claymore from the throne, glaring down at him. Her other hand shot out and grabbed him by the front of his robes, hauling him from the throne and tossing him to the floor. He let out a soft grunt before looking up at her with a small, mocking smile beneath his silver bangs.

'How fierce. You're certainly more brutish than I remember.' Florian pushed himself to his knees.

'Your existence threatens the lives of everyone.' She lifted her blade once more, pausing when she felt it quivering in her hands.

Ah ... I'm shaking. Eden grit her teeth in shame, trying to still her hands. Florian watched her before sighing.

'Look. My heart is right here,' Florian pushed his heart closer to the tip of her blade, 'I know you've always wanted to be a hero. Slay me and that's what you'll be.' He smiled, 'My hero …'

Eden froze. His gentle smile from her childhood memories. Her own lips began to quiver, her face crumpled.

Florian remained kneeling before her, staring expectantly before sighing again. 'My Eden. You're far too kind. Come, join me in a gentle prayer.' He hummed the offer, as if they were back in the wooden pews of their early years.

There was silence before Eden cast aside her blade, falling to her knees before him.

'It's disgraceful. That I would hold affection for you still.' Her lips curved into a pained smile, tears building in her eyes. 'I must be a demon. To have built the hope of everyone so high. For I cannot bring myself to end your life.'

Eden pushed her forehead against his, her breath mingling with his as they whispered worship to one another.

'Oh gentle one; harken to our prayer.' Florian murmured against her hot flesh, uncaring of the blood and sweat that clung to her. His slender fingers cradled her cheek and his pink lips gently pressed against her eyelid, before slowly doing the same with her other one, smeared with the blood from the gash on her forehead.

'Oh gentle one; recall a tiny wish and bend your ear.' Eden's voice had slackened into a soft rasp, but she performed her part. Gently kissing his left eyelid, his silvery lashes damp with tears, she cradled the side of his face and moved to his right eye. Her coarse lips dragged themselves slowly from his lashes to the mole below his eye, lingering gently.

'We bring to you a gentle prayer and pray for our kindly world.'

They both whispered the final passage before embracing as friends once more.

The Wheel of
Ash and Iron

Michael Hutchins

Corvin Blackthorn danced across churned mud, his rapier sliced silver arcs through chlorine-gas fog. Machine gun tracer fire tore the night air. Soldiers slumped on razor wire like stringless puppets. Artillery shells hailed, spitting earth and limbs in every direction. Screams for medics and mothers drowned beneath the thunder of guns. Shadows in great coats surged through no-man's land and spilled into trenches with glinted bayonets.

Corvin spun through their midst, laughing. He ducked beneath a bayonet thrust, plunged his dagger between twin filters of a gas mask, then twisted away before the man dropped. He touched his lighter to the fuse of a grenade and tossed it into the fray. The blast sent steel splinters, scything through soldiers, breaking the charge. A red flare shot into the sky and whistles blasted retreat.

Silence.

Corvin crouched in the blood-stunk trench, cigarette smoke curled from his lips. Loneliness clawed his weary soul. He had fought on many battlefields. The aftermath was always the same: comrades lost, lives stolen, friendships ash. He reached into his coat pocket for his hip flask. He spilled a shot onto the earth and then raised it. 'We fight for a better peace,' he said to himself and drank.

Through the lull, a melody teased the air. Jolly, discordant, like the Pied Piper gone mad. Corvin rose to his feet, tracing the sound like a mime with open palms. The air rippled. He stood before a tent. Corvin stabbed with his rapier and cut open a flap. Steel hissed. Sulphur dripped in flame. Smoke plumed.

Corvin stepped through.

A rusted monkey cranked a street organ. Its teeth bared in a vampiric grin. Steam hissed from its seams and coal dust littered from its joints like dandruff. It lashed out with a clawed hand then strained against the chain around its neck. Corvin sidestepped onto iron tiles. Before him, stretched a grand gate. The sign above was smithed with twisted letters: *In Heaven as it is on Earth.* Beyond, a circus spread for eternity. Gaslit through smoke, steam, brass and iron. Everywhere, street-urchins shovelled coal into boilers that powered machines. A carousel of gargoyles rasped a circle. Eccentric characters, their faces painted to conceal hollow eyes, dressed in Victorian garb, pressed in crowds. A Ferris wheel labouring under the weight of centuries groaned in the distance. Beside it, a clock tower displayed the date 2025.

'I've travelled 100 years?'

Corvin searched his hands for wrinkles. He looked over his mud-soaked boots and blood-spattered clothes. He surveyed the faces around him who mocked his appearance. Corvin's hand moved to grip his rapier. *I've stepped off a battlefield where your grandfathers died for your freedom to wear thankless smirks.*

'Move aside,' said Corvin, in a tone that expected to be obeyed.

He raised his bloody forearm and pushed sideways into a crowd that reared in disgust. He brushed against a velvet wall that was once royal purple but now hung in tatters. The big top rose before him, its roof copper-plated and soldered like dragon scales. Inside, trapeze artists soared above in steel harnesses, never falling, never free. A lion tamer cracked his whip at a beast of pistons and claws. A strongman, his muscles bulging, lifted impossible weights with the aid of sprockets and levers. Corvin spat in the dirt. His lip curled into a disgusted sneer.

'You pose and pretend to be the people you know you should be,' he said.

Corvin shoved his way out of the big top into a smaller tent. A hall of mirrors stretched into endless refractions. He stepped in front of a mirror, but instead of seeing himself, he saw a window into reality. He saw millions of people carrying small screens that monitored them day and night, blaring propaganda. Men and women stood on soapboxes shouting lies in unison, spilling filth into eager ears. Other mirrors showed placard-carrying crowds clashing and leaderless politicians following each other in circles, making decrees that might get them popularity and power.

Then Corvin saw himself.

A dozen versions: Corvin dancing in mud, lashing his rapier amongst bayonets; Corvin on horseback, leading a charge into the rear of men wielding shields and spears; Corvin sprinting at soldiers firing muskets while his comrades spilled to the ground around him; Corvin on a soapbox inciting a crowd. He raised his fist to smash the mirror and his reflection raised its fist at him, smiling wider. A scream caught in his throat. He tore away, but his reflection screamed on without him.

He stormed from the tent, pushed through crowds and smoke until he stood before the Ferris wheel. Like the wheel of an ancient chariot, it tore a furrow, crushing tents beneath it. Behind it trailed a clock tower the size of a cathedral, on wheels. Brass angels trumpeted from its roof. Around it, reliefs of kings and beggars whirred past on polished brass gears. A door opened at its base, spilling light onto Corvin's boots.

Inside sat a woman, her skin as thin as papyrus, tattooed with runes, her fingernails as sharp as talons. A tray of knucklebones lay scattered on the table before her. He stepped inside.

'You're late,' her voice rasped like tearing cloth.

He sat opposite her. Beside them, a crystal orb pulsed red like a living heart.

'What is this place?'

She smiled with gaps where teeth had been.

'In heaven as it is on earth,' she said. 'I am Hetty, keeper of the wheel.'

She pressed two fingers to his wrist. No pulse. Only the steady tick of a clock. Hetty smiled. She leaned forward over the crystal ball, waved her fingers upwards to coax the currents within. She commanded an incantation in a harsh dialect. The orb flared. Images conjured in its haze: armies unborn, cities black with smoke, crowds kneeling before idols of light. She spoke without raising her eyes.

'You have fought for Alexander, for Hannibal, for Napoleon,' she said. 'You think yourself free, yet you are a cog like all the rest. The wheel of history turns and none escape its circle. War strikes and from its fire rise men of iron. From iron comes peace and plenty. But men grow weak as wax. From that weakness, war rises again to bring more suffering.'

Corvin clenched his jaw. 'Then why summon me?

'My time is done,' she said. 'The mirrors spoke truth. Men have become slaves to devices that control their thoughts. Leaders have become followers of groupthink. The media manufactures the narrative in the interests of the wealthy few. War is sure to follow. The wheel must have a keeper to steer it through its cycle, one forged in war who brings peace, like iron from the ash.' The orb blazed.

Sparks leaped between her fingerbones and his rapier. Visions seared his mind: oceans slicked with oil, balls of flame exploding across cities, great armies crumbling under greater weapons.

'I'm tired of fighting the wheel,' he said.

'Then drive it,' Hetty said. 'Take the wheel.'

Hetty drew back a curtain. Behind it loomed a throne of iron and ash, perched at the heart of a colossal mechanism. Gears shrieked, pistons hammered, and the busts of rulers turned in endless procession. The throne pulsed faintly, as if waiting for a heartbeat. Corvin drew his rapier. It burned in his hand. For the first time in centuries, laughter did not come. Memories of fallen friends. Good times that became ash. His memories laughed without him. Corvin stood at the foot of the throne, buckling under the memories of centuries of struggle. The iron seat loomed above him: more prison than chair. A trap of rusted teeth waiting to devour him. His fingers flexed around the hilt of his rapier, as if he could cut a path of refusal against fate. For a moment, he hesitated, unwilling. A soldier who survived too many campaigns to crave another. The wheel's grinding pulse drew him closer; each beat felt like cowardice.

The iron groaned as he lowered himself onto the throne. Corvin's chest throbbed tick, tock. The wheel shuddered. Sparks rained over the circus. The crowd cheered. In the mirrors, another war began.

The Death of Innocence

Carrera Garcia

I t's been exactly three hours since the Starchild had died.

When the moon reached its peak and the stars glistened in the night sky. When the Starchild took her final breath. No one had been prepared.

The Basilica's sanctum was sealed before sunrise, its great bronze doors barred from the inside. The air was dank, heavy with incense that clung to the back of the throat. Tall candles hissed faintly in their sconces, spilling thin light over the marble slab at the room's centre.

Upon it, lay the Starchild.

The Starchild had been small in life—no taller than a child, her bones so fragile they might shatter at a single touch. Her skin, once faintly luminous, now looked like glass cooled to a dull sheen. No blood had pooled under her; it was as if her veins had emptied themselves the moment her heart stilled. And that final garment, said to be woven from clouds, lay folded at the foot of the slab, its purity sullied by a streak of shadows from the crowding figures.

The priests bowed their heads, but not in mourning. Their eyes, when they looked at her, were hungry in different ways: some for the miracle, some for the power it might bring, others for the closeness to her body they never had in their lifetime.

Bishop Wayford stepped forward first. His voice was smooth, patient, the voice of a man accustomed to bending others to his will with words alone.

'We cannot consign her to the ground,' he said. 'The earth consumes what it owns. She belongs to us, and through us, to the faithful. She must endure.'

The other priests murmured in soft agreeance, their hushed voices echoing through the chapel. So soft, it was as if they feared that the Starchild would rise from the slab and strike them down for even agreeing.

In the shadows near the altar, Cardinal Sera's arms were folded tight. 'And by *endure*, you mean—'

'I mean,' Wayford cut in, 'that her body must be emptied, preserved, and made holy through division. Every chapel, every monastery, will keep a piece. She will be everywhere at once.'

Sera screwed her mouth shut and said nothing more. She knew the Patriarch, seated high in his gilded chair at the edge of the chamber, would not intervene. He barely realised this meeting was going on, that the very divine being he confided in mere hours before laid dead by his feet. But his silence was not ignorance; it was consent. The Patriarch just lazily waved his hand, and at that very moment Sera knew she could do nothing to stop them from defiling the divine being's body.

So, it began. Two attendants came from the shadows and hurried to untie the silk ribbon from the Starchild's hair that spilled over the marble in waves. Long and silver as starlight. The first cut came without hesitation. A pair of golden shears whispered through it, severing locks that had once fallen over the shoulders of kings and cradled the heads of the dying. The bishops and priests scrambled to have their piece, each gripping a sheath of strands and waiting for their bit to be cut. Each piece was bundled and tied, bound with red ribbons as those lucky enough to grab some precariously wrapped it in linen and sealed it away in their robes.

The sound of greed was quiet, but it was the kind of quiet that made Sera's jaw tighten. When the Starchild was alive, she prided herself in having luscious locks—it was the one thing she was able to control in her life, something so trivial and yet so vital to her spirits. And now, it was taken from her by the very men she swore to serve. Her once beautiful hair untouched by man, now haphazardly cut into a short, uneven bob that would've made her weep if she caught a glance of it.

Then, the blade was brought out—a long knife forged from meteoric iron, the same one used when she was anointed before the crowds. That same edge pressed to her palm in the blood-oath of her ministry.

The first incision was drawn from the hollow of her throat to the base of her belly. The flesh parted without blood. Instead, a pale, shimmering dust rose from the wound, curling upward like smoke.

'Stardust,' the surgeon-priest breathed, holding out his palm to catch it in awe.

'Do not waste a single grain,' Wayford ordered. 'The smallest relic can bind a lifetime of faith.'

The congregation clambered to clean, to keep, to harvest. The dust was swept into crystal vials, each stoppered and sealed with wax. Each priest, bishop, and cardinal was blessed with one. Even the Patriarch, who sat silent, had his very own vial filled with the insides of the Starchild. Some kissed the vials; others placed it against their forehead and prayed to the goddess lying in front of them.

Hands entered her then, slow and deliberate, rummaging through her empty carcass like parasites. They lifted her heart from its place, revealing it to be black and faceted like obsidian, jagged enough to cut the lips of the priest who pressed it to his mouth in a kiss of reverence. Blood welled on his skin—his own, not hers.

One by one, they took her organs: lungs pale as glass, liver gleaming faintly, kidneys marbled with some strange light. They moved with ritual precision, speaking the old preservation prayers between each removal. Each time the hands went in, there was the sound of soft tearing, of something once whole being undone.

Sera looked away, but the sound clung to her. It was the same sound she'd heard years ago in the confessional when a sobbing woman had spoken, haltingly, about the night she was 'blessed' in private by a priest; how he told her she was chosen, and how she'd lain still so the 'holy work' could be done. Now, as the Starchild's body was emptied under candlelight, the same language was being spoken. The same violation was being cloaked in robes and scripture.

Her bones were drawn out carefully, the marrow scooped and replaced with resin that smelled faintly of lilies. Each rib was polished until it shone white under the candles. Her head was kept for the Basilica, the rest to be divided among the outer churches. But for now, her body was to be kept intact for the reveal.

Her skin was treated next; bathed in saltwater from the Sea of Glass, anointed with myrrh, coated in resin until it no longer felt like flesh. It was the skin of an idol now, not a woman. Through it all, her face remained still, her closed eyes unreadable.

When there was nothing left inside her, they began to fill her again—not with what she had been, but with perfumed cloth. They packed it into the hollowed cavity, pressing it down until the swell of her body returned, until she looked whole. The emptiness beneath did not matter; the shape was enough. Wayford stepped close, brushing his fingers over the body to test his work. His hands reached not in blessing, but in inspection. Touching her limbs, her sides, her stomach, with the detached focus of a man handling something that could not object. He decided to rest his hands on the cusp of her breasts while the attendants worked.

'She will endure,' he said again, with a satisfaction that made Sera's stomach twist.

The small star etched into her forehead—the first indication that she was descended from the stars, a symbol never dimmed or wavered—was fading now. The priests painted over it with gold, layer upon layer, until the dull light was hidden beneath brilliance.

Her hair, or what remained of it, was braided and bound with silver thread. Her hands were folded over her chest; fingers entwined with a rosary of meteoric beads. She no longer looked like a person. She looked like something made—crafted for the eye, for the altar, for possession.

***

When the last prayer was spoken and the incense urns extinguished, the doors of the Basilica were thrown open. The plaza outside swelled with people, thousands pressing forward, candles raised high. Bells rang from the spires, the sound tumbling down into the square like molten bronze. The Patriarch stepped onto the balcony, the hollowed Starchild's body lying behind him on a marble altar, veined with gold.

'My children,' he proclaimed, 'behold the vessel of heaven, made eternal among us. She walks no longer in the flesh, but her presence remains in every fragment, every relic, every altar.'

A great cloth was drawn away, and the crowd gasped. They saw beauty. They saw proof of the divine. They did not see the emptiness sewn beneath her skin, the resin where marrow had been, the cloth where once there was breath. They did not smell the saltwater in which she had been washed like a fisher's catch or see the glint of the knife that had first undone her. They knelt and they wept for the Starchild's return.

And in the shadowed sanctum behind the altar, where the last grains of her stardust had fallen to the marble and been left uncollected, something faint began to hum—low, steady, and patient, like a breath waiting to be drawn again.

Fey Lights

Natasha Ives

The Sun Rising: Andrew

The warmth of the flame tingled the tips of the Bishop's fingers as the candle glowed to life, joining the pairs at the bottom of the large statue of the Holy Father erected in the centre of the Church. In the Father's long shadow, Bishop Andrew remained on his knees, the polished beads wrapped around his palms clinking together as he prayed. He was due to perform every sunrise and sunset and he was known to offer a prayer more than what was asked, but he needed the Father's guidance more every day.

'Good morning, Bishop,' a soft voice gently whispered behind him before the soft rustle of clothes joined him on his side. Sister Hera always arrived before the rest of the flock, straightening the pews and brushing imaginary dust from the paintings along the halls. Andrew never discouraged this behaviour and hoped the other Sisters would follow Hera's lead, but this notion has not borne fruit.

'Blessed Morning, Sister Hera,' Bishop Andrew spoke once he had finished his prayer, slowly rising to his feet, his hands smoothing down the front of his robes. Age had worn down his patience and softened his heart. The flock he had gathered had become his family and he cared about them as he believed the Holy Father did. Yet, some mornings, he would wonder if his prayers filled the empty spaces in the people's hearts, naked to the human eye.

'Do you need help preparing for this morning's service, Bishop?' Hera bowed. Her hair was neatly tucked into the white woollen cap on her head wrapped with a bone yellow ribbon. The rest of her attire matched her cap, as was the dress code for the Church.

Andrew's clothes were equally brightly coloured, minus the red leather wrapped around his neck to signify his position.

'Could you finish lighting the candles around the room, please?' Andrew stepped down the polished stone steps before the Holy Father's statue. He stopped to stand behind the large wooden lectern, his papers and cross resting in waiting.

'Of course, Bishop,' Hera bowed once more before pulling a rock and flint from the pouch attached to her belt. Her heeled boots tapping against the stone floors as she left to work.

As Andrew read through the morning prayers, more of the sisters trickled through the large oak doors of the Church, their hushed whispers tickling at his ears. A small smile curled his lips, but he remained silent as the day started, the first few of his flock arriving for Morning Prayer.

Bishop Andrew spoke softly to those wishing him a good morning, updating them on their daily happenings; another child was born to be bathed in Holy water, and an elder stricken with sickness needed extra prayers—a growing list of favours that he would gladly fulfil. The pews slowly filled with more people, from both the inner walls of the capital to those who live further out, all coming to one place to pray together. The sight always warmed his heart, thanking the Father that he was able to serve the people.

The warmth of the growing crowd filled his heart, chasing away the cold depression that descended on him on this day every year. The reminder of his faith and duty to his flock made him forget about the family he no longer had, whom he could no longer love. His sister's memory would be honoured and remembered today, but the most faithful and the Holy Fathers' teachings filled him with purpose and meaning.

The last of the flock settled down, their scripture ready open in their laps as the morning bell rang, the gong shaking the foundation of the Church.

Morning Service began and the sound of Andrew's voice, full of love and faith, echoed through the open doors of the church for all to hear.

New Day: Fae

Unfortunately, the soft prickle of wooden splinters pressing against her palms was familiar. It marked yet another day when she was shoved down onto the ancient floors of the long-forgotten town hall, which was now a school for the children born to unwanted families. Muddies the rich water, the sisters say, looking down their mouse-like noses at us.

Fae always thought they were bitter because they were left to teach us, forgotten children, rather than stay in their pretty chapel in the capital, where their meals were always warm and beds always soft. Life was hard here, just like the hard floor Fae now lay on.

Fae clenched her jaw hard enough that it almost made the pain in her hands and knees which had just taken the brunt force of her weight after being pushed through the classroom door. *Honestly, they could not have waited till the afternoon,* Fae bemoaned to herself, as she let out a long, slow stream of air from between her tense lips. This tumble had become an almost daily activity for Fae since she had been the main target of bullying from the local gang of kids, young and old. Pick the odd one out. *So original.*

With a practised motion, Fae pushed herself from her knees, she brushed her skin with a stiff flick of her wrists. She made her way towards her seat. It was set in line with one of the back windows, often bathing her in the warm morning sun.

The room was filled with the thumping of feet, hushed whispers of gossiping children, and the scratch of chair legs against the wood. Fae sat at the back of the class making observations on who was early, who was late and noting who was absent.

Rosie was sitting at her seat front and centre, her hair pinned tight to the top of her head, her crisp shirt clean and pressed. Rosie was one of the few kids whom the Sisters liked, and it showed. Fae could not say the same for Josh, who sat slumped in his chair, head resting heavily on his desk. Fae knew the boy had trouble sleeping, but not the reason why. But even Fae saw the bruises, the yellow the same shade as his teeth;

the deep, dark marks under his eyes spoke of not just a lack of sleep, for it didn't hide the redness of his tears.

Everyone was different, but also not. Some had love sprinkled over them, just enough to set the real dirty children apart from the rest; the inequality of value of care, but no one spoke up, challenging the unfairness of it all, for they were the dirty little children in this dirty little town, full of secrets and hushed whispers behind dirty hands.

Fae hated it here. She hated how people would leave their children in this broken-down building, leaving them with Nuns who barely followed their beloved Father's teachings. The same Nuns would preach their teachings to the children, always reminding them to do better, to do as they were told and they would be loved.

They lied.

Their lies spill like muddied water down a raging river, smearing and tainting everything it touched, making the fresh water undrinkable. Fae had stopped drinking their lies a long time ago. She knew that no matter what the Nuns said, what they promised, she would remain unloved by them. They would sneer and point at her bright red hair and green eyes, whispering about the 'old ways' having touched Fae's family.

One day, they would not point and sneer at her anymore. One day, Josh would come to school with a smile on his face, his skin free from bruises and cuts. One day, Rosie would know what it was like to be unloved for no fault of her own.

One day, this town will regret forsaking them. The desire burned brightly in Fae's chest, her nails digging into the wood of her desk as she finally knew. She knew what she must do, what she had to set into motion.

The dark revelation, the dark promise settled into her head as the final ring of the Morning Bell, the last of the stragglers scuttled into their seats before the morning classes began, and all conversation stopped. The familiar heavy weight of dread settled heavily over the children's heads, many slumping under the pressure.

And thus the day began.

Crystal Balls Cause Cautious Mediums to Catastrophise

Karla Heigers

In hindsight, spending the majority of her Monday morning staring into a crystal ball was probably not the best way for Victoria to fight off the vibrational doom echoing within her for weeks now. Unfortunately for the future-telling, tarot-card-reading nutcase, her anxiousness only worsened when she used her psychic powers—powers which she was addicted to using. Victoria had always been psychic, so not using them was completely unfathomable—especially for reasons as *nebulous* as 'mental health'. So instead, she suffered for months feeling like a cat about to be bathed, until eventually busting out her trusty, dusty crystal ball. Victoria last relied on the thing as a teenager, experiencing what was essentially an acid trip into the future—or perhaps the past. She couldn't know, of course, when—or what—she'd seen, only that it either had already, or was going to, happen.

Victoria's most loyal customer, Gertrude, *insisted* she keep using it.

Only if you paid me double time ... Victoria would think to herself. That was until she'd begun feeling this supernatural warning and decided to try it again.

So, there she sat—tripping balls—eye's erupting in bright lights. Bits and bobs floated around her apartment, her once clear crystal ball now fraught with ashy-coloured clouds. She'd become well-adjusted to the feeling of her eyes rolling back into her skull and random, uncontrollable limb movements when she was younger. To an onlooker she'd seem possessed—a wild-eyed woman with outstretched fingers and flailing arms. But in her mind's eye, she felt completely at peace. Swimming through the bright colours and images of time and happening, she suddenly felt her soul pulling to something more tangible.

A burning pain blistered through her temples—

She came to drooling on the fluffy carpet, sun already set, crystal ball shattered by her side. Groaning from the images of pain and suffering—a pumping human heart and echoes of choking amid flashes of green—a clicking sound took their place in her mind instead.

With a jump, Victoria desperately sifted through slivers of crystal in hopes of remembering anything else. The scattered shards sat pearlescent, milky, and shiny—until she touched them. Victoria felt the essence—or rather, *the soul*—of the ball evaporate. It was just ordinary glass now. All she could do was ruminate on snippets provided to her. That dreadful choking ... *sound?*

The pounding heart...

Green flashes...

Fighting the urge to throw up, Victoria tried to make sense of what she'd seen in the crystal ball, searching for any clue that could clarify her future.

There was only one *obvious* answer, really—she was going to die soon.

She spent the next half hour frantically deadbolting doors and closing windows, before meticulously attempting to death-proof the rest of her home. Powdery lavender incense tickled her nose as she cleansed walls and halls of her house. Sweeping through room after room, she collated clothes, trash and crystal chips strewn around her apartment—mitigating tripping hazards. She shut off gas to her stove, unscrewed lightbulbs and tossed suspicious-looking food from her fridge. Momentarily satisfied, she allowed herself to do what any other rational human would do—completely ignore the problem until it went away.

It began with the slow drip of a tap. White noise that would've soothed to her once before, became a sign of something supernatural. The unfixable tap became an unfindable scraping noise. The unfindable scraping noise evolved into an all-encompassing cacophony of threatening and unsourceable noise. Her mind began to wonder to friends, family, and clients—none of whom seemed capable of murderer.

When did she start to suspect her cause of death to be murder? Perhaps the accusation arose from her own ego—what kind of stupid did she have to be to get into a freak accident? Some other person must be the reason. So, from now on, she'd carry a rabbit's foot, practice good omens, and cancel with customers she believed capable of murder.

Two knocks on her front door cut through the silence, beckoning Victoria's complete attention. Fear relaxed its grip around her throat as she recognised the rhythmic and precise knocking of her six o'clock client—Miss Gertrude Hicklethorne.

A distraction! Victoria thought, relief flooding through her body.

She sprang into action excitedly, grabbing, and pocketing, the gift she'd made for Gertrude.

'Sorry to keep you waiting!' Victoria called out, clunking open the many deadbolts on her door.

Gertrude waited patiently by the door for the final bolt, wrapped in a neon green raincoat. Almost everything she wore was woollen, so she had to take care of it, even when it was perfectly sunny.

You never know when it could rain, she'd say.

'Hello, dear.' Gertrude's voice was without her usual anxious tremor, giving Victoria hope for her current mental state.

Perhaps our sessions are finally paying off.

Gertrude Hicklethorne had been a loyal client ever since seeing the Facebook ad Victoria bought a year prior. She was both fascinated, and terrified, of her future. Every appointment she arrived a nervous wreck, obsessing over potential threats lurking in the future. But, after every appointment, she'd leave, no longer afraid of what was to come—though how long Gertrude's confidence lasted, Victoria never was sure.

Her obsessive fixation on the future wasn't healthy—anyone could see that. Who comes to a psychic just to hear 'No, really—everything *will* be okay!' over and over again? Regardless, Victoria was excited to see Gertrude, and, more importantly, to give her latest attempt at providing Gertrude with long lasting peace a try. A voodoo doll—with that, *hopefully* the old lady could gain some comfort out of having some spiritual control. This control, Victoria thought, could calm her in the present, so perhaps she might feel better equipped to deal with whatever came in the future.

Victoria began the reading, pulling the death card twice, and hiding it from Gertrude to prevent agitating her anxiety. Shuffling the deck once again, she sensed the beginnings of her old dread come back. Currently, Gertrude was worried about whether she truly loved her dogs, and if she would one day hurt them as her unwanted thoughts had convinced her she would. Victoria could tell, without her psychic abilities, that Gertrude did not, in fact, possess the evil within her to necessary to hurt an animal. But turned to the tarot cards for Gertrude's peace of mind anyway. Drawing the death card for the third time caused Victoria to pause, she couldn't hide it now without drawing Gertrude's suspicion—and where there's suspicion, there's anxiety.

She placed it on the table.

'I've never gotten that card before. Does it mean I'll hurt my dogs after all?' Gertrude asked. Once again, her tone weirdly absent of anxiety, her eyes far away in thought.

'It normally signifies transformation, change, new beginnings ...' Victoria listed absent-mindedly, eyes fixed on the death card sitting face up on the table. 'It's metaphorical, think relationships ending, severing ties—'

'I've been coming to you for a year, now.' Gertrude was staring intently at her.

A dizzying panic ebbed in Victoria's mind.

'My goal is to keep giving you clarity on your future,' Victoria added automatically.

'It was so you could help me.' The way Gertrude said it, so full of venom, made Victoria feel sick. She met Gertrude's eyes. Her face was warped, her eyebrows furrowed and arched, the corners of her mouth pointing steadily down as her bottom lip trembled. 'But nothing has worked. In fact, it's only gotten worse.'

Victoria had thought she was helping. Her heart began to beat in her ears, and she couldn't help but picture the heart from her earlier vison. She touched her fingers to the voodoo doll in her pocket. She was going to gift it to Gertrude after the session, but now she wanted something to calm the unhappy customer down. 'I made something that I thought would help—'

'I don't want your help anymore!' The shock of Gertrude's raised voice sent alarm bells ringing through Victoria's body. 'I ask you to tell me about the future, tell me I won't crash my car even though it feels like I will. I don't even know what's real anymore unless I ask you!'

A flash of neon green rang in her subconscious mind, and a white-hot panic filled Victoria's body as she heard a soft click under the table. 'Gertrude, I only tell you the truth of what I see, nothing else.'

'I think ...' She seemed calmer.

Victoria held her breath, praying that she'd gotten through to her.

'I think that it all got worse when I began to see you.' Gertrude slowly pulled the revolver out of her pocket, her delicate, wrinkly finger shaking above the trigger. Victoria felt the hot, salty tears flood her eyes. Her lip was trembling now, and she tightened her grip on the voodoo doll.

'I just want to be okay again,' Gertrude admitted, her voice sounding similar to the kind old lady Victoria once knew. Victoria's grip on the voodoo doll tightened. Gertrude's eyes widened like marbles, staring through Victoria, as her grip on the revolver loosened. Gertrude opened her mouth to say something. No—to breathe! The revolver dropped to the tarot cards below, sending them fluttering to the ground, as Getrude's hands began clawing at her neck. Victoria couldn't take her eyes off the horror in front of her. Still, she continued to grip the voodoo doll's neck in her fist, closing it with all her strength. However, she flinched and blinked away when Gertrude's veins began bulging from her wrinkly neck. With a silent cry, blood gurgling from inside her throat, Gertrude collapsed to the floor.

Strangely, standing over the body of Miss Gertrude Hicklethorne—the almost decapitated murder doll still squeezed tightly in her hand, death card face down by her shoe—Victoria finally found herself at peace.

Pursuit of Perfection

Wade Baker

Painter awoke from his trance, lying naked on a bundle of paint-stained sheets. His room, made of peeling wallpaper and rotting wood, was cold, in body and in spirit. Stripped bare, aside from opened half-empty bowls of his paints and piles of ruined canvases towering around the room. The fat spider in a fortress of webs and dust in the corner being the only sign of life, aside from the living corpse of Painter.

The world spun as the scent of clean air overwhelmed Painter, his brain burning and trying to escape his skull. He felt an eternity pass as he opened his eyes, a faint dawn light assaulting them as he did so, while a piercing chill followed, invading his bones. Groaning, he flung his arm around, grabbing a fistful of sheet and wrapped himself up before rising.

Following the scent and biting chill, he stumbled his way towards an open window, struggling against the light that continually barraged his eyes. Fumbling, he tugged at the window, his skeletal fingers unable to make the frame budge. He sighed, making his way to a pile of canvases. Grabbing the most intact one, he stuffed it in the window, leaving only a few slivers of dim light to permeate through. But it stopped the chill, leaving the room only a numbing cold, better than it was.

Shedding the sheets, fresh paint stains like handprints covered his ghastly body. Painter stretched, his body creaking and cracking, the minor exertion rending him into a coughing fit that brought him to his knees.

The fit grew worse and worse, and his vision became splotched with black; blood mixed with saliva as he coughed. Painter felt cold hands press upon him.

Her hands.

A whispering of their old wedding song echoed in the room as her hands wrapped around him, unwilling to wait for him any longer.

But it was not yet time. Focusing, he drew a deep breath and held it until the fit ceased before he gasped for air. Clutching his chest, the pain the culmination of a lifetime of smokes and fumes. When poison became vital and clean air an antidote, there was only one result. Yet poison remained poison no matter the necessity, and would kill him in its own time.

Her cold hands grasped him tighter, tugging at him, pulling at him ... pleading at him. *Soon*, Painter promised. He would finish their promise soon, then she could have him once more, together again. *Forever.*

Rooting through another pile of eviscerated canvases, he dug out an old oil lamp. Fiddling with it for a moment, he managed to light it. A dim, amber light stretched through the hovel, barely more illuminating than the scattering of light from the window. But her pull, and their song, still present, but now faded like the shadow of a ghost. Finally comfortable, he made his way to the far edge of the room, containing only an easel and canvas with a half-finished painting of a mountain, his materials, and a stool.

Seating himself on the old stool, he grabbed his brush and began to paint.

Time passed. Instants became ages, and eternities became moments. Mountains rose and rivers formed. The painting became a world complete, as Painter became the painting. A single stroke encompassing him as whole, all of himself into every brushstroke.

***

Painter fell from the stool. Without the strength to move, he laid there, feeling his stomach twist and churn in pain, his lungs sedentary in his chest, shrivelled and failing. A sickly-sweet smell overwhelmed him, flowers but wrong, vanilla but not, a lulling rot, death encroaching, the smell of himself.

Eventually a creaking sound came from behind, him, a door opened and something came close. Small and delicate hands held him. The small hands rolled him over, his wife, no ... not her, but almost her reflection, yet the eyes were his own. And her hands were so warm to his skin.

She pulled him close and whispered words he could not hear, gave him a look he could no longer understand. Holding him with a tenderness he didn't deserve. She held him, bringing a small bowl to his lips and forcing him to drink, even as it dribbled down his chin and onto the rotten floorboards below. Only stopping when he began to cough. A new look came and left her face as she held him. She pulled at him, helping him stand, ushering towards the door.

But Painter refused.

He resisted her hold, futilely squirming against her as best he could until she let go. He had work, wearily making his way to his stool and sitting before his painting. Painter watched it, the paint was still yet to dry, but it was finished, as close to perfection as anything made could reach.

But a failure still.

She stood beside him, a hand on his shoulder as they watched the paint dry. The amber light flickering and fluttering, their shadows dancing even as they remained unmoving. She turned to him and said something before leaving, but he remained unmoving even as the light winked out.

So, he sat alone in the dark, staring at the painting, a silhouette of black amongst the darkness. The details once there, now gone, but only to Painter's eyes, unseeable but undeniable. Even as his eyes adjusted to the dark, a blurred shape was all he could make out. Yet it struck him as bizarrely beautiful. The darkness swirled and rippled, shifting as a living creature, moving as they do but in ways they could never. It was mesmerising.

But in his reprieve, the song returned louder, and he felt them once more, cold hands tugging at him, wanting him to embrace her, increasingly impatient. He tried to hold them, but only felt the chill, but no substance. The sound of creaking and faint light came from behind him as he did so, getting louder as a light grew brighter every moment. Mustering all he had, Painter spoke, his throat tearing as a creaking voice emerged. *Soon*, he promised. He was almost there, perfection was close, he'd find it this time. But he was tired, the coldness was inviting, unrelenting ... irresistible. Painted felt himself slipping into it—

The small, warm hands shook him, and after a moment, embraced him. The petite figure held him, trembling and screaming. Painter couldn't understand the sounds she made, he tried, but their meaning was long out of his grasp now. But he looked into her teary eyes, seeing a reflection of himself, and for a moment, he *saw* himself. Struggling, he raised a hand to her face. Which she grasped and held in her tiny hands, she spoke softly to him, but the meaning never arrived, which only seemed to make her smaller.

Yet still, her hands were warm.

After a time Painter's mind wandered, shifting from her hold, Painter used the light she brought to look upon the canvas. He stared; the painting was well done. That could not be denied. But not perfect. A complete failure. Painter looked around the room, all the previous failures, a lifetime of failures. The haunting of his life. Painter's pursuit of perfection.

Painter drew his gaze back to the small figure beside him, smiling to them. Their face changed in ways Painter couldn't understand, more words spoken that he couldn't understand, but she seemed happy. He tried to smile but the ghostly hands gripped him tighter; the song now growing deafening, from the subtle hymn to an orchestra within his mind.

Unable to waste a moment, Painter stood in front of the canvas, uncaring of the cold—a mountain? Was it one he had gone to? Or perhaps dreamed? Maybe it wasn't from anywhere but simply the idea of a mountain. But as he watched it more, Painter now detested it. Reaching behind the canvas he pulled out his knife and took it to the painting, ignoring those indecipherable sounds.

After a few swings he was left gasping, the canvas now like all the others. Painter stared at it, the way it looked now was better, but still not perfect. A failure equally. He tossed the ruined canvas with the others and grabbed a fresh one, or an unpainted one, at least. He stood there, staring at the blank canvas. One more chance, that was all Painter had. He could barely think, barely move.

Perfection cannot be borne by human hands. So he became Painter. More. Less. Perfect. Imperfect. Yet still, found only failure. Nothing Painter made had become more. She was never satisfied, unwilling to wait for it any longer.

The swirling darkness, a void, a shadow against the black, and the blurry reflection of himself in the eyes of another; all of it came to the mind of Painter. His left arm reached forward to touch the canvas.

Perhaps it was already perfect, but it was not yet made, not yet Painter. The culmination of a life into a painting, Painter's perfection.

Painter looked at the arm touching the canvas, and looked at the other holding a knife. Without wasting another moment, Painter cut.

***

Painter sat on the floor, trapping a mortar between his thighs, left arm ending at the elbow and bandaged, while the right used the pestle to grind down a white powder. Even as Painter's breath became laboured, and the crying of the petite figure in the corner faded to sobs, Painter continued, unable to spare a thought for her anymore. She ... was inconsequential now.

Once the powder was as fine as could be made, Painter put aside the pestle. Holding the mortar, he emptied it into a bowl of black paint. Using a piece of the floorboard Painter had pried free, Painter mixed it together, reaching a hand into the paint and smearing it over the canvas. Again, and again. Until the entire canvas was covered.

Thus, Painter sat there, an amber light filling the room, his head filled with an old wedding song, and heart wrenching sobs coming from somewhere unimportant. Left arm covered in bloody bandages and right arm covered in black paint. Eyes focused on the painting, if it could be called such, merely a canvas smeared and covered in a thick, uneven and messy, gunpowder black layer, barely visible beneath the flickering amber glow, yet it existed, observable or not.

Painter looked *into* the painting, seeing a darker shadow reflected into it, the shadow of Painter. For whoever would look into it would see a void, a shadow, and ultimately themselves. The only perfection a human can produce.

Cold hands wrapped Painter's chest, freezing his lungs, and as the hands shifted to wrap around his neck, his breathing slowing until not a breath more emerged.

His heart slowing.

His mind fading.

Painter sat, unbreathing and unblinking, he smiled, looking upon his pursuit of perfection. Reflecting within the canvas for just a single moment the image of a young man and woman smiling serenely at one another, before fading away.

Together again.

The Last Man
on Earth

Dan Aleckson

Hi, thanks for seeing me at such short notice. I bet none of your lot are keen to talk to me, especially today. Don't be nervous; it's not like I'll stab you. See? Cuffs.

Hmm? Oh, the blindfold? I asked for it. I don't want to know if you're one of them. Not today. I ... need to talk to someone, even if they're not real.

Yeah, well, like I said, I don't want to know. Now, where to begin? The first sighting? The first death? The first time I found out about them? How about I start there? The first time I found out they existed. It was about a year ago. I had just finished a podcast from The Dail— huh?

Well, that's just nonsense. There's no way I've been here for three years. Don't be stupid. Now, as I was saying; I had just finished listening to a podcast and I'd hopped onto Discord to talk about it with my friends. I loved talking to those guys. I hadn't actually met any of them, of course, but they just got me, you know? Anyway, one of them, I think it was Jog, started talking about running into his old high school friends that day. He said that one of them, I think he called them 'Jake', was, and I'm quoting here, 'such a fucking NPC.'

I asked Jog what he meant. I had only ever heard the term 'NPC' be used in reference to video game characters; I'd never heard anyone say it about a real person before.

'You know,' he said. 'A non-player character.'

I told him that I knew what the term meant but still didn't understand the usage. Then he told me about how some humans weren't really people. They walked and talked and looked like real people but had no internal life. 'The set dressing of the universe,' he said. 'Empty husks that just looked like people.'

It made a lot of sense to me. I would always run into those sorts of people online. The fake, almost pre-recorded sounding woke bullshit they constantly drooled about immigrants and all that crap. They would always say the same things over and over again, like they didn't have any thoughts of their own, just reciting a script.

Anyway, I asked him how he knew how to find out who was real and who wasn't.

'The eyes,' he said. 'Real people have that spark of intelligence in their eyes. NPCs don't. Next time you're out, pay real close attention to people's eyes. You'll see.'

So, I did. It wasn't easy, I was never really comfortable looking people in the eye, but I really made an effort this time. When the cashier at the local pizza place asked me for my order, I made sure to look her in the eye when I gave it. And I saw.

Her eyes were a bright white against her dark skin, but I noticed that they were lacking something. The little light that shines in people's eyes when they have thoughts wasn't there. She—no, it—just stood there blankly, saying the same things on repeat. 'Welcome, what can I get for you?' or 'That'll be $15.95, please,' like a ... well, like an NPC.

I mentioned it to Jog and the others that night, and one of them, Gobel this time, asked a question that piqued my interest

'What do you think they do when they leave work?' he asked. 'Do you think they just walk into the back room and stand there all night?'

'No way,' said CKing. 'They get stored in apartments. That's why housing's so bad, you know.

Because all the apartments are being given to those damn things.'

My curiosity had thoroughly grabbed me by the balls. I had to find out, so I vowed that the next day, I would wait for it to leave, assuming it did, and follow it to wherever it was stored.

I showed up to the place it ... operated a few minutes after opening and spent the whole time sitting in a booth at the corner of the restaurant, positioned so that I could see it while it was at the counter without having to look directly at it. I couldn't let it get suspicious, after all. After about nine hours and a lot of leg aches, I saw it disappear into the back area, then reappear again wearing a jacket over its red and black uniform before walking out. I got up almost immediately, took a second to rub my sore butt, then followed it out.

Luckily, I had parked right near it, so I was able to get to my car and follow it closely as its own vehicle pulled away. I followed the thing for about twenty minutes, until it pulled up in front of an apartment building, parked on the street outside, and got out. CKing had been right, they were using up housing that could be going to real people! That made me fucking furious, I was able to barely restrain myself from attacking it right then and there.

I took a moment to calm myself down. Obviously, not everyone could see that these things existed, and I didn't think any witnesses would look fondly on a skinny white guy attacking some black chick in broad daylight. Even if its skin was just a mask.

I still needed to know, though. I needed to know what kinds of conditions these things existed in. So, I followed it at a safe distance into the building. It took the elevator up, so I took the stairs. At the fourth floor it exited. I watched from the door of the stairwell as it crossed the hall and approached an apartment door numbered 4B. Then I returned to my car, and I waited.

For hours, I stayed there, until afternoon turned to evening, and evening turned to night. It looked like I had gotten lucky yet again; its apartment faced the street, and I could clearly see the lights of the thing's bedroom from where I sat. After those lights finally winked off, I got out of my car and approached the building.

Getting in was shockingly easy. The lock on the entrance was old and flimsy. I retrieved a screwdriver from my car and grabbed a loose brick from the stoop. Fitting the screwdriver's head into the keyhole and giving it a solid whack with the brick, the fragile mechanism shattered and the door swung open. I took the stairs up slowly, back to the fourth floor, and approached the thing's front door. Another forceful blow to the back of the screwdriver sent it spearing through the apartment's lock even easier than the front door. A twist of the handle caused it to swing open gently, connecting with the interior wall with a soft *tap*.

I don't know what I expected when I entered the apartment. Computer terminals, data readouts, maybe a human-shaped robot docking station? I'm still not sure if I was relieved or disappointed when I walked into what seemed to be a completely normal apartment. The floor was strewn with discarded clothes; the kitchen sink piled with dirty dishes. I was turning to leave when I heard a soft creaking sound. My head snapped to where the sound came from.

The NPC was standing in pink pyjamas, locking eyes with me from less than two metres away.

It opened its mouth, probably to scream, and, in a panic, I lunged forwards, ramming my shoulder into its chest, sending it and myself tumbling into the bedroom. I couldn't let it alert anyone, or anything, that might be listening. I scrambled to my feet and leapt on top of it, clamping my left hand over its mouth. The screwdriver—which sat heavy in my right hand—rose above my head before plunging down into the side of the thing's neck. It's desperate flailing intensified, scratching at my hands and sending its grasping at my face. I pulled the tool out of its neck and drove it in again. Again and again, I did this, three, five, ten times, until the thing's skin was cold and its struggling had long since ceased.

Without another thought, I got up and ran. I was covered in blood and had deep gashes on my hands and face, but it seemed like nobody had heard the struggle. I was able to make it out of the building and into my car without anyone seeing me. The sound of screeching tires marking my hasty exist.

So yeah, that was my first, but I'm sure you know it wasn't my last. I spent a long time questioning whether it really was some non-human thing, or if I had really lost the plot, but after a few weeks, I happened to see another one at the hardware store. I followed it into the car park and cracked it in the back of the head with the hammer I had bought just minutes before. It pantomimed pain and simulated cries of agony and begged me to spare the life it didn't have, until one more blow shut it up for good. There were plenty of others after that, of course. The next was a kid who— what was that noise?

Ah, the 6pm alarm. It sounds like visiting hours are over. I'd love to keep going, but we're out of time for today.

The guards say I'm going to die soon. I don't know if that's true, but if it is, I can't just let everything I've learned die with me. I need *someone* to know the truth. And I guess you drew the short straw. I'd say I'm sorry about that, but I doubt you'll appreciate the sentiment.

Thank you for listening to my story, or ... pretending to, at least.

A Bleak Day for All of Us

Hayley Sams

Levi died, and naturally, we were all devastated, but I had this feeling, like something wasn't adding up. How did the fire start? Why couldn't he get out in time?

Poor Ashley was there when it happened, the fire and wreckage. Not that I blamed her, but she hadn't spoken since.

I was supposed to be doing a eulogy, my first one … and hopefully my last, because I was no teacher. I could not stand in front of large crowds and give public speeches. What could you even say at a funeral about someone who was still supposed to be here?

Sometimes I wonder if Ashley saw more than just flames. When she looks at me with her wide and unblinking eyes, it feels as if she's seeing something else besides me, like a wall of bricks are separating us. I remember catching up with her the morning of the fire. She seemed happy, which was so refreshing considering she was usually a pretty mellow person. It was good to see her smile, Levi too. I remembered it had always been us three. Three teens sitting next to each other in class, squeezing together in photos and playing beer games when we were sixteen. Remembering this made me realise that even though Ashley and I have been friends for years, I didn't know that much about her. We only became friends because Levi's mum talked to him about his behaviour towards her and insisted, we make it up to her.

It was the day of the funeral; I had been a wreck all week. I woke up, laid out my suit, showered, put on my aftershave and cufflinks, and stood in front of the mirror. I told myself: *I got this*.

At the funeral, when everyone's heads were bowed, I gazed over at Ashley, sitting in the front row closest to the aisle She kept her distance from everyone. This was typical Ashley; she'd get upset and go off on her own.

BANG!

One of the large wooden doors swung open with a gust of strong wind, rattling the very foundation we stood upon. The service carried on, but I knew the guests felt the same sense of unease as I did.

When it was time for me to stand, everyone had turned to look at me like I was in a room full of programmed robots. As I reached the altar all I could picture was Levi's body burning slowly in that house. I opened my mouth and spoke.

'How to begin? I've been thinking very much about how I could address you all today and leave a lasting impression of Levi's legacy. Levi never struggled with putting words together. He always knew how to fill rooms with laughter, noise or chaos. His fire has gone out, but the ashes he leaves behind will forever hold that memory. Silence has a way of spreading. I think I can at least speak for myself when I say we don't speak the way we used to; some of us not at all. Grief changes you; sometimes it completely remakes who you are down to the bone.'

After I finished the speech, she sat there rolling her eyes and looked away from me as I walked back down the aisle to my seat. *What is her problem?*

After the service concluded, guests said their condolences outside the church. I watched Ashley. She had not cried, blinked, yelled, or shown any sort of emotion today. I knew I had to check on her. I walked up and gently whispered, 'Hello, Ashley.'

Strangely, whilst she didn't say anything, I smelt the lingering aroma of burnt ash. It made me question if she had gone back inside that night to save him. But lately I'd smelt it everywhere. Smoke in places where it shouldn't be. I thought it must have been grief, playing into my senses.

'Did you see him … die?' I murmured. The thought had lingered upon my subconscious since his death. I had thought she must've watched something so traumatic for her to completely shut down like this.

Finally, her eyes met mine with a sharp and perplexed look. She leaned close to the rim of my ear, and as her breath brushed against my lobe, she told me something that had spooked me.

'Let's go back inside,' said Ashley.

After arriving at the chancel and ignoring all the creaks in the floorboards, we stood at the altar, looking over Levi's coffin. The silence was eerie.

'You see this hand? This filthy hand is the reason he's dead.'

'What do you mean?' I asked her.

'Don't play dumb, you know what Levi did. The night he died was the last night that he will ever touch anyone!'

'I don't know what you're talking about,' I replied. 'Ashley, what do you mean?'

'After we'd become friends, Levi would come round to my house after you'd gone home. At first, it made me feel special, but then he would get in my bed and force me to do things I didn't want to do. The night of the fire I was in my bathroom, and I decided enough was enough. I pushed the candle on the bench and lit the carpet alight locking him in my room. I ran out of the house as soon as I could. I let him die.'

'Oh, Ashley, I had no idea.' I tried to take in what she said. She murdered him. He raped her. How had I missed all this?

'Liar! You had to know! You can't be that fucking oblivious.' She grabbed his burned hand and wrapped it around my mouth making it hard to breathe. Her grip was colder than the wooden floor beneath us.

'Wait! Please! Don't—' I blubbered as I tried to cry for help. Suddenly, I could no longer feel the warm ambience of the chapel's candles. Rather the cold bleakness of death. Before my eyes softly closed, I saw her grin.

'Now my secret will die with you,' she whispered. There is no longer an *us*.

Dolorum

Lachlan Leahy

What do you want from me? What more could you possibly want from me now? My hands and feet ache. Cuts and bruises coat my flesh from head to toe. My walls are covered in crimson and other bodily substances such as pus, excrement, and urine, some of which isn't even mine. Every room I walk into reeks of iron. It has gotten so bad that going outside feels funny to my nose, but that is simply because I smell the absence of blood. I'm surprised my neighbours haven't confronted me about it, let alone called the police.

How—how did this happen? I was healthy ten weeks ago. There wasn't anything wrong with me … No, I know exactly what happened. It was that fucking psycho outside the clinic. It was when he laid his hands on me, when he pulled out his knife and started cutting me. I didn't think about why he was attacking me. I just wanted him to stop. I can't remember how, but we eventually ended up grappling with each other on the road and ... well. I was lucky enough to have moved out of the way in time, but he wasn't.

Good.

Afterwards, due to the freak's actions, making my case for self-defence was fairly easy. So, I wasn't criminally charged. My cuts from that fight were still there, but despite them being a royal pain, that's all they were. I got back to my work the moment the trial concluded. I just wanted to take my mind off the fight and the freak. The whole thing left me perplexed. Why attack me? Why do any of this? I shouldn't have left it like that, but I did. I ignored what was happening, and it grew out of control.

It was small at first, small enough that I didn't know it was there. Just feelings of irritation towards someone, like a rude customer at work or a maniacal driver on the road. Nothing too big ... then it got worse. My temper worsened. I had to restrain myself before I started shouting at people. After that, it was the images. Jesus, the images. I couldn't get them out of my head—thoughts of injuring and mutilating people, sometimes outright killing them. It got so bad, so disgusting. I told my manager I wanted to take sick leave and clear my head.

I was granted a week's leave, but the images and irritations never faded. In fact, without anyone else to channel them towards, they turned their focus to the only one around: me. Every knife or razor in my house became a mental battleground between reason and urges. Every night gave me a vision of a potential death of my choosing. Every waking morning was a prayer that someone would come to the door so that I didn't have to worry about myself, the implications of which I didn't give thought to, like at the clinic. I just wanted an escape.

But no one came. I was alone with these images, and they were becoming enticing. Disgusting and repulsive, but still morbidly enticing, regardless, and that's when I first let it out.

The first urge I gave into came when I was shaving. I was looking in the mirror, but all I saw were missed whiskers and my repulsive face. Then it came, and my razor dug into my cheek. I remember shouting in pain and then throwing the razor across my bathroom. I applied pressure to the wound, and could only stare at myself in the mirror and ask:

'Why?'

My answer came to me soon after that. The following day, I went out to a pub with a mate. He saw my cut, and he suddenly changed. He smiled widely, his posture shifted, his demeanour changed.

He lowered his turtleneck shirt, revealing a deep cut across his neck, telling me.

'Here's your answer!'

I just looked at him, sickened, before a drunkard came over to our table. My recollection is largely blank regarding what happened next, but my next memory is of my friend gouging out the man's eyes, as if something possessed him to do it.

I bounced after that and went home. I tried to forget about it, but I knew I couldn't. I cut off contact with anyone outside my house aside from phone calls, but my impulses remained.

No.

Not mine, they are not my impulses, this is ... something else. The psycho from that day, maybe he caused it? No, that doesn't explain my friends' actions, outside of contrived coincidence. Is this some pandemic, s-some psychological phenomenon? I don't know, I don't know! I wasn't like this! I'm not like this! This isn't me! This isn't me! This is not me!

But then he arrived the next morning. He knocked on my door. A deliveryman is dropping off a package. It was normal. A normal occurrence, and then I opened the door so he could hand over the package. As he did, another image invaded my mind. I was slamming the door on his arm.

I didn't do it, but then something took over, and whatever it was, it slammed the door. It pulled the deliveryman inside as he yelled in pain. It grabbed a knife, silenced the man's pain, and continued playing with his corpse like it was a present.

How ... How did that happen? Why did I do that? I ... I had a dead man in my house. I murdered him. I want to say that something made me do it. I know something made me do it ... What made me do that? Why so randomly? No rhyme, no reason, no motive, just that fucking urge to kill that man.

Shit. Someone's gonna come looking for him, someone's gonna find out I did this. Even if I told them that something compelled me, they would think I'm insane, like that madman from before.

How long until they came searching for him? Six days? Six hours? Six minutes? That answer was six seconds, when someone else came knocking at my door. A colleague or policeman wouldn't be that quick to respond. A neighbour? ... Fuck. They probably heard him screaming. What do I do? I'm soaked in blood, and I can't clean up fast enough, so there was no way I could let him. But I didn't need to, due to my neglect to lock the door. The deliveryman's murder was more of a priority. The door opened up, and I heard disgusted gasping.

Several minutes later, I'm here with the deliveryman and neighbour's corpses lying at my feet. For some reason, I can remember my neighbour's murder this time. Every detail, every yell, every cut and every impact. Why was he different? Am I used to it by now? ... Maybe. That thought makes me feel numb, but then why did I attack him?

He was a threat. He would have informed the police.

My other neighbours probably heard the skirmish, likely both of them. They would have called the cops anyway.

Then why did you kill him?

... I don't know.

Maybe I can answer that.

I get off the couch and make my way to my bathroom, sliding open the door before immediately spotting my reflection in the mirror. Instinctively, I turn the light on.

Keep it off. I need you to see me.

I listen and turn it off. Approaching the mirror, I continue to stare at my reflection. With the dark lighting, I swear that half of my face belonged to someone else.

Grab your razor off the floor, and I will answer.

I listen and pick the razor off the floor. The man in the mirror smiles.

Dig into yourself.
I listen.

He awoke in a body bag and spent several moments trying to crawl out. Eventually, fed up with the outside-facing zipper, he tore a hole in it, finding himself in a compartment next to several dead bodies and a metallic drawer at his feet. Opening it and crawling out, he looked around the room for a reflective surface, but with little patience to look for something akin to a mirror, he settled on the metallic cabinet drawer he had crawled out of. In the reflection, he saw both his face and mine. As I looked at our wounds, he spoke.

To answer your question, 'Why did I attack him?' You did it because you chose to. Nothing more, nothing less. I didn't force you. I am every thought of violence you ever had, the desire to make people feel misery in both flesh and mind. When there is no agony and torment, I starve. You tried to make me starve. You tried to bury me, with little thought as to why I was there in your and every mortal's minds to begin with. I am of pain, and to you I say: Thank you for indulging me. You spoil me.

Passing Through

Terry Joseph

Jim took in all the details of his wife and two children's faces as they packed their picnic baskets and headed to the front door.

'Goodbye, Dad.'

'We love you.'

Jim forced a smile as he waved from the couch, the front door slowly creeping shut. A wave of heaviness rippled through his body. He retrieved a rope from a dusty basket in the garage, lugged it over his shoulder and climbed onto the kitchen dining table. Heaving it over a thick wooden beam, he tied it off and wrapped the noose around his neck before tiptoeing to the precipice of the tabletop.

He pondered how he got to this moment. He had kept a roof over his family's head, but he didn't have a lot of money or big ambitions. His wife had an optimistic passion for life, while he dreaded waking up to face each day. Still, despite dying inside, he did everything to be the best dad and husband he could.

Jim often felt insignificant, drowning in his father's lofty expectations. They were on speaking terms now that his dad had mellowed out, especially after the cancer diagnosis. But Jim couldn't help but look back at his strict militaristic upbringing as the catalyst for standing here. He tightened his grip on the rope as he hovered one foot forward into the empty space. As he felt his weight start to transfer forward, a magical sphere, the size of a bowling ball appeared next to him. It pulsed with dark purple energy before exploding into a mystical doorway. Through violet smoke, an arm extended out and ripped Jim within.

Jim awoke, lying on the ground. He frantically felt around his neck, but the rope was gone. He was helped to his feet by someone who looked exactly like him, but with an added ghostly blue aura surrounding them.

'Am I dead?' Jim said.

'Take a good look around,' his ethereal twin said.

Jim felt a rush of familiarity as his eyes perused his surroundings. It took him a few seconds to realise he was standing in his childhood bedroom.

'You wanted to know how you became the man you are, Jimmy?' the twin said.

'You know I hate that name, right? Only Dad calls me that.'

A young boy played with his action figures, quietly narrating the battle. His sister barged into the room, slamming the door behind her. She grabbed her dolls and joined the action, squealing and laughing as they played. The children froze as the bedroom door was hurled open, a burly man wearing army camo pants created an imposing figure in the doorway. Even though Jim was close to forty years old, seeing his dad in a fit of rage still petrified him.

'Get your ass out here now, Jimmy. I told you to play quietly!'

'But sir ...'

Jim's dad stormed the room, lifted the boy by the arm and dragged him out, before taking off his belt and whipping him. Jim clenched his fists as his fear turned to anger.

'Dad always went overboard with the punishment. This is what made me nervous, shy, reserved. People at school bullied me, called me a *weirdo* because I kept to myself and found it hard to make friends,' Jim said.

'Maybe he just wanted the best for his kids. Wanted to teach you to be disciplined, well-behaved, good members of society. Maybe his heart was in the right place, but his methods were wrong,' the twin said.

'The only thing I learnt from him was what *not* to do as a father,' Jim said.

The twin turned away and clicked his fingers, manifesting another magical door. The translucent figure passed through the portal with Jim close behind. As they exited, loud music started thumping, mixing with the sounds of cheers and laughter.

Teenagers littered the suburban backyard, all with alcohol bottles in hand. Groups congregated and chatted while others ran around. Some pushed each other into the pool.

'Underage drinking ... always ends well,' the twin said.

Everyone was in their own world, having a good time, until a silhouette of a boy appeared on the roof of the double-story house.

'Everybody, listen up!' the silhouette said.

Loud conversations turned to hushed murmurs as the boy gained everyone's attention.

'Twenty bucks says I can cannonball into the pool!'

Cheers erupted from the crowd.

'Who the heck is that guy?' a girl whispered to her friend.

Teenage Jim took five drunken steps back, hunched into a runner's stance and bolted towards the edge. As he leapt, a roof tile slipped under his foot, tanking his momentum. A sickening crack echoed as his legs hit the concrete. Teenagers screamed in horror.

'How could you be so careless?' the twin said.

'I was a boozed-up outcast. I wanted to be noticed,' Jim said.

'Well, you sure were after that.'

'Dad was so pissed at me when he got to the hospital. Did he ask how I was or question if I was in pain? No ... he only screamed how stupid I was, that I couldn't play soccer anymore with two broken legs.'

'The papers did say you were a promising rising star ...' the twin said. With a snap of his fingers, a new doorway appeared. This time the pair walked into a hardware shop.

'You've always loved working with your hands,' the twin said.

Jim walked down the aisle, hand grazing the timber and admiring the power tools.

'This was my dream job. I'm so glad Reginald gave me a chance to work here,' Jim said.

'And when Reggie passed away, you took over the business and learnt to be an amazing leader. You really listen and empathise with the staff. And you used those skills to become a great father too,' the twin said.

'I learnt that from Dad. He always came in half-cocked, screaming, dealing out punishment without knowing the facts. I always knew I'd do the opposite,' Jim said.

'Speaking of your dad ...' the twin said as he unveiled another portal.

On the other side, a woman was humming and swaying to a tune as she washed dishes. A young boy ran around the kitchen, holding a toy plane up high while making the appropriate whooshing sounds. The front door busted open as an overweight man came stumbling through. He knocked the toy plane out of the boy's hand and stomped on it with a chuckle. The boy stamped his foot and raised his fist. The man backhanded the child to the ground. He grabbed the boy's throat and lent his face down real close, breath reeking of booze.

'No use dreaming of flying, boy. You'll never leave this god forsaken town.'

'Is that boy ... Dad?' Jim said.

The scene shifted. Jim's dad was older and wearing military attire. Now he was the one standing over the drunk, fist raised.

'If you *ever* hit mum again, I will fucking kill you!' Jim's dad yelled.

'I never knew Dad had it so tough,' Jim whispered.

The vision dissipated. Memories of a younger Jim and his dad spending time together formed many scenes: kicking a ball, playing board games and being taught how to use power tools.

'When I think back, I can only remember the bad stuff. I forgot all of this,' Jim said.

'Where do you think your love of soccer and manual arts came from?' the twin said.

The memories disappeared and a new scene formed. Jim's dad sat at a desk elated, a pen in hand. In front of him laid a contract from a professional soccer team, they wanted Jim to sign to their youth squad. Before he could sign, his phone rang.

'Jim's hurt bad, you need to come to the hospital right now!' Jim's mother said.

'So that's why he was so pissed at me ... I had no idea,' Jim said.

'He kept the burden of what-could-have-been to himself.'

A new portal opened, but this one glowed with an angelic white light. As Jim went to pass through, he glanced down at a ghostly arm stopping him. When he looked up, the twin had morphed into his dad.

'Listen, Jimmy. I know I made a lot of mistakes, but I always wanted the best for you. Times get tough, but I never gave up, and neither should you. I wish things were better between us now. And I want you to know one last thing ... I'm proud of you, kid.'

Jim's dad walked into the bright white light—it exploded and engulfed the area, blinding Jim. As he refocused, he realised he was standing on the table in his home. As he took the noose off, he wanted to call his dad, but the phone rang first. After pulling it from his pocket, he heard his sister's shaky voice.

'It's Dad ... he's dead.'

City Without Shade

Ellie Holtby

The city is on fire this January. Baked concrete slowly roasts the nine-to-five commuters. UV rays violate my skin, kissing all over except for the pale triangles left by my plum-coloured bikini. It is our basset hound's first summer, and most of the time I find him in the bathroom, melting into the terrazzo floor. Ice cubes in his water dissolve to a tropical slobbery soup. We spend the days alone. Cleaning the bar cart or counting the red cars that drive by are our favourite pastimes whilst Henry is at work. That is until the painters show up.

Last month, the Queenslander next door was stripped naked. The sound of scaffolding clanging outside our bedroom wakes me one Monday morning and I look out my window to see the backs of two men in white caging the Queenslander in metal. I slump back into bed, pissed off at being disturbed, sleep in the city is already hard with all the honks, sirens and not-so-sober shouts that repeatedly soil our bedrooms' slumber. I doze until noon only waking when my basset's bladder begins to bulge and he nudges me to get up. I grab my pack of cigarettes, open the front door and sit on the steps, analysing how many pearls the succulents have gained overnight.

'Hello there,' I hear someone say. Looking over, I see the basset reaching his paws as high as he can along the short fence as one of the painters scratches the top of his head.

'Oh, sorry about him, he's too friendly. Lugsy, get down,' I say.

'He's all good … what is he? If you don't mind me asking?'

'A basset hound. They're basically bloodhounds with dwarfism,' I say.

'Hmmm,' he responds. He is tall and lanky and his skin-kissed even more than mine. A silver earring sits in his left ear and a thick brown beard blankets the perimeter of his lips as he speaks.

'You're painting the house then?' I ask.

'Yeah, my boss and I.'

'How long will that take you both?'

'Ahh, we estimate about two weeks for each side so about eight weeks tot—sorry, where are you from?'

'Oh, I'm from the UK, up north. I left when I was two, just got the accent from my parents.'

'Knew you were a northerner, I'm from Southampton.'

'Star-crossed lovers we shall be then,' I joke. He smiles, his dark eyes swallowing me whole—only to spit me back out, saliva bubbles fizzling on the hot cement. I stand to go back inside, not wanting to interrupt him from his work any longer.

'I'm Matt, by the way,' he says.

'Charlotte,' I reply, 'and that's Lugsy.' I turn around, ashing my cigarette butt against the banister, its smoke drifting up into the city's already screaming ozone.

'Guess whose home,' I say to Lugsy as I hear Henry fumble the front door key into the lock.

'My loves!' he says with arms outstretched for an embrace.

I hug him gently; he smells of champagne and Kerastase kisses again.

'Busy day at the salon?' I ask.

'Oh yeah, the girls and I were run off our feet. Then bloody Amanda forgot to put the order in, so we ran out of toner halfway through the shift.' He pours himself a scotch from the freshly polished bar cart and I stir the bolognese that is beginning to stick to the bottom of the pot.

'There's scaffolding next door now. They must finally be getting that place painted. Did you see anyone there?' he asks.

'No, Lugs and I just stayed cool inside today, never went out there. Do you want any garlic bread with this?'

'Ooh, yes please, baby.'

'Okay, well, would you mind getting it out of the freezer for me then?'

'Sure thing, oh, did I mention we had a new girl start?'

I place the garlic bread into the 180-degree oven and close the door a little too hard behind it. 'No, you didn't,' I say. 'Is she any good?'

'Yeah, I think she will turn out really good, she's a friend of Kaitlyn's—you remember Kaitlyn? The one that did your blow-dry for my sister's wedding.'

'Yes, I remember Kaitlyn,' I snap, the small searing kitchen beginning to squeeze me now.

'Yeah, so we will just have to wait and see, but I have high hopes. Anyway, how was your day, baby?'

'Have you followed her on Instagram yet?' I clench my jaw. Keeping my eyes on the watery sauce that I haven't stopped swirling.

'No, why would I?'

'I dunno, just asking.'

'Don't start this again.'

'I'm not starting anything. Dinner will be ten minutes, were you going to pour me a drink too?'

'Yes, of course, what would you like?'

'I'll just have some of the leftover wine your mum got me—it should be in the fridge door.'

'Sure thing.'

'One of the painters next door is from Southampton.'

'Where's that again? Near where you're from?'

'No, the opposite end.'

'Ah, how cool, so you did get talking to them then?'

'Yeah, Lugsy just went over to say hello and we had a brief chat.'

'Lovely. They must be fuckin' hot painting this time of year.'

'Yeah—I think I might ask him for his Instagram account,' I say, knocking back my last drop of birthday wine.

The dash of his car is littered with dehydrated receipts and scattered paintbrushes. I'm not sure which part of the windscreen to place the note, in fear that it won't be found. He is no longer anywhere in sight, presumably painting the far side of the Queenslander now.

I lift one of the Hilux's stiff windscreen wipers. A gust scatters a few brown leaves as I tuck the note beneath it with a clunk.

The fence has been painted a charcoal grey; I look up briefly as I turn to head back to my car parked around the corner. Our old bedroom window—the one that used to let too much noise in. For a second, I think I hear Kaitlyn's snores somersaulting through the city air. But then I have to run, the clanging of paint tins nearing closer behind me.

Denial, Anger, Bargaining, Depression and Acceptance

The Legitimate President of Suburban Australia, the dis-Honourable Dr. Sam Maker—Astronaut

Taking stock of the ciggie-butt collection expanding by my front steps—then adding to it—I briefly wonder whether the wine's painted itself over my smile yet.

Fuck it.

Spinning and grinning, I take further stock of the expansive human collection in front of me, and—adding myself to it—begin waxing nonsensical about the environmental merits of *Industrial Society and its Future*. It almost blows up in my face when the trust fundees of the world unite and counter with the *Communist Manifesto*, but they're swiftly supressed. The same savage nobilities skip across Orwell and Huxley without reservation, while I freely admit to preferring the latter's utopia (I was raised epsilon). Eventually an amateur (online) historian (Nazi) brings up the possibility that perhaps not *all* of Adolf's policies had been terrible—but it's a little out of Mein Kampfort zone.

'I guess even evil people can have … good ideas?' I concede, 'broken clocks en' such—'

'And good ideas can still be evil!' someone furiously quipped as I fled the front.

That they can … the rioja seemed to say, and I topped myself up in solemn acquiescence to such higher truths.

The minutiae of bitcoin crops up by the bog, clogging my inbox with shit I'll never watch and probably forget to wipe. We inevitably agree gambling our dole on code seems infinitely preferable—and infinitely more profitable—than honest work in our post-retirement, post-housing, *post-apocalyptic* society.

Petty theft rears its pretty head next, but I shut it down—much like facial and gait recognition did for me—instead professing my strict adherence to what I lovingly referred to as the pleb diet. Appropriately, we've moved to the kitchen, and I quietly pray the pantry moths don't hear me or I'll starve.

'I shit you not, I got forty kilos of lentils and split peas off the internet for thirty-five bucks! Potatoes are two-fifty a kay-gee, and I mince discount mushies to supplement meat.'

Everybody laughs.

I think they think I'm joking.

'Nah serious—I been eating the same shep pie for a week, one meal a day—your gold! I credit this system for tonight's wine and tomorrow's hangover!' This gets a few laughs and more than a few looks of genuine concern.

We move on to the big five—

'—Like the shit you're not supposed to bring up on a first date? Politics, religion ee-tee-cee?'

More laughter.

'No, no! The *big* five.' A cumulonimbus of bong smoke insists.

'You can't *will* meaning into existence by repeating it, ya ding-dong.'

'I'm gettin' there! Fuckenell! Y'see—it's—well, ahh—*it's the big five*! Lions, elephants, rhinoceor-i, giraffes, hippos—'

'—Oh yes *the* big five how silly of me!'

We're yelling at each other across the kitchen now. That thing's happened where we've become accustomed to an abrasively high level of music cause everyone's given up remembering how simple it is to turn down.

It doesn't help we've perched up damn near on-top the thing.

'*Mate*, all I'm sayin' is—giraffes don't really put the fear of God in me like the other four do!'

'But they're large! They're dangerous! You've seen 'em fight!'

'*Egg—zactly* brother! I have seen 'em fight— swinging necks en' shit—it's ludicrous! That's the crux of it! A cheetah or somethin' should have its spot.'

'Yeah-nah, I get what you're sayin' but cheetahs ain't that big though!'

'Yeah *but*—they're *dangerous*, they're *scary*, they *take out gazelles*. I mean, fuck—I'd take a giraffe ove'ra cheetah any day!'

'Yeah, but it's the *BIG* five! Not—*which one's a worse surprise*—five!'

'Well fuck, I'd assumed it was synonymous for danger! You lead with a lion, they're not that big comparatively—but they're fucken dangerous! Even *BIG* as in, like, the most known five!'

'Well, if it was pure danger—we'd be talking mosquitoes!'

'True, malaria's no joke.'

'Dengue!'

'AIDS!'

Everyone laughs.

Somehow all this suffering and death is hilarious.

In the morning my head is suffering and death. I try to find some Valium, but I'm worried I'm still drunk enough to black out and do something incredibly stupid if I indulge.

I sit at the computer instead; start to write.

It's good stuff, I think.

But then again, maybe it isn't—*who gives a fuck*.

Maybe it's the same set of libated rubbish everyone carries on with. I'm mildly concerned the future reader'll think we're a somewhat unhinged and insensitive bunch, perhaps even borderline psychotic (not that some aren't), but I guess I'll just trust you to see the wood from the trees—or however that stupid fucken turn of phrase occurs.

Fuck it.

I take the Valium.

A Panadol.

Some aspirin.

And a lonely tramadol I found loose in the overflowing medicine bucket.

After all, why not?

I've always believed in moderation, and my

hangover required immediate moderating. But the drugs offer no immediate relief.

Juice!

I'm onto a winner now, but as I hobble up the street it doesn't quite feel like it. I round the corner and am nearly cleaned up by a P-plater in a Golf (the worst kind). I curse the both of us drawing the ire of the post-congregation congregation huddled on the church lawn in front of me.

Fuck.

'Morning!'

Fuck!

Their disapproval of my life choices is palpable.

'That maniac nearly killed me!'

Their eyes keep burning.

'He had a river to the sea bumper-sticker?'

Salvation. The crowd goes wild.

'*Those people*, don't care about anybody!'

'*Bastards!*'

I really hate to invoke a genocide, but I'm too tender to cope with their collective condemnation at the moment.

'God bless,' I wave and continue walking, '*deez nuts.*' I finish under my breath.

In the servo, the aircon's genuinely freezing.

Noice.

It's the first thing that's gone right today, and I'm pleased, but not as pleased as the attendant—who's fucken stoked, apparently.

'G'day mate, how are we this morning!' And before I can even think, 'What can I help you with today, bud?'

'Uhhh ...'

'I see you're eyeing off the sports drinks, big night uh? Well might I recommend ...'

He said more—*a lot more probably*—but I gave up listening as quick as he'd started. His beverage selection is immense, but I know from experience what to get. The one with the most vitamins, the one that tasted the most shit, the one that stained my mouth, and all its faculties, the most vibrant hue of blue.

I get two.

It's just that kind of day.

The bloke is still going by the time I hit the counter, so I sum up some of my most convincing AUSLAN. Miraculously, it works, and as I turn to leave I hear him talking to the woman behind me in the line.

'Poor fella's deaf *and* retarded, just signed my cat goodnight.'

Of all the fucken ...

'How dare you!' I hear her scream.

I pick up the pace, crossing the street immediately, mostly to lay down some distance, but also to avoid bothering the Presbos' again.

What a day.

I keep trudging away, avoiding their eyes—which no longer burn of hate, having shifted more towards a glowing ember of solidarity. This freaks me out even more.

I notice movement in my peripheral and see an arm shoot up into wave—a wave that begins walking towards me.

Fuck.

He makes it halfway across the street before almost getting slumped by a Tarago.

'Sorry!'

Old mate, who's now so pale he's almost translucent, crosses himself and wobbles back to his flock.

The driver turns to me.

'HELL—O!—I,' she points at herself, 'WAS BE—HIND YOU,' pointing at me now.

Fuck me ...

I feign ignorance.

Shake my head.

Keep walking.

None of it works. She's rolling beside me

pointing, shouting and over-mouthing her words at me out the window.

'AS I,' pointing at herself, 'WAS SAY—ING, THAT MAN,' thumb over shoulder, 'WAS BE—ING VE—RY RUDE, TO YOU,' at me, 'I DON'T KNOW IF YOU,' at me again, 'HEARD,' at her ears, 'HIM.'

The penny drops.

'*Ohmygawd!* I'm sorry—I didn't mean! *Ohmygawd!*'

I look at her, scowl, and shake my head.

She floors it.

Tyres shriek.

Bitumen flicks.

The *Little Wizard on Board* sticker disappears round a corner.

'I'MM SoOooOOOooRRrY!' echoes down the street.

A smirk ripples across my face.

All's well that ends well.

Except it hasn't—

'Some flamin' galahs' out today, bloomin' heck!' a young man in his Sunday best— complete with Akubra—says to me in his best, un-ironic, Alf Stewart impression.

'Yeah mate, I'll say.' I do say. To him.

'Probably another one of those pro-Palestine nut-jobs, only good at driving *EXPLODING* cars!' he cracks himself up.

I shake my head in disbelief, but he's too focussed on not shitting himself laughing to notice.

Fuck it.

'Yeah, I'm absolutely sick of 'em,' I say, 'like don't they know it's been Israel's land for thousands of years?'

He stops laughing, taking to vehement nodding and affirmative grunts instead.

'Tens of thousands even,' I add.

There's fire in his eyes and brimstone on his breath now. 'Too right, cobber! Flogs like that reckon those terrorists are right to roll in an' rape an' murder like it's their false-Gods' given right! Actin' like they bloody own the place—entitled cunts!' he finishes—momentarily forgetting where he is and looking around sheepishly.

'I know, mate, it's ridiculous!' I say. 'It's just like what the crown did to the Indigenous peoples here!'

His eyes widen.

'Well now I don't ...' he stammers.

'Nah, I'm just kiddin', cobber,' I say.

A relieved smile creeps onto his face.

'Nah, about everything,' I continue. 'From the

river to the sea, buddy. Fuck Israel. Fuck the crown. And fuck you.'

The five stages of grief flash across his features.

Denial.

Anger.

Bargaining.

Depression.

Acceptance.

And he rolls right on through again; finally coming to rest somewhere between denial and anger.

But I've already accepted it and moved on.

And a smirk ripples across my face.

GRWM: To Leave the
World Behind

Eva Timmermans

7:00am

I long for a life I have never known. A life that belonged to my ancestors before me. Of balance; light and dark, sun and moon, life and death. My heart races as my eyes snap open, I hear the familiar screech of my alarm. For me, sleep equals happiness— my only chance to live through my subconscious. I dream of a primitive life in nature, a life that the tangled roots of my DNA still remembers. A hunger my great-grandmother had instilled in me when I inherited her journals. I translated and read her journals religiously. I experienced epiphanies, lived vicariously through her and reflected on my own, uninspired existence. She would have created the most original GRWM content—Get Ready With

Me—the modern-day journal, for the internet to devour and discover the rawness of uncolonised life. As I brush my teeth and shake out my bed hair, I wonder if there would ever be a time when the human race forgets its lineage. I eye the bag in my wardrobe, packed and ready to go but I am not ready. I don't know if I will ever be ready or brave enough to leave the world behind.

8:32am

A university education, an office job, a white-walled apartment: the construct of comfort is agonisingly intolerable and void of meaning. Looking around I see the familiar sea of bent heavy heads staring down at phones on the train. The disconnection to my peers strengthens my dissatisfaction with 'normal' life. I ponder my own affinity to nature and the non-human ...

Journal Entry:

> *Wisdom of the ages, passed to me from my mother, from our ancestor's past. Knowledge from the Earth is a sacred currency and knowledge must be earnt through time and*

dedication. I am speaking about today, my sixteenth birthday, a monumental occasion for me as a woman coming of age and earning my place. My family couldn't have been prouder of me today during the celebration of my passage to adulthood and my decision ceremony where I chose to be a guardian of a sacred animal: the whale. During my life, I will be a warrior for the whales. It was an honour for me to be accepted by the elders into this guardianship. Imagine, what it would be like to have a heart as mighty as the whale.

11:07am

Ugh ... only two hours into my workday. This is the most pain I have ever endured, the feeling of having your soul sucked from you like a mosquito finding a juicy ankle artery. Eight hours a day. Five days a week. How can this even be considered living? Technically, I am still breathing and my heart still beating but every cell in my body is screaming at me to flee ... But I am paralysed. I look around the office space at the dull, but familiar faces and the time, it's not even midday yet. I tilt my head skyward—all I see is the ceiling. The water stain from last month's plumbing drama is still evident. I close my eyes and imagine the ceiling collapsing around me and a brooding storm washing me away in a flood of freedom.

Journal Entry:

> *The thunder cracks in the sky and is illuminated by lightening. I cannot sleep for my sister is fretful and requires constant attention during storms. I couldn't believe it when an elder told me to be home early for she sensed a storm coming. Alas, she was right, and my gathering excursion was interrupted by the rumbles in the sky. It had been such a magnificent morning. Turquoise ocean lapping on the hot sand, only a gentle sway of the palm trees, the palms which are now parallel to the horizon on account of the fierce winds.*

Sometime During Lunch

'Geez, you're a good girl. Must be trying to lose weight are ya, darl? You're already too skinny, wouldn't worry about a diet.'

I catch a strong waft of what's-his-face's putrid body odour. Why does he always have to make a comment about my food and body? My simple lunch consisting of real food, apparently categorises me as on a 'diet' these days. Why shouldn't I listen to him though? Clearly the pinnacle of human health, with his beer gut and uncontrollable sweats from taking the stairs. Why am I being condemned for choosing to source my food, real food, from the earth? I didn't always use to feel like an outsider but lately I feel a deep yearning to be removed from this society. Why am I the one feeling like an outcast when so many thrive in this environment? My thoughts are out of control as the embers of my anger flares again, sparked by questions I'll never stop asking. I glance up from my lunch and look at the faded poster on the break room wall: Live, Love, Laugh. I want to scream.

Mid-Afternoon

While at the copy machine, I notice two of my colleagues exchange sombre words while pointing at their screens. I peer over and catch the title of the article: 'Female Fatalities: two women died in the crosshairs of public brawl.' I hurry to my desk to read the article. Two women, friends. Shot down in the prime of their lives through no fault of their own. I have so many questions that the article leaves unanswered. How did they live their lives? Do they have regrets? Only two people can answer my questions, but they are voiceless in the matter. My chest tightens and my breath quickens. Selfishly, I can't help but reflect on my own meaningless life in the wake of their tragedy. I fear I am wasting away, and my fate is one braided in regret.

The news rocks me to my core, but the knowledge that I will be going home soon to be alone calms me. I am counting down the seconds on the desktop clock. I wonder what it is exactly that I looking forward to going 'home' to. An empty, sterilised apartment ...? Only to repeat this loathsome routine again tomorrow? This cannot be my life. But it is my life— the one I chose to pursue. What have I become? The answer looms and lingers around me like a predator stalking its prey. I am too cowardly to face it head on, but I know that if I don't, I will die from exposure. If I go out on my own, do I even have a chance? The what ifs are endless but what I do know for certain is that I can no longer endure these conditions that so many thrive in. I do not accept the terms that were agreed upon. I will not be misled by the false promises offered by westernisation again.

Almost Home Time

I know what I must do, the time on my desktop

reads 4:59pm. I've waited too long. I've waited for the right time, a signal, a sign, but none came. Perhaps I wasn't looking for the right one? Maybe it was there all along? A reason to live.

10, 9, 8, 7, 6, 5, 4, 3, 2, 1: Goodbye.

Who needs time anyway. I mean tick tock time. It is just a human construct and is not needed where I am going. All I need is the kind if time the sun keeps— slow, patient, endless ... I jump on the travel app and quickly book the flight; this may very well be one of the last times I ever use my phone. Good riddance!

I bound up the stairs to my apartment like a migrating salmon and grab the one bag I will be needing for my trip, a bag that has been packed for years, waiting. My one bag, holding just the essentials for a trip home, and I mean *home* in every sense. The home of my great-grandmother and her mother before her. A place where I can realise my longings and appreciate the gift of life, of instinct and impulse, unrestrained and untamed. I am finally going home to plant my feet in the Earth and nourish my mind, body and soul.

The journey itself is ordinary—baggage, customs, transfers—but for once, the destination means everything. When I arrive, I settle on a temporary location. No need to get too established. Tides, winds and seasons change, then so must I.

The view is like nothing I have ever seen before. Better than any 'wish you were here' postcards and, let's be real, I am very glad that there isn't anyone here. Sitting on the shore, I start to fashion a fishing basket of sorts from the local plant life as described to me in my great-grandmother's journals, watching the waves slowly crash onto the sand. The ocean is a transcendent being and I know it will be a peaceful and fearsome friend of mine in the moons to come. The shimmering sunbeam on the horizon makes me smile. The little avalanche of sand that my footprints leave behind makes me smile. The dominant sound of the wind in the trees and the chattering birds makes me smile. I cannot remember the last time I genuinely smiled. The comforts that Westernisation has to offer won't lure me in again with their false promises—this, I vow.

I am free.

Wails From the Deep

Maisy Robson

Death seemed to surround my family. It was only fitting the cycle ended that way.

I remember passing the graveyard. It was one of the more dismal stretches of the journey. There were no neat rows, no flowers, nor names etched into stone. Just rusted carcasses, half-buried, sagging beneath centuries of silt—memories of war jutting out from a desolate plain. Nothing grew there anymore. We never lingered. Only drifted silently.

We had completed this trip every year with the entire Humphrey family for as long as I could remember. But this was our last. We had always travelled north with the changing seasons, but the heat had grown unbearable. So, we decided to move south. Permanently. Only, there were less of us this year. Mama said some of the family moved to a new neighbourhood. But her words were thin and fishy.

Now I was older, I noticed the wary glances shared between the adults. The extra wrinkles that swam along Mama's forehead. The hushed voices: the ones coated in terror that would rattle in the background whilst I looked over the young ones. I noticed the missing were not one or two—no, entire bloodlines had disappeared out of the blue.

I think we slipped passed the City of Gurang next, but it had looked different. Once, it had been magnificent: collections of castles that towered over us like a rainbow barrier, dividing us from the red mountains beyond. We never went too close; we didn't have to. It was probably visible from the stars. But it had been redecorated in shades of bone and ash. Over half of it had been reduced to skeletal remains; jagged silhouettes gnawed down and splintered like a shattered ribcage. Development, they said. Yet, the locals had fled.

And in their place came the strangers.

They were ... odd looking, that's for sure. Small, narrow-hipped things with slick, dark skins, giant glassy eyes, and grotesquely oversized feet. I couldn't help but stare. They carried metal shells on their backs that hissed and gurgled like some irritated parasite. Where they fascinated me, they terrified my grandmother. She would stare too, but it was with a haunted and distant glare. She spat curses at them as we passed—foreigners, devils, desecrators. Mama too, yanked me back whenever I drifted too close, trying to catch the tails of their strange language.

I didn't understand why they hated the strangers so much. Maybe because they were so unusual, so unknown. Maybe because even Grandmother, the ferocious war hero she was, seemed to shrivel in their presence. It irritated me. I was almost an adult, and my parents were still bound in their bubble-wrapped ways. There was always some rule to break:

'Don't get too close to that', 'don't make too much noise', 'don't stray too far'.

Don't! Don't! Don't!

They worried too much. But curiosity is a tide, and tides are hard to control.

The last memory I can recall was travelling through Phantom passage. A vastness that stretched beyond boundaries. Where strange shadows resided in the sky, casting eternal night over the path. Grandma told us ghost stories, warning us to hold our breath else the shadows might hear. Though I knew them to be tales, to keep the younger ones at bay, I would secretly strain to hold mine—just in case.

It would be a lie to say the trip was completely safe. Mama said other travellers had been snatched up and sold piece by piece. Uncle said it had already happened to our cousins, the Baleens. Perhaps—I hadn't seen them in years. But Mama was such a fusser—we completed the trip every year, and nothing ever happened to us. What if these were JUST stories; shells of truth distorted by fear?

Tendrils of shrouded sunlight would sometimes slip through the veil as we travelled along the passage. I remember how it illuminated the strangers sauntering by the shadows in the sky. I remember, under the cover of the dimness, how my curiosity excited me. How I began to stray from the herd. I remember how, for a moment, I was free ...

And then I was sheltered under Mama's arms once more. Her voice broke through the darkness.

'Marina, for the sake of this family, stay in the shadows!'

I huffed and glanced towards the strangers, growing further away as Mama dragged me back towards the others.

'This entire trip you have been ringing my head in. Can you just do what you're told for a while longer.'

My eyes never met hers, only watched the shifting shadows, needing to know what they were, why the strangers were there. Why couldn't I? I had played by her rules for too long. Whether I was agitated from the trip, or had finally found some stupid courage to channel, I breached.

'No! I can't do this anymore. I'm an adult, please just let—'

I heard her jaw clench; the scarred, blemished skin stretching and squeaking along the bone.

'Keep your voice down!'

Her eyes grew wide with something unsettling, as if a nightmare had crawled across them. Deafening silence descended upon us. Not from our quarrel but from ... something else.

'Just—you'll understand when you're older, when you have your own family,' she hushed, ushering me deeper into the dark.

'You still don't get it! I don't—I want to be free! Away from this family!'

I fled. I remember the immediate regret.

How guilt had called out, telling me to look behind. But as I did, where I expected to see Mama on my tail, furious and seething, a kraken-sized form thundered down from above. Its colossal force sent me rolling backwards as it imploded into the earth. Shards of sand, stone and soot whipped at me, carried on the winds from its impact. The faint shrill of Mama's voice wilted through the atmosphere, like a sorrowful, haunting farewell.

At some point, I finished tumbling. I searched back, blinking away the dust, and saw a pale stormy wall. The landscape and passage had disappeared. I called out to Mama. To anyone. Nothing roared back.

What was that thing? It was as if one of the shadows from above had collapsed and was chasing away, growling and shrieking like some feral, hungry beast. It mustn't have seen me. Luckily. But if it had seen the others ...

The twirling in my mind slowed. My throat seared in panic. My heart pounded with dread. Why couldn't I have just stayed put. At least I would still be with them. My family. Oh Mama. I am sorry.

I looked up, as if praying to the sun that appeared in absence of the shadow creature, and saw one. A stranger, not too far away. What if they weren't demons, but saviours? They could help! Maybe they saw what happened? I hurried towards them, crying out for aid. I had to trust them.

They turned to me, stunned. Fascinated. My strides steadied, my bravado diminishing as a familiar sinking feeling consumed my gut. Their arm extended towards me. An offering of help. I thought I had been right about them, that I was safe. And so, as the last sip of air fizzled out of my lungs, I leapt, past the stranger, and broke through the boundary of the water's surface.

Everything was one vast breath of blue—the sky a shimmering echo of my home's own endless hue. I looked around eagerly, hoping my family had surfaced too.

A piercing crack split the sea air, and I felt a sharp, agonising jab in my back. I reeled around in haste. I saw the shadow monsters that, from the surface, stretched high above the ocean with rigidity, painted in the colours of my skin and blood. Painted by the gallows that suspended the entire Humphrey family above. All dead. Below them, a giant net overflowed with neighbours and friends I had known. I cried out, waiting for Mama to sing her song back to me. But I only heard the dribble of her blood as it slapped the water's surface. Something from within me stirred as the truth came crumbling down. Mama had been right, they all had. I had been too oblivious to listen. I whipped back towards the stranger, the sting of my back bleeding past my skin and into my soul. Cheated. Disheartened. Disappointed. I looked deep into the eyes of the stranger. They were as empty as the abyss. Devoid of the light I once craved. I stared deeply into that void, before expelling a final wail and letting darkness claim me, like it had my ancestors.

I am not angry. I am patient. I have swallowed gods, cradled continents and now I hold the slow, acrid dust of destruction. As reefs die and currents shift, I speak in tides to those who listen—children, lonely researchers, my kin, leaving stories and warnings in shells and wrecks. I am not a metaphor, or a muse. I am a mirror. And although I am wounded, I am alive. My memory will outlast you. When nothing of you is left but echoes along the breeze, will it all have been worth it? I have produced megalodons and krakens, still, you do not grasp the power of the ocean. How dare you wrong me. Will you ever listen? Will you ever learn?

The Calf or Huí Guāng Fǎn Zhào

Ella Woodborne

For you, little one, who fought until the very end.

I had truly hoped you'd make it through the night. You arrived to me as a sack of misshapen bones, awkwardly assembled beneath the loose bind of your coat of freckled black and white, still soft from the fluids of your mother's womb. Your hooves had hardly congealed when you came stumbling from the back of the neighbour's truck, knees twice as wide as your forelegs and hindlegs slick with bloodied faecal matter. You hardly made it onto the bed of hay I laid for you in the barn, tucked away from the wind in the corner of the grey cinderblock construction, with its roof of corrugated iron so old, corroded holes around the bolts permitted speckled glimpses of the cloudless sky.

Your neck was hardly strong enough to lift your head to take me in, a tall, two-legged stranger who regarded you with concern equal to the wariness with which you regarded me. I'm not even sure you could see me through the milky patches of white tissue over your eyes, like the imprints of cloud wisps upon your sweet brown irises.

It elicited within me something some may call basic empathy, but it was more. Somewhat indescribable, the feeling was a deep and primitive one that we women feel deep in our chest—this *feeling*, more powerful than hunger and thirst, to protect and to nurture. Be it the hen in her laying box, settled over unfertilised eggs, or the fox coiled around the kits in her den, we share the desire to take the small and innocent into us, swaddle them in our warmth, and keep them there until they are grown and fat.

You were very skinny. Devoid of a sucking reflex, you refused to take to the teat, though I don't blame you. No one would want to suckle from cold silicone. I resorted to rubbing the milk mixture along your gums, trying to have you swallow a mouthful, even just lick your lips—anything to prove you wanted to live. Forcing that syringe down your throat felt so cruel I scarcely had the strength to pry your mouth open and push it past your grey, rough tongue.

I am a childless and educated woman, and logic knew you were not mine, but filaments of code in my mammalian cells know only a simple equation: all babies need milk, you were hungry, and I had a bottle.

Admitting defeat, I let your head fall onto my lap and stroked your forehead, your ears, your neck, just like your mother should have done. With my head resting against the wall, watching the sunset through the gap in the barn door, I heard the approach of footsteps on gravel. My mother poked her head through with her greying brows knitted.

'How are you doing, Bub?' she asked.

'I'm fine, Mama, thanks.'

'And the little guy?'

'Hardly sucking.'

'The neighbour said the mother isn't even bellowing for him,' she said.

I looked at you with your wide eyes and your glistening nose, and I could feel your exhaustion in the weight of your head upon my denimed thighs.

'She really didn't call for him at all?' I asked.

'Not once.'

You looked most poorly on the second day, having hardly unfolded from the furled ball of knobby knees and protruding vertebrae you fell asleep in. We took you to the yard so you could doze beneath the sun, and we hoped the warmth of the early spring breeze might carry away whatever pestilence lived within you. But not even the stirring of the gum leaves nor the warble of the magpies roused you as you lay curled in the puddles of midday sunlight. You refused the teat again, but I couldn't bring myself to force the syringe down, so my mother did it instead. There was a confidence in the way she pulled you under her arm, hand supporting your chin—a knowing gained only through experience. While she fed you, she smiled; she had the *feeling* too. Feed, keep warm, grow. I sat beside you, cooing your praises as you managed gurgled swallows.

Your third day was the turning point. In the pale dawn light, you lifted your head to greet me with broad ears perked. I balanced your head on the mound of my chest and held the syringe to your nose, your lips parted, and you took the milk in small but determined mouthfuls. We fed you about five times throughout the day. In the afternoon, you trembled as you rose, but you stood.

My stepdad, brutish and cross-armed, despite his characteristic pessimism, broke into a thin smile. 'He might just make it.'

As the world quieted into dusk, you'd brought yourself to sit beside me, so I lay on the grass with arms open to you. Flopping against my side, you fell asleep, and I held your frame close to mine to keep you warm. The *feeling* hummed in my chest as you slept for half an hour, only awaking when the dog came to lick the milk residue from your muzzle. You took a final glance to the setting sun, rose from the earth, and made your way to bed.

I should have known it at that moment. The way you gazed at the sky, alight with its vibrant oranges and pinks and purples, and the sun perched atop the undulating horizon, it seemed like you were drinking in every detail of it, like you knew it was the last thing you'd see. I'm not sure how much you could see of it, but in that moment, when the horizontal slits of your irises met mine, I knew you could see enough to know it was beautiful.

When I came to wake you on the fourth day, you did not raise your head to look at me. Your ears were limp. Your nose was cold. Your legs, unfurled from their safe positioning against your abdomen, were straight and stiff.

There was an uprooting in my chest, like the *feeling* which had stitched itself into the fascia of my rib cage was being torn from me, fibre by fibre. The concrete of the barn felt cold as I collapsed by your side, my tears eroding furrows down my cheeks as you regarded me with your eyes, empty of all light. How I wished you'd blinked.

My anger began to rise like the waves of a great sea storm, first directing itself at my neighbour for bringing you to me so late. Too late. Then I blamed your mother for rejecting you, whether she did it out of selfishness or because she knew you were already gone when you were born.

I blamed myself too, telling myself that I should have done more. But I'd no idea when I tucked you into bed last night, with the milk already mixed in solution. The bottle is still full and cold on my kitchen counter.

My stepfather came to collect you for the burial, tight-lipped and silent. The dog did not wag her tail. Prying my hands from you, slow tears trailed down her cheeks as my mother held me, assuring me that I'd done all I could. With her heart space flush against mine, she patted my back and tried to soothe the grief with soft whispers. She knew this feeling too.

Amongst the Tibetans, they say *Huí guāng fǎn zhào.* It means something like, 'The final radiance of the dying sun' and refers to when the sun has set, but still lights up the sky with its golden fire reflecting off the bottom of the clouds. Medical practitioners say that before people pass, they are often gifted a day or two of energy before their demise. They feel more energetic, more optimistic, like they're getting better.

But they're not.

Whether it's cancer or an infection, whatever enemy the body is fighting wins. The immune system concedes, and signals to the rest of the body's tissues, *Don't bother keeping your reserves. We don't need them anymore.* So, the body stops trying to heal itself, and instead, donates its remaining energy to the enjoyment of its final hours—to stroll, dance, or behold a sunset one last time. The dying sun burns bright until the very end, and then, after its last luminous flash, it's gone.

I'm glad you spent your final few hours beneath the sun, little one.

I know I was never a substitute for your mother, nor you a substitute for the children I do not yet have, but for those three days my cells did not differentiate us by species. It was simple. You were hungry, and I had milk.

I don't know when it came for you, but I hope you didn't notice when you stopped inhaling. I hope you were warm and oblivious, and that your belly was full when it stopped rising. I hope that despite your blindness, you were overwhelmed by the beauty of the fields you were dreaming of, abundant with bovine friends and loving mothers with full udders of cream.

I don't know where you are now, little one, nor if you can remember me wherever that may be, but I want you to know, it was a pleasure loving you until the very end. To be honest, I was scared for you, but also for myself—we are both just knitted flesh and braided veins after all. I saw within you what lies within me, in all of us, of fur, feather, or fin—a fear of the end. Separated by all means of evolution, there was a recognition of each other as living beings, united in one suspended moment against the vast backdrop of eternity. To witness each other, facing the evitable mortality of our lives, in shared understanding.

I see you, your eyes seemed to say to me.

'I saw you,' I whispered to your corpse.

When the grief softens, I think I will continue loving, bright as a thousand suns, until it is my turn to burn out, and then I too shall paint the sky gold, just as you did, little one.

Thank You for Leaving

Harrison Cobham

I forgot to connect my phone to the car on the ride home. The silence in the car was shattered by a guttural internal scream, fracturing my emotions into tiny pieces, all for you. You'd had an accident the night before. You seemed dazed, unsure of what was happening or where exactly you were. I had managed to get you to the doctor as early as possible the next morning; however, the diagnosis provided no comfort. Dementia.

So, in the car we sat. Deafening silence. I felt numb to the world, subtle bumps and turns barely register as I drove on autopilot. Then, an unavoidable pothole startled me, clearing my mental haze. Before I could steel myself, a single tear rolled down my cheek, carrying with it the silent scream echoing in my head.

'I love you, Lilly.'

'I love you too,' you replied softly. 'I will never stop loving you.'

Now the diagnosis was confirmed, I knew you wouldn't get better. Your mother had suffered from the same thing. And her mother before that. We knew it was a possibility—but fear of that reality kept us from truly confronting it.

Pulling into the driveway, a familiar barking rose from the fenced-off yard. Rufus, reminding us both that he was still there. Your spirits immediately seemed to lift. I remember seeing that familiar, warm smile spread across your face as you ran towards Rufus who pawed relentlessly at the fence, reaching over it in his desperate need for attention. I remained in the car a while longer, swallowing my emotions each time I made the mistake of remembering this morning's tragedy. By the time I willed myself out of the driver's seat, you were still throwing around Rufus's ratty old tennis ball that he loved so much, but I couldn't meet your eyes. The fear of falling apart was stronger than I was, but I had to be strong for you.

Walking into our small suburban home was a reminder of our time together. We were high school sweethearts. Since Year 11, 15 years ago, we were inseparable. Golden beams of light shone through the kitchen window, illuminating the warmth that we had worked so hard to create in our home—a task that I could never have completed alone. You made it look effortless. The love you infused into our home rejuvenated me, allowing me to briefly forget about the tragedies of our new reality. Indulging in all the mementos, curios and trinkets that you had used to reflect your soul onto the house filled the hole in my chest with a bittersweet love. I knew then that whatever lay ahead, we would face it together.

The obnoxiously pompous cabinet I inherited from my grandfather—filled with commemorative liquors from the places we've travelled together— remained sealed, as neither of us drank. The needlefelt figures you made of all my favourite characters, along with my own poor attempts, standing proudly next to them, that you insisted you loved even more than the rest, just because it was from me. And my most prized possession, a shoebox filled with letters you wrote me. Two for every year together: one for our anniversary and one for my birthday. I always did my best to reciprocate the beauty and kindness of your cards, but my creations could never match yours.

You refused to waste what lucidity you had left, wallowing in despair, so we stayed up. Despite everything, you were glowing, radiating the same loving warmth that you always had. We both knew that this would soon fade, but at the time, I was lucky to still have you.

The next few months were rough. Your mental state spiralled. Reading your cards carried me through the darkest times. Your bouts of delirium were growing longer, more severe, but I stayed with you through it all, refusing to let you suffer alone. Rufus and I did our best to look after you—with unwavering devotion and frequent trips to the beach where we had our first date, the botanical garden where I proposed ... all the places you loved most when you were well. I held myself together for you, despite how hard it was to get through your particularly frantic delusions.

Things changed a few years after that. Your delusions became the norm, lucidity an increasingly uncommon reprieve. Most of the time, you didn't even recognise me. I felt like a stranger around the only person I ever loved more than myself, and it broke me. The home that we had created together all those years ago was starting to feel like a prison. My life felt like some cruel punishment for a crime I didn't know I had committed. My days were spent caring for a temperamental stranger in my wife's body. Rufus kept me sane. He seemed to do the same for you, even though you couldn't call him by his name; he spent every night sleeping by your feet, providing some warmth to a house that felt colder than it did when you were well.

Then Rufus passed. I'm glad you didn't have to go through that like I did. The house felt it had lost what little warmth remained. You slept a lot after Rufus passed. I suppose you didn't have all that much to get up for anymore. I was the same. I managed to pull myself off the couch only when I needed to get you food or your medication. The house felt frozen; the sun no longer brought warmth into the living area but instead highlighted the innumerable specks of dust floating through the air, a reminder that the place that was once our home is now dead.

The house was mostly silent now. The obnoxious liquor cabinet sat empty, its door slightly ajar, unclosed since I had last taken the remaining bottle in an attempt to fill the void in my chest. The needlefelt characters almost appeared greyscale because of years of dust building up on them, neglected. A shoebox sat atop the kitchen cabinet, caked in dust, all but forgotten. I was trapped in a prison of painful reminders of the love I once had. The house was a constantly dark place despite our presence; it was lifeless. The warmth of our love had long since waned, both of us trapped. You were trapped in a prison of your own mind and body, and I was trapped by my love for you.

A few months after that, I lived through the most painful day of my life. The television was playing static, white noise drowning out the depressing silence of that empty house. I peeled myself off the couch to check on you, make sure that you were alright and give you one of your small white capsules that was meant to slow your mental decline. But your room felt even colder than usual. Stiller than usual. Quieter than usual. Your pill bottle was already on your bedside table, cap ajar, and the bottle was empty. A note lay under the bottle.

I never stopped loving you.

The months after you departed were the hardest of my life. The grief that engulfed me nearly destroyed me—more than once. I had to move somewhere new to sever my ties to that house and the darkness that lingered with it. I spent some years travelling abroad after that. It took a long time to work through the trauma of saying goodbye to you. Experiencing a world outside of that cursed house, however, made it possible.

I have met someone new now, someone who makes me feel a similar peace to what I felt when we were together. It took me such a long time to get over how things ended with us. I used to hate you for leaving me all those years ago. I couldn't understand why you would leave me alone in that house, after everything I sacrificed for you. But now I know that you truly never did stop loving me. You saved me from that dark place. Even though I have found someone else to share my life with, I will always hold you in my heart. Lilly … thank you for leaving.

A Greyhound, a Golden Retriever and the Irish Setter

Chelise Robinson

'**B**anjo sit. Sit. Banjo, sit. Siiiiiit. Banjo here, here Banjo, look here! Banjo sit.' The gesturing is unbearable and embarrassing at this point. 'Oh my gosh. Okay, fine. Go, just go.' I open the gate for the fanatical dog, just in time for him to almost bound completely over the fence with anticipation. I watch the Irish Setter weave in and out of the dogs who have approached the new attendee, welcoming him with wagging tails and delighted barks. He takes off in a contagious run across the park once the greetings have subsided.

Fanatic vibrating drags my eyes away from the commotion and down to my phone, where a missed call lingers on the screen; a message follows shortly after.

Hi Cassidy! Sorry I missed our phone meeting earlier today. I'm free now though if you're still wanting that interview for the paper? Give me a ring back before four, thanks!

I glance at the time: 3:58pm. Yeah, not happening. A common tactic those in political positions like to use—not returning calls until the very last minute of the work day on a Friday, because they know you're already out of office and into the weekend.

Bastard. I really need those quotes.

I pocket the device after turning it fully off. I'm so done with that part of my day.

Approaching my usual spot in the corner, I'm relieved to see the old, rugged bench unoccupied, given the amount of people and their dogs here so late in the afternoon. Usually, coming just before sunset yields less people in the area, but I don't blame most of them for staying out in this weather a little longer. The soft chill on the air is reminiscent of the winter just gone. An inviting smell of jasmine from across the field wafts into the park, like the wind is gently coercing spring to come out from winter's cold clutch and fully immerse the world with its warmth.

I tug my jumper a little tighter and sit down, letting the creaky boards take my weight from a heavy day, allowing it to become an extension of myself, resting into its inviting embrace. This spot gives a perfect vantage point for me to see the entire fenced area and keep an eye on my mahogany dog, bounding through the lush grass with his friends. I swivel slightly around, adjusting my view, before a familiar pair of paws grace my linen pants.

'Percy, no! Oh my gosh, every damn time you come in here you just have to put your silly muddy paws on Cassidy! Bad dog,' Annie yells from across the yard as she hurries over to where her golden retriever's front legs sit happily atop my lap. She shoos the enormous dog away before sliding in next to me.

'It's fine, it's fine. You know I'm used to it by now. It's my fault I always forget to change before coming here.' I smile gently at Annie as I wipe the splotches of dirt away.

'The jumping up is the one thing I can't seem to train out of him. I swear one day he'll knock over a small kid or something and the parents will never forgive me.'

'He has already done that.' I let out a small laugh remembering back to the first time I met Annie, when her dog decided playing fetch with a toddler was a good idea but once the kid was knocked to the ground, the unrelenting licking-of-the-face started and my dog, unfortunately, decided to join in on the fun.

And there was us two—embarrassed owners trying to pull our stupid dogs off this poor baby while the parents scolded us for not 'having control' of our animals. I mentioned the fact that it probably wasn't a good idea to bring their almost infant child into a specifically designated fenced in area for dogs. Especially considering they didn't appear to have a dog of their own.

Jonathan—a regular park-goer who I'd previously seen here a few times—had quickly intervened, as he'd watched the whole ordeal unravel from his spot on the bench and helped us wrangle our dogs away from the now aggravated couple. He also threatened legal action against them when they'd hinted at the mention of contacting council about 'rabid dogs' being allowed in the area. That quickly de-escalated the situation. They stormed out and, coincidently, I've never seen them here since. But my friendship with the girl and her huge golden retriever and the man with his old greyhound, has only blossomed since.

'Oh my gosh, yeah you're right.' Annie giggles softly and glances at her phone for a split second before scrunching her nose, letting out a heavy sigh and placing it face down on the bench between us. I reach into my pocket and do the same, putting mine directly on top of hers. A small gesture between us, we're now ready to be fully invested in the present. I glance at the entrance gate and to the asphalt carpark beyond, hoping to spot a familiar face.

'Jonathan's not here yet?' Annie asks, looking in the same direction.

'No, I haven't seen him. I'm a little worried about Charles, actually.' I think of the aged greyhound who accompanies Jonathan everywhere he goes. 'That man won't survive without his dog.'

'Yeah, he's really starting to show his age now, the poor fella.' Annie's face falls and her spark seem to fade at the thought of something terrible happening to Charles. I push the negativity away; there is still plenty of time for them to join us.

I often think what would happen to the three of us if that day was to ever come. Our friendship was confined to the fence before us. I didn't have Annie's phone number, nor Jonathan's—I didn't even know their last names. I went against my better instincts to do a deep search for them online; I didn't want what we've created to be hindered by anything that lies outside this fence. We'd fabricated our own little world right here in the present of each afternoon. To think that one day, when our dogs pass, that'll be the end of us too. We'll know from the absence of each other, that what we have is over, that the change in something so small is so consuming of our lives. People dwindle away not slowly but suddenly. Life—it's not gradual, it's instant.

Annie and I chat the afternoon away. I ask about her job; she tells me it's nothing but the usual—preparing her patients every day for the inevitable: death. Updating the family members with any information worth noting, making sure the place of occupants is ready to be quickly but effectively dispersed upon the patient's passing whilst remaining the one calming presence in the person's life for however short it may now be.

I like to imagine her as a lingering spirit—waiting, watching, caressing the person into finally feeling like they are able to leave this life into the next. A segue between worlds, taking their hand and letting them cross into the imaginary white light. I don't envy anything she does, but I respect the times she's entered these afternoons we share with such a weight on her shoulders; no conversation can ever take away what she carries with her.

I find myself glancing at the gate every few moments, itching every time someone new enters, only to see it's not who we're waiting for. Even our pups stop what they're doing each time they hear the click of the latch as a new member walks through the fence. They deflate upon the realisation it's not their usual friend; I share the same feeling. Their playful antics seem foreign and misplaced with only the two of them.

Annie asks me about work, and we exhaust our usual topics of conversation: updates about her crazy ex-boyfriend, my annoying loud neighbour, how that bastard of a politician didn't get back to me in time to run his interview in this week's paper. We speak about Jonathan, too; how in the first few days of knowing one another it took my elaborate journalistic know-how and interviewing skills to coax any sort of information out of the shy, stoic man. We learnt that Charles was gifted to him by his grandfather—who had raised Jonathan sense he was a child—and he was a lawyer, which explained the reason for the suits he wore each day to the park.

We watch in sorrowful silence, the sun slowly dipping behind the trees and the breeze picking up, rustling the leaves overhead, catching our breaths on the cool air still lingering, refusing to disappear along with winter. Occupants of the park have trickled out slowly while the light continues to fade from the darkening sky. I know we should get going, but neither of us dare to move as it goes unspoken that we'll just wait another five minutes; and then another.

The dogs have abandoned their playing and now lie in shelter under the bench, the gaping hole between them, a devastating gesture to loyalty.

'I'm so sorry, Cassidy, but I've got to get started on dinner.' Annie gathers her things and clips Percy to the lead. She gives a me a gentle, reassuring look, one I can only imagine she's given many people before. 'I'll see you tomorrow.'

I wave her off and wait another ten minutes in the dark that now coddles me. Banjo wines below my legs. 'Come on, boy, time to go home.'

We make our way out into the world, leaving the fenced in area behind.

Flowering

Juan Tatis

A s the last shred of weight left my hands, it felt as though my being no longer existed.

I had come to spite this tireless effort—the incessant lifting and hauling, the clumsy movements, the letting go. Hours went by, cardboard boxes full of memories leaving my hands in a blur, and yet I seemed no closer to seeing this monumental task to its conclusion, even after my arms and back grew sore from exhaustion. Lift, carry, let go. It was, perhaps, this mundane act alone that kept me tethered to myself. Like a lone flower, standing proud under the dying sun. Somewhere along the way, I found myself quite pleased. It was easy to carry all those boxes around. Although simple, it gave me purpose. I felt strong, useful. Most of all, however, I felt closer to her. Because however straining, however numbing, for as long as it bore upon my arms, this weight meant that she was not yet gone.

With the trunk of her pearl-white SUV fully shut at last, she let out a sigh and walked back from our driveway. She wore a gentle smile and prodded her feet on the grass, pleased by the long-awaited conclusion to our shared plight. The light evening breeze bore a deep sense of relief which filled her words.

'All right, that should be everything,' she said.

'Yeah,' I replied. 'Was a bit of a pain, but we made it in the end.'

'Sure did. Though you certainly didn't pull your weight.'

'Please. You might as well have not even been there.' She hadn't broken a sweat, mind you. Ever the hypocrite—though I knew it was in jest, and so didn't shy away from biting back.

'Mean,' she said, pouting. And ever the schemer …

She shot a fleeting glance at the plain two-storied house behind her. The dusty porch, the worn woodwork, and the unevenly cut lawn we stood on. The sight of it all reminded me of a dilapidated painting—its colour gone, its canvas dusted, yet still bearing hints of once undeniable splendour.

'Can't say I'll miss it,' she said. 'Cramped kitchen, creaky floors, boiling our arses off during the summer.

Honestly. I don't know how we put up with it.' She seemed amused by her own matter-of-fact tone, as if proud that she could acknowledge such vexing things with such silly detachment. 'And the rent was a bitch too.'

'Yeah. Real bitch.'

Perhaps my voice wasn't convincing enough in its inflection. Perhaps her mind naturally stumbled upon this next step in our conversation. Or perhaps she possessed, as I had always suspected, some strange form of clairvoyance.

'How are you feeling?' she asked, piercing right through my words straight into what lay behind them. I could tell her question was laced with genuine care.

'About how you'd expect,' I replied. I figured my answer was honest enough for her to deem her concern acknowledged, yet just the right amount of unassuming to dispel it entirely. 'And you?'

'Well ... I'm not sure.'

'You seem a little giddy.'

'I am. It's a big day. If anything, that's why I'm actually kinda worried about you,' she replied, wearing a timid smile.

I fell silent at her remark, and my thoughts began their noise. No longer convinced I had wormed myself out of reach from her worries, the panic of not knowing what the hell I was supposed to say bore its fangs anew. I rummaged about for the right words, for the right expression, but all I stumbled upon was an overpowering thought—the sort of tiny oddity that plants itself within your heart and, before you know it, takes root in your being, straying you from any thought or feeling other than itself. It was a cruel affliction. And it begged the question—why was it that I sought to hide away in the first place? What is it that lies beneath me that I deemed far too unsightly for her to see? Was my willingness to remain unseen truly a display of selfless virtue, or was it a deceitful, egotistical act of cowardice? But my desperate plea for an answer was shushed away in a moment, drowned out by the pressing need to speak. And I did so the only way I knew how.

'We always knew it would come to this. 'There's nothing to worry about,' I said.

She frowned. I could tell she didn't mean to.

'You sure?'

'Yeah.' Always measured. Always composed. Always, at every turn, strong. I wondered ... what did she make of that?

'... I'm happy to hear that.'

Yes. That's exactly what I needed, what I wanted to hear. Yet as if willingly contending this, after a brief silence, she began to giggle.

'What is it?'

'Nothing. I guess maybe I am a bit too giddy.'

'It's a big day.'

Clever. She laughed, twirled, donned a bright smile. I played along, muted. As she wandered off merrily into her own mind, I caught a glimpse of a flat object peeking out from her pocket. A picture, torn and wrinkled, yet one I dearly recalled us taking not long after we came here. We went out to celebrate some special occasion with a couple of friends. She drank a bit too much. Me? Probably a bit too little.

'I see you chose to keep it.'

'Oh, you mean this?' She took out the picture and displayed it proudly. 'Yeah ... I know you told me it'd be better if I didn't, but I figured it wouldn't hurt. I don't mind holding on to small memories like these.'

'I thought you wanted to let go. Wouldn't keeping it just make that harder?'

'Maybe, maybe not,' she said, attempting to form a smile. What that attempt had amounted to, I did not fully know, but when she spoke next, I could hear a faint sadness whisper itself alongside her words. 'I just feel like, somehow ... as long as I hold onto this, things will be okay, you know?'

You know?

What did I know? What could I, after all this time, have possibly ever known? There was nothing for me to know, nothing for me to say, because whatever I did, it would inevitably push the two of us even further apart. I was blinded, aimless, stumbling over and over again upon my failures, upon my own incompetence. I could never find the words nor the answers that she needed. Now more than ever, I fell prey to this parasitic feeling. To the curse of understanding my own weakness.

But what did that matter? The fact that things go, the fact that things change is undeniable proof of this world's cruelty. To see this change as a blessing is nothing but a farce—a lie we tell ourselves to ward off the haunting feeling of the end. So, hearing her tell me these things, even if she didn't mean to—that everything was okay, that better things would come, that part of her invited that end—was it childish of me to feel terribly hurt by it?

A flower is not beautiful because of its pretty colours or its pleasant fragrance. It's beautiful because it can be destroyed. But should it? Does its transience mean it should be left to wither? Would it be better off alone and unkempt, unable to embrace the life it would have led had it fought just a bit harder to claw its way to the sunlight?

But what if it wouldn't? What if a single droplet of water were all it took for that flower to bloom, to sprout up into the skies and bathe the entire world with its beauty? What if this silence, this fear, were wrought from the very thing that keeps our hearts bleeding and our souls riddled with senseless loss? In the end, all I had, all I knew ... was myself. I knew what lay beneath. I knew what I wished to say. *I don't want to leave. I don't want to move on. The truth is, if I were to remain in this one moment forever, I would be unimaginably happy.*

Could she have wished for the same? It is a beautiful thought, isn't it? But then ... I suppose there was always one more thing I've always known. I know that, however much I wish, however much I feel, it all turns to dust beneath this crushing weight. I know I am not the man to fight back against it. And I know that, however much I try, I shall never be strong enough to carry it.

My hands stopped trembling as I nodded, smiling. And the words never reached you.

Becoming Her

Nykayla Dux

Wednesday, 11:17am.

A bar where lovers meet in secret and lone drinkers pay in cash. Low light. Eyes down. You press your fingertips together, feeling for that foreign thing lodged in your flesh—the splinter answers with a sharp throb. You can't remember how it got there, only that it's been bothering you all week. Swirl the olives in your drink, then rip their flesh between your teeth one by one. Your throat burns in delicious anticipation of dissociation. The pain in your thumb recedes a little. It's your third time here this week—work doesn't need to know. Another sip and the ever-present internal turmoil declines to a gentle churn. Contemplating life here has become a ritual of self-pity disguised as self-reflection.

A man sitting nearby throws back a vodka, then another. He catches you looking.

'What are you staring at, bitch?'

You swallow the word. *Nothing*. You are not like him. You are not like anyone here. And you especially are not like *her*.

You order another drink.

On your phone, a headline: *Good bloke pushed too far: pillar of community 'lost control' loving his family to death.* Bile rises in your throat. The splinter demands attention again, a steady heartbeat in your finger. You dig into the soft pad of your pointer finger and peel back the skin. Deeper than you thought. Squeezing, until a bead of red rises, and then—there—something hard and black pushes free. It pulses. Maybe that's your pulse. Don't breathe. You put your finger in your mouth, savouring the sweet metallic taste.

A woman in the corner has been on the phone for twenty minutes, too loud for this room.

'I'll pick my washing up this afternoon. Need anything on my way home?' her shrill voice slicing through the hushed rhythm of the bar.

You press harder on your finger.

'All right, Mum. Bye.'

Your stomach hits spin cycle. The bile in your throat all but ready to come out. The wound the splinter left behind is now shooting electricity up the palm of your hand. The room goes black at the edges.

Push up from the table. Walk. No—run.

Shove the battered blue stall open. Drop your bag against the back of the door, a weak protection against the broken lock that leaves you vulnerable. Graffiti climbs the tiles. A fluorescent light spits and buzzes overhead. You check your reflection, desperate to anchor yourself in reality. But there is something dark wedged in the delicate pink of your tear duct. You lean in closer, pressing a digit to your eyeball. It squirms, withdrawing into the hollow of your skull—tickling, like someone gently licking the depths of your socket. Rub your eyes and check again.

Nothing.

Just tired, you tell yourself.

Sleep hasn't come easily. Dreading this day. Sitting on the closed lid, you wait for the sweet spot of the second martini to kick in. Your finger burns. Looking down now, the splinter has returned—but longer and burrowed deeper. The skin on the tip of your finger has turned an ominous plum hue that spreads under the nail bed. Is there something burrowing inside? A worm, you think. Making a home out of your flesh. You hope she finds it comfortable, safe. You shake your hands. Wet your face. Gum. Go. It's time.

The meeting spot is brighter, with nicer-looking people.

You don't feel like you belong here. But neither does she.

At the sight of her face, your heart simultaneously flutters with longing and a heaviness that only comes from heartbreak. Her face is tired, cheeks hollow, eyes yellowed in a way that tugs at a memory you can't quite place. You can tell she's made an effort though: a new top, curled hair.

'It's been a while,' she says. 'You all right?'

'Yeah, I'm good. You?'

'Yeah. All right.' You hug.

Her body trembles, violent and uncontrolled. The perfume is cheap, fighting a losing battle against the sour tang of her lifestyle. You sit. The worm in your finger is still there, making herself comfortable at your expense. Digging. Growing. Feasting.

'I ordered us vanilla lattes, your favourite,' she says.

That hasn't been your favourite in years.

'Thanks.'

Her eyes: yellow. Yes. You've seen it before—in her mother, in those final days.

The last time you saw her mother, she looked so small in that wooden box. Nothing like the lady with the soft belly and purple hair you remember from childhood—the one who begged you to dance with her around the cramped apartment, barefoot on the Elvis rug, ice rattling in her emerald Tupperware cup. She'd call you 'bug' and ask for a refill from the box in the fridge.

After the dancing, the two of them always fought. At the time you couldn't understand why she was so upset with her mother, and why she never wanted to see her. Maybe she didn't like fun.

The symptoms were always there, but after her mother died, the inevitable *becoming* accelerated, engulfing the woman you knew. What followed was the inherited rotation of inconspicuous bruises and men. She started dancing in the afternoon. Then the inevitable fighting.

You grew up. And dancing in the living room was no longer fun.

'How are you, anyway?' she asks.

'Good.' You hesitate. 'What've you been up to?'

'Not much.' She pours water into the glasses unsteadily, splashing on the table. 'What about you? Are you good?'

'Yeah.'

'Oh well, that's good.'

You stare at each other, waiting for words that never come. The truth: you barely know each other. She holds her hands beneath the table like she is hiding something. And then you see it. It's subtle at first. But something writhes beneath the skin of her forearm. Like a snake coiled around the bone, looking for an escape out of the deteriorating skin suit. She tugs her sleeve down.

'So, how's work?' she says.

You're certain she doesn't even know what you do for a living.

'Good,' you reply.

There is an undeniable burning sensation of something taking root beneath the skin of your hand now. You, too, hide your arms under the table, suppressing a wince. Neither of you can look each other in the eye. Her question cracks something open—the mountain of anger you can never summit, no matter how much therapy you go to. You remind her too much of what she could have been. And she reminds you too much of what you don't want to be. The heaviness of generations of women reverberates in the quiet between you.

'I'm not well,' she says, voice meek.

Silence.

This day was always coming, but in many ways you've already mourned her, as if she isn't here sitting in front of you. She looks fragile, and a desire to protect her rises in you. You reach out to touch her hand. As soon as skin connects, something claws at your insides, screaming for sedation in the form of another drink. She feels it too. But she wouldn't in front of you, nor you in front of her.

The café hums with chatter and clinking cups. Pain is radiating in your arm which is now the shade of midnight. The air is static, like at the foreshore before a tsunami.

Vines begin corkscrewing from your fingertips, leaving the skin raw. You glance at her. Beneath the delicate skin of her chest a deformed face presses outward. Its mouth open, as if screaming—summoning the splinter that lodged inside you back in the womb, calling it home to its creator.

A moist ripping sound fills the room as her skin tears open and the darkness, wild and ravaging, pours out. The vines from your hand scuttle toward hers, intertwining like old friends, splattering ichor onto nearby tables.

The lattes arrive. The waiter doesn't notice. Around you, conversations continue.

The darkness ravages the both of you. Talons in your lungs, stealing your breath. It pushes harder, forces its way out through every crevice. You look at each other—through bulging eyes, as the darkness swarms out from beneath your eyelids like thousands of ants fleeing their water-doused mound—with the same desperate recognition that you would sacrifice everything in this moment to numb it. Sludge lands on the waiter's white button-down. He turns, unbothered, shoes squelching as he walks away.

Looking at her face now, you see your own, only fifteen years older—you imagine it cut off, left out to dry, then stitched back on. You've never felt closer to and yet further away from her, her mother and every woman before that shares the inherited disposition for dysfunction that contaminates your veins. A contorted catharsis settles over you.

In the stillness, something ancient exhales and whispers for you to stop resisting.

Sisters

Elena Betschwar

They say some houses look like faces. The terrace house down the lane had a telling face: unwashed, tired, a large, red front door and arching windows that rose high on each storey. Creeping vines etched their history over the exterior like wrinkles of time. The apex of the roof bore dirt and decay from an age of neglect. This was the home of two sisters.

The neighbours never met Jane's sister. Even more peculiar, the lease only records Jane's name. However, Jane's sister is always at home. In fact, she never leaves. She is never seen nor heard.

Jane's sister sits in the corner: silent, watching and waiting. From where she was set, she could see sunlight pouring in through the window; shadows of vines crawling along the floor. She couldn't, however, see outside the window. She longed to watch people on the street as they strolled past. She wondered what it would feel like if the sun kissed her long, blonde locks. She hoped to see her sister again soon. Jane was so pretty—she had light hair, and the bluest eyes, just like herself. Her body held gorgeous curves—her skin clear and fair. Jane's sister marvelled at her beauty any chance she got.

Footsteps crept down the hall towards the room. Jane's sister buzzed with excitement as she watched the door ... it clicked open and there she was, Jane. The silky skin of her perfectly round cheeks blushed pink as her sister walked past. She tried to call out to her, but no sound escaped. Jane acted as though she wasn't there, her eyes stared so intently at the floor it nearly bore a hole. She hurriedly gathered what she came for and scampered away.

Earlier that day ...

'I, Jane Pudley, am capable of entering a room in my own house,' I told myself in the downstairs bathroom mirror.

Saying it out loud didn't make it any more believable in my head. I get anxious going in there, but I left my makeup bag on the floor like an idiot. I knew she would be there waiting ... watching. I crept up the stairs, each step feeling an age. I tiptoed down the narrow hall, trying desperately not to make a sound. *Perhaps she's sleeping and I can avoid her.* I was wrong, as always. I slipped open the door, careful to not look straight ahead. I could feel her gaze burning into me. I stared straight down, not daring to let my eyes drift. I knew exactly where my bag was. I clasped it in one hand and turned on my heel, the door closing behind me. I knew I'd have to go back in there soon. It's not her fault she is the way she is.

With my makeup done and my outfit freshly pressed and slipped on, I made the trek back down the hall. I knew I had to look at her this time. I pushed open the door, lifting my gaze to that damn mirror. I see her looking back at me, her hair sitting perfectly, her body so small and sculpted. I looked her outfit up and down, it matched my own, but it was her that caught my eye.

'You look beautiful,' she mouthed at me.

I turned away. *What does she know about makeup?* She could never understand the work I have to put into my appearance. She was everything I wished for—everything I was not. I reached into my makeup bag, searching for anything I could grasp. I pelted whatever I could find at the mirror, again and again. The girl looked scared and confused.

'Why won't this damn thing break?' I panted between each object I threw.

Exhausted and shaking, I grabbed a blanket off the floor and covered the mirror, the image of perfection disappeared. I felt a pang of guilt in my chest, but I had to do what was right for me.

Jane's sister became enveloped in darkness, enshrouded by the deep black of the blanket Jane had tossed over her. She realised Jane is cruel to herself and full of resentment, unable to live up to the high expectations of the perfect image in the mirror. Jane had no idea the fortune she had; to live life in her body. She focused on her sister in the mirror, rather than appreciating all the good in her curves, creases and her smile. There was beauty in her freckles and moles and that imperfect hair that wouldn't quite stay down. Jane never appreciated her own amazing sense of humour or intelligence. It was all wasted away with this fixation on becoming an even better version. It felt like she was staring into that dark abyss for years.

Two days later ...

I can't take it anymore. The mirror is eating away at me. I went back to the room, the door slightly ajar from when I left in a hurry. One step at a time, I slinked to the mirror and pulled the blanket away. There she was, smiling back at me, except her eyes appeared red-raw from crying. Even still, her features mocked me: the symmetrical close-lipped smile and the button nose. I reached a shaky hand toward her, moving nearer to the glass. Her hand mirrored mine. Just an inch away, we stopped … I didn't know why. Her eyes darted from our hands that almost touched, to my face, pleading. My hand slipped away as the reflection and I fell to the ground in unison.

'I'm sorry,' I whispered, unable to hold my tears any longer.

'I'm sorry,' she mouthed. The same, but different.

Sometime later, I rose from the floor. My sister had fallen asleep; her cheeks still stained with tears as she lay on the floor. I mustered my strength and dragged her mirror to face the window, settling down beside her. The movement must have shook her awake, but she didn't seem to mind. Her head rested on the edge of the mirror; her glassy eyes shone with crystals of happy tears as she gazed into the street below. My head matched hers as it leant against the glass too.

As people passed by, entangled in their lives, the vines suffocating the window began to recede. The old terrace house let out a sigh of relief, though some would call it the wind. The sun shone through the windows, illuminating the golden in the girls' hair who were matching at last.

Dogshit

Finn Gallagher

Bones defecated on the puppy pad in the Northwest corner of the living room. His Human of Choice—the real estate agent and former child actress Margaret Rochester—was out touting a tumbledown duplex in Carseldine, but his Other Owner Lenny Rochester, the one that never smiled and forgot to fill his food bowl every second night, smelled the turd from his wardrobe-turned-office down the hall. Lenny wrinkled his nose.

'Fuck me dead,' he said to himself. He attempted to rise from his chair, calves straining under a recently acquired beer belly, and then fell back into his seat. The crap didn't smell *that* bad, and besides Margaret would be home any minute now. She was a maddening old cunt, that Margaret, but she knew how to keep the house in order. *Only thing she was good at.* That and chewing through his salary like a cashed-up crack addict. And staying out late. And fucking other men behind his back.

Just then Lenny heard a thud that could only mean Bones jumping off the sofa or a lounge chair, and then the patter of paws making their way towards the front door.

'I'm back, Bonesy!' Margeret trilled from the veranda. *Speak of the devil.*

He rose from his chair again, dusted potato gem crumbs from his blue-and-white striped jacket, straightened his tie and moved to stand at the office entrance.

'Bonesy Boy! I *did* miss you, I *did.*' Margaret was crouched down at the doorway, ruffling Bones's hide and giggling as the mutt licked every square inch of her skin. *Bones was licking a dead toad earlier today*, Lenny recalled, and nearly chuckled out-loud. Hopefully the toad in question had been a toxic one, one of those neon-yellow creatures with poison skin and an exotic name like the African Odabunga or the Guatemelan Natashitsu. Hopefully Bones was coating Margaret with the poison at this very moment, and the two of them would croak it in an hour or two. *Now wouldn't that be nice, killing two birds with one stone.*

Margaret was returning to her feet now, and she finally noticed Lenny standing down the hall. Her smile faltered, slightly, and then re-formed as quickly as it had vanished. It looked forced, painfully so

'And how has your day been?' she offered. Lenny flashed his own plasticine grin and rolled his eyes in his best *aw shucks I'm just a no name freelancer that hasn't worked a jot in the last month* impression.

'Oh, you know. Bumming around the house … I revised my resume like you told me to. I removed the university accolades section. It looks more professional without it, you were right.'

Margaret nodded her head slowly, smugly, like she knew all the secrets of the universe. 'That's what I've been saying! It was *really* taking away from your other accomplishments.'

'Yeah. Yeah, it was.'

'Well, I'm glad you got rid of it.'

Lenny nodded. A not-entirely-comfortable silence fell between them. *She's calculating ways to bring up her agency sales without sounding like she's bragging*, Lenny thought. He decided to set up her punchline.

'How was your day?'

Margaret grinned again, and this time it was wide and sickening and genuine. 'Three offers,' she announced. 'I got *three freaking* offers in one day! All serious buyers, too.' She tilted her head and arched her eyebrows; waiting, Lenny assumed, to be showered in praise. He wanted to reach over, wrap his hands around her leathery neck and squeeze it until the arrogance slipped from her eyes. He wanted to run her head through a lawnmower. He stretched his arms wide. 'Come here, you!' Margaret fell into him, releasing a near-inaudible sigh as the supple of her breasts brushed his chest, and the two embraced.

'I'm proud of you, honey,' Lenny murmured. 'Proud as a lion.' Margaret placed her hands behind his neck and stroked it; her talon-sharp nails sending lightning bolts down Lenny's back.

'And how proud is that, exactly?' she whispered. Lenny reached down below her waist and began undoing the zipper of her business trousers.

'This proud.'

The next morning Lenny awoke with a startling realisation: Margaret needed to be taken care of. And not the kind where you feed a horse carrots and brush its fur, but the kind where you lead it behind the barn and shoot it. He waited patiently as Margaret painted her face for work; she rushed out the door at 9am, and Lenny noticed with considerable disgust that Bones's shit from the morning before was still sitting on the living room puppy pad. It was now black and shrivelled like skin after a bad sunburn, and the smell rising from the remains singed Lenny's nostrils. *That layabout cunt*, Lenny thought. *The only thing she was ever good at was keeping the house in order. Too busy thinking about her condo commission to bother with that, I guess.*

Lenny listened as the engine of Margaret's 2017 Camry faded off into the distance and then retrieved a piece of paper and pen from underneath his desk. *Ways to kill Margaret,* he wrote at the top, and a wave of relief washed over him. He imagined this must be how depressives felt when they finally decided to top themselves. It didn't matter how desperate or depraved the situation; it felt good having a plan. *Stab her,* he wrote near the top of the page. Simple. Effective. *Blunt.* Too blunt, given modern forensic technology. The cops would find one drop of her blood and one strand of his hair, and he'd be sitting in jail until Trump's great-grandson had taken office. It was a shame, because stabbing her would feel oh-so-satisfying, but the puzzle pieces just weren't connecting.

Poison her? he jotted. This idea was far more appealing; slip some Rat-Be-Gone into her nightly Rosé and watch as she groaned and gurgled to death on the back patio. And he'd call the police straight afterwards and tell them in his most convincing shocked-husband voice that Margaret had collapsed out of the blue, and they'd believe him, at first. But of course, they'd run an autopsy on her, and they'd find traces of arsenic or aluminium or whatever, and the cops would be knocking on his door before one week of Margaret's death had passed. Sure, it would keep the 5-O busy for a while, and his prosecutors would tear their hair out compiling evidence against him, but they'd nail him in the end.

No. Margaret's death needed to look like an accident, to *be* an accident for all intents and purposes. She needed to die in a manner so freakishly random, so unequivocally distant from himself, that the lawmen would arrive at the scene, nod their heads a few times and close the case the very next day. *Margaret needed to kill herself.* He pondered that last chestnut for a few seconds and began to smile. It would be a frosty Thursday night when Margaret descended into hellfire, Lenny would make sure of that.

Over the next few days Lenny watched Bones like a hawk. Every time the mutt barked, every time it sniffed and sneezed and shat, Lenny would poke his neck out of his office and look at it. He had a dog collar tucked away in his bottom desk drawer, one of those heavy-duty, neoprene-padded ones designed for a labrador or a golden retriever, and a vial of sleeping agent nestled up alongside it.

He hoped he wouldn't need to use the sleeping agent; in a perfect world, Bones would start growling and walking in circles, and Lenny would simply slip the collar around the mongrel's neck and lead him to Margaret's bedroom at the rear of the house. In a perfect world, Bones's rabies wouldn't kick in when Margaret was in the house at all.

That was the only thing that could throw a spanner in the works, Bones spitting and foaming at the mouth while Margaret was nearby, because every other aspect of Lenny's plan was damn near watertight. He'd brought Bones to the bat caves near Marulba Falls on the 21st of July, a balmy day by even Queensland standards (he'd read somewhere that bats were more aggressive in hot weather), and had let Bones loose in the maze of tunnels underneath the dried-up waterfall. Bones had looked at him, eyes wide and shining, mouth open and smiling, and Larry had said, 'Go, boy go!' and Bones had run into the caves without a second thought.

The dog exited the mouth of the cave an hour late, covered in scratches, whimpering, and there was a bite near his left eyebrow that had drawn a considerable quantity of blood. 'Good boy,' Lenny had said, and the dog looked up at him with his unswollen eye and licked his hand.

An hour later, Lenny had washed Bones off under a public shower ten minutes from his house, and the dog was looking far more put-together, all things considered. Bones's left eye was still half-closed, but the swelling had faded, and the bite mark above it was now completely hidden under the dog's generous matte of fur. Bones had been scratched about twenty times, Lenny estimated; he was relatively confident that the dog had contracted rabies at some point during his cave expeditions.

And now here he was, three days later, waiting for Bones to show the smallest symptom of the disease. The second Bones so much as coughed, Lenny would take him to their shared bedroom, where'd he'd promptly lock the door and wait the few hours for Bones to metamorphose into a bloodshot, bloodthirsty devil dog. And that's when he'd take off his shirt and ask Margaret if she was up for half an hour of bedroom action. He'd open the door and motion Margaret to step inside. Ladies first, and all that.

Till Death Do Us Part

Cayley Berridge

Till death do us part. The five words we spoke to one another on our special day, the five words we promised with tears streaming down our faces and shaky hands intwined. The same hands I still hold, as though I can keep you here. As long as I don't let go.

Fuck cancer.

We were so happy building our little lives together. We were so naïve. Our white picket fence has begun to peel and rot. Food given from friends and family, now turn green in our refrigerator as we sit in the hospital waiting for results from the endless tests.

Every little thing reminds me of you and you're not even gone. The flowers wilting beside us reminds me of the ones from our first anniversary.

What flowers do you want next to your casket?

I know I shouldn't think about the funeral so often but the logistics plague me every minute I'm awake. Who should I invite to mourn your cancer ridden body? People who wouldn't even lift a finger when we got the diagnosis. Do you want your body burned to ash, filling an urn on the mantal, or would you like to be buried for the worms to feed off you until all that's left is bone? Oh, how I wish you would tell me.

The stale hospital room assaults me with sterile light and beeping monitors—I clutch your icy hands; I won't let go.

Two young nurses in the reception outside gossip about a new good-looking doctor. My heart pumps faster as anger begins to boil. How can they talk about something so useless while you are dying in a bed just across from them? Tears burn my eyes. I know there is nothing else they can do. We've tried everything: chemo, natural medicines, even religion. But no amount of money or praying could stop the cancer as it creeps into your brain.

I think back to happy moments, reflecting on the times I was not thinking about the outrageous price of lilies and other assortments of flowers for the funeral. I think of the day you asked me to be your girlfriend, the day I moved into your small one-bedroom apartment. I think of when you asked me to be your wife. As I sit and wait in the musty hospital room, our memories flood over me. One memory quickly pushes past them all: The day we met. We were so clueless.

I sat at the front of the traffic lights, waiting for the light to turn green. My leg bounced as I glanced at my watch. It was my first day at my new job, a receptionist at the city's largest law firm. Dad's best friend Jason was the CEO. I'd known him since I could walk. He'd given me the receptionist position, because he felt bad about what had happened at my last job at the café. The owner, Lilly, had been a mother figure to me since middle school. She had to close shop as her heart issues had become worse. Everyone from the café urged her to sell sooner and look after herself. Maybe if she had, things would be different. She passed away in her hospital bed only a week after selling. That was the first time I had *really* experienced grief. She'd always been there for me, wiping away my smudged mascara when I was having trouble with boys at school. She was even there the day I graduated, sat in the crowd with my dad, bawling her eyes out. She always said how proud she was of me.

I miss her. I wish she was here now to help me get through your sickness.

I went to look at my watch again, but something slammed into my car, and I was vaulted forward. I could hear the screeching sound of metal crashing together. My chest was forcefully crushed against the steering wheel. All air pushed from my lungs; I gasped for breath. Suddenly, I felt sharp pains running up from my spine causing an instant headache. I opened my eyes, dust from the airbags distorted my view, blurring the sight of my dashboard.

I remember thinking, *Fuck.*

The driver's side door flung open so hard it could have come off. I winced as I craned my neck slowly to see who almost ripped apart my already mutilated car.

'Holy shit! I am so sorry. That was totally my fault, I wasn't looking where I was going. What can I do to help? Please let me help you,' a deep voice said beside me, words frantic and worried. I finally managed to turn my neck. I saw a tall man around my age. Handsome, with dark brown hair that flopped slightly over his deep blue eyes. Thick stubble framed his jaw; his thin t-shirt pulled taught against his muscular body. A small trail of blood dripped from his temple down the side of his face.

'That's going to need stitches,' I said, raising a hand, pointing to his face. He smiled and let out a laugh as he dabbed away some the blood with his shirt.

'I think I need to go to the hospital.' My voice sounded like gravel. He managed to lift me out of my seat like I weighed nothing. He set me on the ground next to the car, shrugging off his jacket to drape over my shaking shoulders. I looked down and noticed my spaghetti strap dress had shifted and was very close to exposing me to this beautiful stranger who just totalled my car. I duck my head in embarrassment as I pulled the oversized jacket tighter around my exposed front.

He averted his eyes—I realised he was calling an ambulance.

'Don't.' I shook my head. 'I'll just call an Uber.'

'Please. It's the least I can do after I basically destroyed your car ... Please let me help.' I looked over at his four-wheel drive, only slightly damaged. His steel bull bar, now quite bent, had taken most of the hit.

'Fine. But only because I won't be able to drive my car there,' I said, looking towards my crushed car.

His face twisted. I could tell he felt horrible.

Once all the mess from the crash was cleaned up and my car was taken away, the ambulance arrived. He helped me up; his large figure loomed over my small one as he gently helped me into the arms of the trusted professionals.

In the ambulance, he continued to ask if I was ok. He was anxious, more so than me. Luckily, we weren't too far from the hospital.

Being rolled out into the hospital on a stretcher was utterly embarrassing. He walked next to me, refusing a wheelchair for himself. He noticed my hands were trembling.

'Are you ok? Is there something wrong?' Worry laced his voice.

Images of Lilly and the hours spent in her hospital room rose to the surface. My voice trembled. 'It's just nerves, I hate hospitals ... horrible memories.'

He scooped my hand into his own.

I looked up at him.

'Is this, ok?' His voice was shaky as well.

It took me a second, but I nodded as a smile lifted my face. We sat in the patient room with hands joined. We just met, but this felt so normal.

He sat with me the whole time, holding my hand while doctors ran tests. He wouldn't leave my side. Even when they stitched his temple back together.

Once it was all over, he said, 'I know this may be weird under the circumstances, but I was wondering if you would like to go out for coffee or something sometime,' as we walked out the sliding doors into the sunshine.

A large smile spread across my face.

'I thought you would never ask.'

I jump as the alarms go off, bringing me back into the terrifying present. Monitors flash red. The two nurses rush into the room, followed by doctors and nurses.

I stand, and your hand slips from mine. 'What' going on? Is he ok? Please tell me he's ok. I can't lose him yet.' Words spill from my mouth. I feel like I'm going to vomit. I reach for your hand.

'Ma'am, you need to wait outside,' the doctor says, ushering me into the corridor. I try to fight my way back to you. Tears flood my vision. Then I hear it: a never-ending beep. The doctor turns and runs back into the room. My chest tightens as I gasp for air. Nurses try their best to calm me down but it's no use.

You're gone.

A Space to Fill

Jayden Marie

This drive used to calm me, feel welcoming, feel like home. But this time, rounding the final bend into town, I only feel a sense of unease. The sun seems to feel this too, as it attempts to blind me through any of the gaps in the trees and buildings it can find. I don't know why I'm here. I didn't mean to take this turn off the highway, but maybe coming back will help.

I was different when we left, when we packed up everything we owned and moved to the other side of the world; when I was a child and understood nothing of the world around me. I thought this little pocket tucked away from the chaos of life was heaven on earth. But coming back, it seems this pocket has stayed tucked away and only watched as the rest of the world drove by.

I slowly pull the car to a stop at the first intersection. I can turn left and head south down the highway, taking me past the parade of fast-food chains just off the main thoroughfare; I can keep heading west out of town, or I can turn right. Right into downtown, past the school, past the church, past so many memories.

I hadn't planned on driving out here, but I couldn't sit through another evening of quiet sobs as my family sat together trying to put together a funeral. The raw emotions and the forceful way memories would come rushing in. It hurt to sit there without her around—she was warm, full of love and the cornerstone of my family. So, I quietly slipped through the front door after dinner, got in the rental car and drove, letting autopilot take over while I attempted to tread water a little longer. I had over twenty hours of travel time to sort through the tidal wave of emotions that threatened to steal my breath, the heartache that hurts everywhere, and the hole nestled in my heart for the last twelve years.

A jarring sound transports me back into the car. The green light stares me down, *left, straight or right*, it seems to taunt. The oversized man in his oversized F350 honks again.

Left, straight or...

Without allowing myself to process it properly, I turn right.

I bring the rental car to a stop in front of the blue and white building. The noise from the highway fades away in the rearview mirror. It's funny; I was too young to drive any of our typical routes before we left, but without thinking, I pulled right into the same parking spot my grandma used to park in every weekday. She'd pull her truck in at 8:30 Monday through Friday, dropping me and my neighbour off. It used to be a bright memory, but it's now clouded in grief. *Remember how we used to rush to get out of the blue truck and then how we'd race Alex to the playground every morning?* The quiet voice breaks through the chaos in my mind, startling me slightly. My lips curve into a slight smile. She sounds so happy, so at ease ... so young.

I slowly step out of the car, heading towards the playground. The gravel around the once bright, vibrant, magical kingdom crunches under my boots, and I pull my jacket tighter as the wind blows yellow and orange leaves across the ground, and I hear her laugh float past me with the wind. I turn to follow the laugh, and there, just in front of the green ladder, I see her watching me. Her blue eyes, my eyes, stare at me. She flashes me a toothless smile and waves for me to follow. I climb the ladder leading into the infamous red tube that connects two platforms of the playground. I squeeze myself into the tube, thinking of all the overly competitive games of Grounders played here. I was shocked when no one in Australia knew about the game. I guess playing blind tag crossed with the floor is lava is specific to Canadian 'culture'.

The shockingly warm space feels oddly like a hug—she's waiting there, smiling from ear to ear as I settle. It's odd, almost like staring into a fun house mirror that doesn't make you taller or shorter, but younger. *Aren't you happy to be back here?* I don't think I can bring myself to tell her ... although, I know on some level she feels it. It's hard to put into words, but this place fills me with a type of nostalgia that brings longing and hurt. Her toothless smile beams at me. *There couldn't be anything better than this*. To her, nothing could be better than being back in the red tube and watching the leaves float in the wind. It's funny, isn't it? How life ebbs and flows, how we change so much, how that change can chip away at memories until they start to fade, slowly falling from our reach. I don't think she can imagine what I've found beyond the barriers of this place. But that's what hurts, that's where the hole started twelve years ago. I miss it here, almost more than words can say, but what I found is better than anything this place has to offer.

The warm wind blows through the tube, blowing gently past me, taking her with it. *Hurry! The Fall Fair is about to start.* I climb back out of the tube, following her innocent giggling back to the car.

I pull the car to a stop at the last empty parking space in front of the optometrist. Its windows full of orange, yellow and brown paper leaves, pumpkins and the infamous scarecrow. *Just like it used to be! We have to get a candy apple while we're here—remember how good they taste?* Of course, I remember; the Fall Fair used to be my favourite 'holiday'. I'd spent the evening running around with friends, eating all the candy apples we could ... and I'd always spend the morning helping Grandma with the window display for the optometrist. A sharp pang of grief hits almost paralysing me.

Well, we're not going to find any candy apples in here. I watch as she floats through the crowd, not looking out of place. I catch up to her in line for an infamous candy apple, and I use the moment to take in everything around me, the smiles, the laughter and the joy. It's hard to be back here, living in what could have been. Life was so simple here—and still is. The little girl standing next to me seems to enjoy the simplicity; she needs it. *There couldn't be anything better than this.* I hope she knows I believe her, that once upon a time, nothing could be better than eating a candy apple at the Fall Fair, but that was 12 years ago.

Walking around Main Street, the feeling of nostalgia is hard to ignore. The pumpkin carving competition happening in front of the bakery, the school band performing on the stage in front of the bowling alley—everything deepens the hole of guilt, hurt and grief. It wasn't just that being back here reminded me of simpler times, but everywhere I look, I see my grandmother. Her warmth in the sun, her love in the fall colours and her strength in the wind. It was hard to leave all those years ago, but saying goodbye to her was the toughest. A few tears break through and slide down my cheeks as the warm wind rushes past again, drying them before they make it very far.

It's ok. I look down and see blue eyes mirroring my tears. *It's ok. I'm ok here, I'm happy here—you can leave me here.* Life was wonderful here when this was home, but now home is somewhere else, brimming with new, brighter memories. It feels unfair to both of us to keep living in what used to be and hold onto those fading memories, clinging to her—to them. *I'm not mad you left. We needed the change. It's ok to let me go and just remember.* She gives me one last toothless smile before disappearing back into the crowd, her giggling filling the air.

I make my way back to the rental car and think of all the memories this place holds, just memories. She seems to disappear in the warm breeze, and I smile. I feel my grandmother in the wind, giving me the permission I need to let go. The permission I need to stop feeling guilty about leaving everything and everyone behind. The feeling of unease and nostalgia remains, but in the background. Opening the door, I allow myself to look back just once, and I finally let her go.

As I pull back onto the highway heading east, the heartache still hurts everywhere, but the hole that nestled deep twelve years ago starts to fill.

Tear

Amy Geraghty

'**P**ush!' the midwife screamed.

Gwen looked down past her colossal belly into the peering eyes fixed between her spread-eagle thighs. The futile father stood pale-faced in the corner of the room.

'Great job Gwen, you're almost there. I've got the head against my palm, I'll guide bub out gently, only a few more pushes,' the midwife said.

Although Gwen was the star of the show, the midwife was the director; she took pride in her work, guiding life into the world and championing women through it. Gwen gagged through the terrifying extent of agony that she'd never known. The collective pain of women hummed through the birth suite like a haunting song.

She pushed.

'Holy fu—' Gwen vomited, fluid expelling from her at both ends.

Splat. The floor. Splat. The bed. Splat. Gwen. The midwife scowled at the father.

'The bag!? I thought I told you to be ready with the vomit bag!?' she snapped, while skillfully holding pressure on the baby's crowning head with one hand and catching shit in a bag with the other.

In the split second of the midwife's inattention to Gwen's vagina, the baby ripped its way earthside, tearing Gwen's perineum with it. The midwife caught the slippery being just in time. The baby let out a healthy cry as the midwife placed the child on Gwen's bare chest and gauze over the gaping wound. Gwen didn't know the extent of the trauma yet, too flooded with adrenaline, oxytocin and the epidural to feel it. Women are so often torn out of love. The midwife washed her hands, trying to hide her disappointment. *That tear was on me,* she told herself. She reached for her phone to call the doctor who would stitch Gwen up. *Six missed calls and two texts.* Her fingers went numb momentarily as she stared at the notifications. *Not now.* Her eyes glazed over as she tried to block out the vicious messages—each one a dagger laced with threats of violence. She called the doctor.

The birth suite was outdated, short-staffed and all kinds of horribly off-pastel greens and blues. A constant hum underlay the sterile air, tainted by the stench of various bodily fluids. But the baby, all cleaned up now, was the celestial life force that kept the place going. Oh, and the mothers.

The doctor sewed his stitches as the infant let out soft coos against Gwen's chest. The father stood over the doctor's shoulder intimately examining every stitch.

'So,' the father paused, cautiously selecting his next words in front of his audience, 'what will the recovery time be like?' he asked.

By recovery, he probably wants to know how long until they can have sex again. The midwife fought to suppress the contempt etched onto her face.

'Well, she'll be out of commission for at least a month, likely longer while she heals. But don't worry, the women I stitch up *and their husbands* are usually quite satisfied with my work,' he replied with an orchestrated chuckle and a pat on Gwen's exposed thigh.

Gwen laughed uncomfortably.

'You must be hungry Gwen, fourteen hours in labour,' the midwife said with eyes directed at the father.

'I'm starving, but I don't want to eat anything too solid yet, my stomach's still a little weak,' Gwen replied.

'All right, I'm all done here young lady,' the doctor said as he placed down his steel utensils and stood up.

'The midwife will go through the instructions of your aftercare, you must follow them Missy,' the doctor said, his finger patronisingly pointed at her.

'Thank you, doctor,' Gwen said sincerely.

He ignored her.

'All the best,' he said to the father, while shaking his hand; both with smug smirks on their faces. The doctor exited the room.

Gwen turned her attention to the father.

'You know what I could really go for?' she said trying to get his attention away from his phone.

'Huh?' he let out without looking up.

'You know my favourite, mango magic, there's a Juice bar downstairs. Can you please get me one, babe?' Gwen asked, as if it were something of a grand gesture.

The father appeared frustrated with an undertone of insecurity.

'Uhh, can't,' he huffed, 'I haven't been paid yet.'

There was a fracture in Gwen's spirit. She'd remained full of grit throughout the entire gruelling labour, but this is what silently broke her.

'But it should come in by tonight,' he said quickly to defuse her disappointment.

'Oh, that's ok,' Gwen forced an appeasing smile.

Was it really ok though? The midwife excused herself from the room and b-lined for the break room. *Not my monkeys, not my circus.* But she couldn't help feeling the pain welling in her. Over a freaking juice. She'd seen so many couples over the years, conventional, unconventional, rich, poor, functional, dysfunctional. She couldn't help but compare them to her own tumultuous marriage and the life-defining circumstance of childbirth. More importantly *who* you birth a child to. It was about so much more than juice. She sighed, sat down and opened her phone. *Eight missed calls, five texts.*

'How did yours go?' her co-worker asked walking into the room.

The midwife locked her phone, swiftly and instinctively, trying to hide her husband's abhorrent text messages.

'She tore, poor thing, but she's a tough cookie. The father though, ughhh,' she said.

'Tell me about it, the father I just had was a total nightmare, walked out for a cigarette and missed the entire thing,' her co-worker said.

They sat in the silent cycle—women with cunning partners, misogynistic fathers, whose daughters would eventually subconsciously choose the same mistakes in men that'd been modelled to them. The midwife's phone buzzed incessantly.

'Jeez, somebody's popular,' her co-worker said.

'Something like that,' she replied sombrely as she breathed into the fresh bruise decorating her right ribcage. She retreated to the solitude of the bathroom to collect herself in private. She began reading through the slurry of text messages she'd been turning a blind eye to: profanity, threats, accusations and denial. Another Tuesday.

Among the cacophonic rant, a few words stood out:

You, slut.

I'll, slit.

Throat, sleep.

Her heart beat in her throat. She dreaded the rest of her shift, but even more her arrival home. She headed back to Gwen's room.

As soon as she entered, she knew she'd interrupted something tense.

'Well did you lose it?' Gwen asked the father.

Her juice sat on the overbed table. *Good*, the midwife thought.

'I'm sorry, babe, I can go look now,' he replied.

'No, it's fine, give it some time maybe someone will hand it in, just hand me my phone please so I can cancel my card,' Gwen said with her hand outstretched.

Oh, not so good, she still paid for it, and he what? Conveniently lost her card? The midwife put two and two together. The father rummaged through the bags while the TV played in the background. Channel 7. Breaking news flashed across the screen. The reporter stood across the street from a harrowing scene. The burnt carcass of a family vehicle. Baby seats, black in the back.

'I—I'm standing at the site ... of an extreme act of domestic violence ...' the reporter said, she was breathy yet frozen still.

'Earlier this evening, a car in Brisbane's Camp Hill was allegedly set on fire by an unidentified man—a mother and three children were inside at the time of the incident, they have been taken to hospital in critical condition', the solemn reporter said.

A family photo of the victims was displayed on the screen.

Hannah. I delivered her last child.

The midwife stared in shock; her eyes glassy. *You cannot start crying at work.* Red and blue lights flashed. *Too late.* A toddler-sized sandal lay abandoned on the bitumen. *Was this what we've come to? Is this us, now?*

'One in four Australian women will be affected by domestic violence in their lives,' she ended the report.

The midwife choked on this statistic—one that included her, though only if she risked her life by reporting it. The degrading perspective and foul treatment of women within Australian society hummed—silently, systemically and generationally— so casually, in the background of our culture.

'I can't find it babe,' the father said, snapping the midwife back to reality.

'Seriously? You can't find my bank card or my phone, you just had them a minute ago!' Gwen said, her patience thinned to a tearing point.

The awkwardness hung in the air. How could someone, responsible for a newborn, be capable of losing two of modern-day's most valuable items in one go?

'Mum's probably been calling me worried, I told her I was going to call her back ages ago,' Gwen started ranting.

'Here, use my phone,' the midwife said as she handed it to Gwen. 'Call it, see if anyone's picked yours up.'

The father shifted uncomfortably, his hands fidgeting around his pants pocket region.

'I'm just going to the bath—' the father began to say, turning away from the reckoning.

'No. Stay,' Gwen said bluntly.

The midwife could tell this must have happened before. Gwen acted with a confrontational certainty, knowing the exact sequence of events to come. As she finished punching in the numbers, Gwen tilted her head, sucked on her smoothie straw and stared daggers at the father as she hit dial.

'You're fucking crazy, you know that?' The father laughed, to soften his malice in front of the midwife.

He kept mouthing off and fidgeting, but the noise faded. The TV, the baby, the distant groans of women in labour—all fell silent. Only Gwen's ringtone remained, blaring from the father's pants.

'Turn out your pockets,' Gwen said with a stern calmness.

He looked at Gwen red-faced, then turned even redder when his eyes shifted towards the midwife.

This was too good to miss. Reluctantly, he pulled the phone out of his pocket.

'I said turn them out,' Gwen commanded him.

He let out a long sigh and begrudgingly turned his pockets inside out. Gwen's bank card fell to the floor.

The midwife closed her car door and sat in the well-earned silence after a twelve-hour night shift. *Everybody's got their shit,* she thought, almost feeling better about her own circus. Her phone buzzed. *Five missed calls, four texts.* She drove home with the nagging thoughts nibbling at the back of her brain, yet they'd become so mundane. *I wonder if he'll scream at me tonight. Hurt me? Kill me? But maybe he'll love me tomorrow.* The humming was back, and it was louder than ever. I wonder, can you hear it?

Hysterical

Elizabeth Chown

In the morning before I left, I peered into Mum's room. Just like yesterday, she was in bed. I knew when I got home from school I'd find her in the exact same place. She had these spells of staying in bed for days on end, practically becoming furniture. Down the hall were my brothers' rooms. My older brother Jimmy was in Year 12 and did all sorts of extracurriculars. Footy, debating, art. Neil, my younger brother, had just started kindy. Since the moment he was born, Mum was always real protective of him. Jimmy had been under the weather all week and Daddy had finally called the school to excuse him, despite Jimmy's assurances that he was fine. Neil seemed to have caught the same sickness so he was out for the count as well. In vain, I called out goodbye to Mum and left.

Kay Johnson was walking her kids out the door, her army of little girls filing through one by one. Next door was Pete Clark and his red Pontiac, gleaming in the sun. I swore he spent more time polishing that car than anything else. I spotted his son Jack in the backseat and he flashed a smile at me. I giggled and looked away as I kept on my journey to my best girlfriend's house. When I arrived, Macy was standing outside waiting for me. I gave her a side-hug so as to not disturb the overflowing pile of books she was carrying in her arms.

'Nancy Baker, as I live and breathe,' she quipped. She must've noticed my flushed face and how I was nervously twirling a strand of hair. 'Another run-in with Dreamboat?' That was Macy's nickname for Jack. She had lived on the same street as him since forever and was seemingly the only girl that was immune to his charms.

'He smiled at me.' I looked down, embarrassed at how much that small gesture meant. 'God, I'm such a geek.'

'So, you're finally wising up to it,' Macy grinned. I shoved her away and we both laughed. We walked to school together every morning but we always somehow found new things to gab about. The one topic we never broached was Mum and I liked it that way.

My first class was science. I was sat in my usual spot in the back corner when Jack swaggered in with his buddies. It was like time stopped whenever he entered a room. Mrs. Kelly cleared her throat and informed us to make pairs. I looked around at everyone forming groups without a hitch and felt my face get hot. I hated feeling like an outsider. That was, until Jack walked up to me.

'I hope ya don't mind. My mates all paired up and I saw you without a partner—'

'Yes!' I cut him off. We shared a laugh at my lame enthusiasm. We worked well together. Mrs. Kelly pointed us out as an example to the class since we were the only ones that used the microscope right.

After school, I saw Macy out front and ran to her, almost knocking her over in all my excitement.

'Guess who my lab partner is,' I squealed. Her eyes widened.

'No way, Dreamboat? I need to hear everything, let's head to the milk bar.' She had already started leading me down the road.

'You don't have to be home yet, right?' I shook my head. I knew Mum would've wanted me home, especially since my brothers were sick, but she was in one of her moods. I figured she wouldn't be awake to notice.

Sunset fell as I made my way home. I swung the door open to find the living room fully rearranged and the house spotless. I knew what that meant. Mum was up and I was in for it; the door closing behind me was her cue and she burst out of the kitchen.

'Young lady, where have you been?' she barked. 'Your father and I have been worried sick.' Daddy was sitting on the couch with the newspaper; he hadn't even looked up. She loved to exaggerate.

'I was out with Macy, Mama.'

'Your brothers are ill and your father's been at work all day,' she huffed, walking to her bedroom and slamming the door.

I sighed and sat down next to Jimmy in the kitchen. I rested my head on the table, trying to remember back to a time before she was like this. Before Neil, she was quite level-headed but since then she was full of nerves. She barely left bed, and when she did, she'd bounce off the walls. I was so ashamed of her. I looked at Neil in the living room playing and felt a pang of irritation. It wasn't anything he did; that was the only way he had known her, after all. Just as quickly as the thought entered my mind, Mum returned to the kitchen for round two.

'I know you're lying about where you were,' she hollered. Blotted mascara and tear streaks stained her face like a watercolour. She would often convince herself that we were all lying to her, even about the most inconsequential things. I took a deep breath, responding to her accusation.

'I'm not lying, Mum. You don't know what you're talking about—' A sharp sting to the face cut me off.

'I bet you were with a boy, you slut,' she snapped. Daddy and Jimmy were out of their seats now; Neil was standing in the doorway, looked on worriedly. Daddy stood in front of me as he tried to calm Mum down.

'Joan, get a hold of yourself,' he said, reaching out to grasp her shoulders.

'You don't tell me what to do.' She shrugged him off and backed up. 'And you, I bet you knew the whole time.' She pointed at Jimmy.

'Known what? You're being hysterical,' Jimmy quipped.

'Hysterical?' she shrieked. That word always set her off. She beelined for Neil, swooped him up and attempted to leave the kitchen. Daddy blocked her exit with Jimmy and I close behind.

'Honey, where are you trying to take him? This isn't settled here.' Daddy attempted to reason with her, he always did.

With her escape plan thwarted by Daddy and Jimmy's doorway blockade, she retreated backwards.

Mum ran at the knife block and unsheathed a steak knife, attempting to ward us off. 'He's the only one in this house that doesn't antagonise me.'

Neil started wailing. Jimmy and Daddy both leapt at Mum, fighting to take the knife out of her hands. The blade sliced through the side of Neil's cheek, and she dropped it in an instant.

'Take your brother away,' Daddy instructed us. Jimmy swooped Neil up and we watched on as Mum crumpled into a pile on the floor.

'Go, now,' Daddy yelled.

Neil's injury was minor, it didn't even leave a scar. But we knew Mum had gone too far. We listened through the door as cars pulled up outside and Mum apologised to Daddy through sobs.

A few hours had passed when Daddy knocked on Neil's door and told us to come out. In the living room stood a police officer. Mum wasn't there.

'Where is Mum?' Jimmy asked. I didn't think I wanted to know the answer.

'Listen, kids, your mum has been taken to hospital for treatment. Your dad didn't think it'd be good for you to see her like that, more than you already have tonight.'

'We'll visit her soon,' Daddy explained. 'They'll help her, she won't be there for long.' Neil continued to cry into Daddy's chest until the officer left.

In the weeks that followed, Mum's incident made the rounds all throughout the neighbourhood. Macy told me she heard her mum on the phone speculating about what had 'really' happened. I didn't want to talk about it. I had to take time off from school to help Daddy around the house; Neil was still getting over his sickness and was a nervous wreck with Mum gone. I missed the end of year dance that Macy and I had been talking about for months and Jack got a new lab partner. All the normal teenage girl things seemed trivial now but nevertheless I grew to resent Mum more than I already had. I felt like she had taken my life away from me.

When we visited the hospital, I expected the worst. I sat hand-in-hand with Daddy, gazing at the fluorescent lights and the deadbolted windows. The whole place gave me the creeps. When Mum came in, she hugged us one by one then sat across from us with a dead-eyed smile like nothing had happened. I don't remember what we talked about in that room, only the eerie feeling, the cold atmosphere and the heavily sanitised smell. I understood the treatment had worked, her nerves had calmed, but it took something away from her.

***

I moved away from home soon after Mum was released from the hospital. Thankfully for Neil, the house was less of a shitshow but I wasn't able to handle Mum's sudden emptiness. Looking back now, all the years of feeling ashamed of my mother have caught up to me. I only wish I could get the time back, maybe try a little harder to understand her condition. But none of us really understood in those days. A few years later, she died of a seizure while Neil was at school and Daddy was at work. The doctor said her brain struggled after her treatment. You don't really understand your mother until you have children of your own. Now mine will only know her through stories.

Into The Shallow Grave

Eli Lister

His phone rang for the fifth time in five minutes. Whatever it was, Jasper would usually let it go to voicemail until he could pull over. But his patience wore thin as his daughter called a sixth time. Jasper shot a glance at the speedometer as he reached for his phone.

'Jules! What is it? Has something happened?' Jasper said, his voice soaked with trepidation.

'Dad! Hey yeah, something happened but not like, well, not bad! Not the way you're making it sound,' Julie laughed, her voice washing away the doubt and despair. Relief flooded into Jasper's lungs and his paranoia hissed out through his teeth.

'Oh thank God. Jules, I'm driving right now, you know that, can't this wait?'

'No it couldn't. Oh, Dad! I was accepted, I'm going to college!' Jasper heard her sweet laugh suspended in disbelief. 'Not even out of school yet, Ma would be proud.'

'Julie, that's great!' Jasper echoed her laugh back to her. Soon he'd be sending his daughter from high school to college, and she'd be all grown up. His little bird out of the nest and into the world.

A deafening crunch, and something sliced through Jasper's chest. Something hard collided with his head, and his vision turned off like a switch.

A cloud of darkness spilled in from beneath the door, slithering across the pasty walls like living, breathing vines. The walls oozing sickly sweet chemicals were swallowed by the curtain of glittering darkness, a void so deep and penetrating, the walls beyond may have vanished entirely. The beeping machine beside the bed shuddered like a sick dog before it fell silent. He tried to sit up but a surge of agony shot through him, his limbs short wired and he fell limp. His dreary eyes drifted to his body. His clothes were gone, replaced with a slinky blue gown that had several large damp splotches. Beneath that, he could feel the pressure of bandages strewn across his body. He blinked, and reality drifted back and forth as if he were floating on the shore of life and death.

'Jules ...' He expected his voice to rip apart his throat, for the breath that followed to claw its way down his trachea, but instead his voice cut through the darkness like a knife.

'Jasper,' something cold and deep rang out from the depths. Hollow rasping and rattling of bone and sinew, its voice sounded like it were strangling the warmth out of the world.

The wall of smoke parted, it stepped forth in a cloak of glittering cloud. Something stared down at Jasper from beneath the hood. He could feel malice squirming beneath its eyes, and a deep, unquenchable hunger in its voice. It took Jasper a moment before he remembered his name, that it—whatever it was—was waiting for him. For his answer. He didn't know how he knew, just that he did. Every fibre of his being was screaming the answer at him in some biological code his brain couldn't decipher. Two small green blips shone out from beneath the hood, like stars painted across the night sky.

'What are you?' Jasper whispered, fear clung to him like sap. He knew who it was before it answered. When it did, another pang of fear rung out like a gong.

'Your people have given me many names— Ankou, Yama, Santa Muerte, Grim Reaper, Death.'

'Death ... I really am ... oh god, Jules ... oh god.' Despair filled his lungs and he sunk deeper into the bed. Just like that, his whole life was gone. And Julie?

He'd left her alone. What would she do without him? Would she be okay? What was he supposed to do now?

'You keep going,' Death's voice cut through the haze of thoughts, capturing Jasper by surprise.

'I ... what?'

'What you are supposed to do now. Keep going.'

'I keep going ...' Jasper repeated. His eyes were curtained by hot tears and his vision swam away. The haze swirled before him and the image of his daughter emerged from the clutter of colour. Her charming smile, her bright eyes, her mother's laugh. 'I can't go, there's ...' But Jasper's voice trailed off, because what do you say to convince Death not to take your life?

'I do not take life,' he rattled, a deep, impatient breath billowed from his mouth. 'I escort you to what comes next.'

'Is there a difference?' Jasper spat, and the idea that Death himself were dragging him from his daughter floated to the front of his mind.

'Quite a difference. If I took your life, it would be mine. You would lack all that is living. I doubt you would not enjoy that. But deliverance ... You will find all you have lost there, and all still waiting to be lost.'

Jasper looked back down at the cocoon of bandages beneath his gown. His body had been wrapped up like a tight meal for a large spider. Blood oozed from the bandages to the surface of his gown.

'What does that mean?' Jasper asked. Death's shoulders shook, the sound of bones grinding and chattering gave Jasper the impression it was laughing.

'You would truly be dead, and I would be living.'

'I can't just … How do you expect me to … I can't just up and leave her, you *must* understand that. How could she ever forgive me, leaving her like that …'

'Must I? It is you whom must come to understanding, Jasper. She will forgive me for delivering you.'

'No, she won't! How would you know? Have you died? Have you lost someone?' Jasper wished he could stand, just so he could pace around the room and shed the anxiety that wrapped itself over him.

'I have,' it said. 'And I have guided the unliving to the next place for thousands of years. I will continue to steer your souls for thousands more, not until the planets and stars have died alongside you.' Death's voice grew stronger, encumbered with finality and impatience. How many conversations must it have had like this, where someone would accuse it of murder, where someone would beg for a second chance. 'Time and time again, forgiveness is asked, but what does forgiveness entail but more tragedy? Mortals spend their lifetimes like the certainty of death is beyond them. Your kind is riddled with carelessness and greed. The weight of one's actions never truly felt until it is bore witness to me and to the beyond. The undead are waiting for you, Jasper. It is rude to keep them, and to keep me, waiting.' Death let out an exhausted rattle.

Jasper's head lowered. Wasn't it true? Hadn't he been the same? Begged for a second chance and shown carelessness when he died? He stared out of the window, to the stars that pierced through the veil of darkness. And then silently, a thought snuck in through the back door of Jasper's mind. A thought Death couldn't see, nor could it expect.

'You said you had died, so you have lived, too?' Jasper asked. The room fell silent. Several seconds passed before Death answered.

'Yes.'

'And you lost someone too?'

'One.'

'Is this person beyond? On the other side?' Jasper asked, unsure if he had been inching towards a line he should not cross, but he felt the fear draining out of him with every syllable.

'Yes,' it said. 'Yes, she is.' When it spoke this time, Jasper could hear it living through the thousand warm memories with that person. Jasper knew this was the right track, and even when Death rattled, 'No more questions,' Jasper had to push. For whatever punishment Death could give, it wouldn't measure up to being taken from his child and failing Julie again.

'If she's waiting on the other side, why are you here and not with her?' Death fell silent for a long moment, and it seemed an eternity had passed. Death's cold voice brushed against him and his heart froze.

'Punishment. Now, come,' Death said, its voice growing more impatient, and Jasper knew why: because Death was eager to see someone he loved, too. To find who had been taken from him. When the glittering dusk spread to his bed and threatened to swallow him whole, he lurched up through the pain.

'I have an offer!'

'I have no—'

'Give me one more chance, one more shot to make things right. Just to speak to my daughter for five minutes. I'll give you my life and embody death, long enough for you to find whoever is waiting for you!' Jasper cried. The dark cloud swirled with a range of dark reds and purples. The green gleam beneath the cloak grew brighter.

'That may take a lifetime.'

'And I'd wait that long to see her anyway. Wouldn't you make the same sacrifice if it meant you could live with your person again?'

And with that, Jasper knew the battle had been won. The smoke retreated, falling back towards the cloak Death wore. The hood fell off, and a skeletal head stared back. Yellowed from time, cracked with age. Moss and vine latched to the bone and flourished like a forest. It was almost poetic, that life existed within death.

Jasper's mouth became very dry, like his throat had been torn up, sliced by a thousand razors. His head spun like he were on a rollercoaster. It became impossible to breathe. When he opened his eyes, he had never felt so much relief in his life.

'Oh, Dad!' Julie cried, tears cut down her face. 'They said you died, but you just ... came back.' Julie hugged him, mindful of his bloodied body. 'I love you, Dad. I love you so much!'

Jasper only expected those last five minutes with his daughter. That was twenty years ago. Today he visited a different wing of the same hospital. He gazed down at his grandson, Daniel Jasper Murkoff, curled up in his mother's arms. Soon, Jasper would lead the undead with a smile, knowing he got to live again, only because Death too had loved.

Final Draft

Megan Edwards

T hey were sun and wine drunk and their feet rested lazily on the railing. June and her sister, Bailey, sat on the veranda of their pink Airbnb overlooking a sapphire bay in Corfu. They spent the earlier part of the evening debating who was more like their mother.

Bailey scoffed, 'I know you think you're not sensitive, but you are. Being emotional and sensitive is in our genetic make-up.'

'I never said I wasn't, I know I'm sensitive, but I just think you're even more so.' June replied coolly, sipping on her wine.

They went on to discuss the men in their lives.

'What about James? What happened to him?' Bailey asked.

It'd been a long time since June had heard his name aloud.

'He's married with a kid,' June replied.

'Do you still talk to him?'

'Nah, it's been about seven years, I think.'

Bailey's phone started ringing; it was her partner, Harrison. 'I'm going to take this, he's completely useless without me,' she said as she wandered inside the apartment, leaving June to her thoughts about James.

James was three years younger than June and she'd met him when she was fourteen. Her boyfriend at the time worked for his father, who lived on the same street. She'd been asked to babysit James and his younger sisters and frequently cared for them on weekends or holidays. Years went by like this and at some point she started spending more time with James than anyone else. Feral and foolish they'd been. She hated the way things ended between them. She hated why. She was twenty-eight now, but she still felt nostalgic for those years. The loss was more like a dull ache now. She thought about the last time they'd been together. He'd been visiting their hometown from Mount Isa. He'd let her know last-minute that he was in town and told her to come for drinks with him and Rob, who was his other best mate. She'd agreed. Too drunk to drive home, she spent the night at Rob's house with James. They'd gotten into an argument about who would sleep on the mattress and who would be on the floor. The tension had been high; they'd slept together so many times before, but only in the purest sense of the word. They shared the mattress and went to bed, annoyed at each other. She'd been barely able to sleep, suddenly self-conscious of falling asleep and snoring and wary of ending up too close. She woke him up early.

'Can you please take me home?'

He groaned, 'What time is it?'

'Um, 5am.'

He rolled over to look at her, his arm haphazardly swinging over the top of hers. Her skin felt hot.

'Jesus, June. Go back to sleep. I'll take you in a couple hours,' his thumb absently stroked her arm.

'Please? I'm sorry.'

James sighed heavily and rubbed his eyes. 'Fuck, okay, whatever.'

The drive had mostly been in silence. About a kilometre from her house, he pulled over and cut the engine. The morning cicadas were loud.

'Can I ask you a question?' he turned to look at her.

'Yeah. Sure,' she replied, struggling to make eye contact.

'Why didn't you ever give us a go? Why can't you?'

'Does it matter? You have a girlfriend, Rob told me.'

'It matters to me. You're seeing someone, too, don't think I don't know why you're asking me to drive you home so early.'

'And look what I'm doing. You don't want me as a girlfriend, James. I'd be terrible, and you'd end up hating me. And what if we don't work? What then? As if we could go back to being friends. I don't want to be strangers.'

He let out a frustrated groan. 'June, we haven't been friends for a long time.'

'Don't say that.'

'I should have kissed you that last time before I moved to Mount Isa. I was so close.'

'But you didn't, and I didn't, and this is where we are now.'

'What if we do work?'

'We wouldn't, trust me.'

June grabbed her laptop. Writing James an email suddenly felt like a great idea. She was pretty sure he had her number blocked, so a casual message was no longer an option. She opened her MacBook and a new email message.

To: jamescaldwell@live.com.au
From: junebrightman93@gmail.com
Subject:

Hello!

I suppose this is totally random, and as I'm writing this, I'm not entirely sure I'll send this to you. I'm not sure you'll want to read it, either. Probably not, considering all my unanswered texts from years ago. I'm in Europe on holiday with Bailey. She's a doctor now. Wild, right? Anyway, I'm not writing to you to talk about her.

I wanted to talk about you.

Or us.

Or something. Mainly, I wanted to try and clear the air about the way things ended between us. You probably don't care by now and this is most likely selfish on my behalf. But that's nothing new to you, is it? Even back then, I'd always been selfish. Anyway. You'd asked me the last time we saw each other why we never ended up as anything. I lied, obviously. I'd told you that you wouldn't want someone like me as a girlfriend and that I had a lot of my own shit to sort through. I guess that part was true. But that wasn't the main reason. I don't even know how to say this. It still makes me sick to my stomach. Every time I think about it, I want to tear my insides open. Anyway, you know how your dad was Matt's boss? Well, I guess when I first started looking after you and your sisters, your dad had my number for logistical purposes. That was the main reason to begin with anyway. We were fifteen and your dad would drive Matt and me places. Sometimes, he would drop Matt off before me, so it'd just be him and me in the car. I guess things started from there. I don't know how it really started, though, nor did I know how to stop it. He was so nice to me. Especially when I compared him with how Matt treated me. It was a very confusing time for me. I don't remember how long it lasted. Even now, as an adult, I still feel guilty, like it was my fault or something I did. There were so many times I wanted to tell you. Tell anyone. I couldn't, though. You loved your dad and I didn't want to blow up your life or your family. Your mum was always lovely to me. As we got older, every time I spent time with you, you were just this bright, warm light in my life. Between things at home, with Matt, and your dad, you were the only thing that felt pure and good. I'm sorry, I always took advantage of that. I'm pretty sure I told you back then that I thought you were my soul mate. Anyway, I guess the feelings you had for me were mutual. I felt them, too. Not in the earlier years of our friendship, you were a brat. But later, I did. I felt them for a long time afterwards, too. That last time we were together in your car. I was so close to giving in. But then I pictured our wedding, and your dad being there, and I couldn't. I couldn't spend the rest of my life with you, carrying that. I could live with you hating me for any other reason, but not for that. Sorry, this is probably a lot. Anyway, it's funny how things turned out. I'll be honest, I've stalked your socials a couple of times over the years. I saw that you married that youth pastor. You also have a kid!!! I love that you still have kelpies. Are you still playing basketball? You honestly deserve all that is good in this world. I'm happy for both of us. I'm glad we ended up all right, even if it wasn't together. I'll always cherish the time we spent together.

Love always,
June

June closed her laptop.

Bailey walked back onto the veranda, two glasses of wine in her hands, 'What were you writing— bloody hell, are you okay? What happened?' she hurriedly sat down beside her.

June laughed, wiping her face, 'I'm fine. I forgot how writing a final draft can bring a sense of loss and closure.'

All We've Got

Jemaja Lindner

White cascading to the floor. Flowers, matching those clutched in her grasp, are woven into her hair. A veil blowing around her like a halo. A crisp white gown standing next to a perfectly pressed suit. The older man, beaming with pride, shares his final words of wisdom, 'marriage is a partnership; trust in your love for one another.' He cups the bride's cheeks, lowering his voice to whisper, 'and if he ever hurts that big heart of yours, I'll break him tenfold.' He winks and the bride giggles. They link arms as the music starts and walk down the aisle.

That will never be us.

We are fractured. Broken and put back together in the wrong places. Veils separating our worlds. I was left picking up your fallen pieces—a child with building blocks trying to recreate your image. But the blocks faded.

The father of the bride kisses his daughter's cheek, shakes the groom's hand and takes his seat next to his emotional wife. I clamp my eyelids shut, concealing my inner turmoil. I'm happy for her. Today, standing next to her loving husband-to-be, she is the happiest I've ever seen her. She deserves this. I'm happy for her, truly. The bittersweetness of the day coats my mouth, tainting the taste of the floral air. She turns, handing me her bouquet. I hope my face doesn't spell out my jealousy.

I don't want her husband. I don't want her life. I don't want this day. I want that nod of support her dad gives, the spark of confidence that springs through her afterwards and the kiss she blows him before starting the ceremony. When I'm standing in white that chair will be empty—just as it was at my birthdays, graduations and every other day of my life. An empty chair, a gaping hole, a vortex pulling everything back to it.

No matter the years, no matter the therapy, everything pulls back to you. I don't hate you; I used to, when I was younger. There was no one to blame, no one to scream at for taking you away. No one to hit and kick until they felt a semblance of the despair sinking into my bones. Although you are gone, there is still ... *us*. You're everywhere and anywhere: a ghost peering over my shoulder, a shadow watching my back, a voice echoing from far away. I can see you now, an apparition wandering the outskirts of the party—always near, always watching.

***

My daughter, with hair falling delicately around your face, I remember when your curls were unruly. The days when they hung in tousled braids with bright clips holding the hair away from your face, a face so young with missing teeth and a beaming smile. Now you're older, and I missed the moments between. I'm merely a presence at your side, unable to pick you up when you fall, my hand falling through yours like air.

'It truly was a lovely ceremony,' says a man I do not know. He knows you better than I do. I was robbed of that opportunity. He asks about your work and life. A life I've witnessed from too far away.

'I'm good,' you smile and say, 'Work's good too. Kellie looked stunning today.'

'She's gorgeous like her mother,' the man says.

'It's nearly half past,' you remind him, 'Time for your big speech.'

'Wish me luck,' he says and heads for the stage.

A father's speech at their daughter's wedding is tradition. Another milestone I have to go without.

But I have things I would wish to say, perhaps the veils splitting you and I would lift on that day and grant me a wish. A wish to tell you all the things I never had time to, but I know you can hear me now. Your eyes are lingering on me as you fade to the background of the group. How I wish you would stand out, shine like I know you can. You were not born to fade into the unknown.

Speeches commence and laughter fills the tent. I still remember the first time I heard yours. The sweetest melody from my little girl. It still sounds the same to this day. The dance floor clears and the married couple sways. A father twirls the young flower girl around.

That used to be us.

You were wild and carefree, following your imagination on a whim. I can see that version of you now, in a pink tufty tutu. With a twirl of your wand, you spin between the sea of legs, weaving onto the dance floor and throwing me a cheeky grin. With the ferocious energy of a lion, you take off, running through the tent. Like a fish on a line, I'm drawn closer. Panic laces my heart when I lose sight of you.

'Daddy, watch this,' you call out. I follow the voice. You throw me a grin over your shoulder, turning around to blow me a kiss before fading into the woman you are now. Where did the time go?

You are older. The set of your jaw is tighter; your shoulders pushed down with the burdens of the world. Your mind a maze of tangled thoughts. Is this what I did? I did not mean to take the joy that made you. I did not mean to be the one who broke you. A father should protect his children, and in that department, it appears I failed ... I am sorry.

But then you smile, and it is still there. That spark of light reflecting in your eyes, the softness of your heart buried behind walls. You look through the crowd and whisper, 'I miss you, Dad.'

***

The party is winding down, the happy couple swaying on the dance floor is lost in their own bubble. Groups have dispersed, chatting the evening away. I gather the wedding gifts for Kellie, piling them into the living room of her hotel suite.

'Are you off?' I ask Kellie's parents on my way back to the party.

'Time for bed,' her mother says, slurring her words, 'You're such a good friend to our girl. Kellie appreciates you so much, so do we.'

'Don't forget to have a little fun of your own,' her father winks at me and they walk away.

I stand there for a while watching them leave hand in hand. I don't remember you and Mum embracing; I was too young for the memories to stick. But I do remember the energy around you both—the playful way she chastised you, saying your name with a hint of laughter when you teased her ... the calm that wrapped around you both in your quiet moments.

'*You'll find that love one day too,*' you say, and I turn to find you lingering between worlds. Close but too far away to touch.

'How do you know that?' I mumble to myself, walking back to the party and grabbing a drink.

'*A father's intuition,*' you say with that enlightened tone, '*It'll be your wedding one day.*'

'Yeah ... but you won't be there,' I sigh, falling into a seat outside the ruckus of the party. A drunk groomsman heads towards me, no doubt looking for a dance; I shake my head. He frowns and moves onto his next option.

'*I'll be there,*' you say, '*You might not see me, you'll be too busy in the moment, but I'll be there. I promise, kiddo.*'

'It won't be the same.' I close my eyes, holding my heart together and pulling the tears back inside. I will not cry at my best friend's wedding. Today is supposed to be happy, not sad.

'*No, it won't ... but it's all we've got.*'

I open my eyes and look at you for longer this time. You're sitting in the seat opposite me, but your face is fading as my memory tries to piece it back together. I close my eyes, remembering your big hand holding mine ... your smile, larger than the world, pressed close to my face when you held me ... and the smell of sweat and dirt that clung to you after work when you'd find me playing hide and seek. Through teary eyes your face comes back into focus.

'What if I want more?'

Rest in Paperback

Tina Ocampos

Gathered here today, whether by invitation or curiosity, we honour my first, truest and longest love. If you expected a person, you'd be dead wrong. Pun intended.

My first love was books.

They didn't have to speak to keep me company. They fit perfectly in my hands. A faithful companion through every chapter of my life.

At six, they were filled with dancing animals and silly rhymes that made my small room feel larger than life. At twelve, when weekends meant packing bags between my parents, they became my shelter in rabbit holes and tea parties, where madness was kinder than reality.

By sixteen, they introduced me to romance— longing glances, tension-filled conversations and confessional letters. I was shocked. I didn't know people could feel *that* much. They could forgive arrogant proposals, manipulation, societal ruin and *still* find each other in the end? My cynical teenage heart thought it was impossible.

Yet, I was swept into their world. Books became my confidant, convincing me I had mastered love and was ready for whatever was waiting outside the pages. After all, what could life possibly throw at me I hadn't already dog-eared and underlined?

Tony.

Life threw Tony at me—elbowed me in the arm, to be exact.

Of course, ladies and gentlemen, our dearly departed set the bar high. Real relationships, as it turned out, were far less polished than the chapters my first love promised me.

Books showed me that not all meet-cutes were flawless, but at least they had some charm. Picture this: two strangers reaching for the same special edition of *Pride and Prejudice*. Fingers brush, the book slips and they both dive to catch it. They clumsily bump heads, laugh about it, then their eyes linger for a beat too long.

But this was reality.

Tony tripped, hip checked the display table and the paperbacks wobbled like dominoes on edge. I lunged forward to steady them, but his flailing elbow caught me square in the arm.

'Ow!' I winced, clutching the spot.

'I—I'm so sorry! Are you ok?' his words tumbled out. His gaze lingered before he flushed crimson. 'I—I should go,' he stammered, retreating so fast he nearly tripped again.

The display rocked one last time but held. I massaged the sore spot and went in search of the first aid kit. The edition had to wait; my bruise could not.

Then I remembered what books taught me: second chances were around the corner. When I returned the next day for the special edition, there he was, clutching a copy like a white flag.

'Hey,' he said softly. 'I'm really sorry about yesterday. I didn't mean to— '

'It's fine,' I cut in, keeping my expression neutral.

Relief flickered across his face. He held out the book. 'This is for you.'

The moment I took it, forgiveness slipped in with it, far less stubborn than Mr Darcy's pride.

He smiled sheepishly. 'I ... was wondering if I could make it up to you? Coffee? Tomorrow?'

My hesitation melted into a soft, 'Yes.'

Books made first dates seem ... manageable. In stories, a coffee date entailed a hug at the door, ordering the same drink, then the barista smiles knowingly as if the universe itself ships them. A giggle here, a shy smile there, then a profound compliment lands at just the right moment to seal their destiny.

Reality preferred slapstick.

When I met Tony the next day, I moved in for a hug, but at the exact second, he turned to open the door. It was just me and the air, locked in a brief but committed embrace. Tony looked back and saw the awkward exchange, but at least he held the door for me.

We sat down and our coffee orders were drastically different. Mine was sugary enough to induce a coma and his was bitter enough to bite. Our conversation was no smoother.

Trying not to drown in the awkward silence, I asked, 'So ... other than romance, what else do you like to read?'

'Mystery, historical fiction, memoirs ...' he rattled off.

Before I could process any of that, he flipped the question on me. I panicked and went into a ten-minute spiel about how Mr Darcy's emotional constipation was either tragic or romantic. Midway through, I realised he wasn't going to stop my rambling. He was just ... well, watching me. Intensely, but a hint of wonder softened his eyes. My chest fluttered, my words stumbled and I felt a strange warmth creep up my spine.

And that's when I saw it … sitting on his upper lip, like the world's least dignified disguise, was a foam moustache. Biting back a laugh, I managed to tell him about it. But he didn't wipe it away.

He just smiled, foam and all, and said, 'You really light up when you talk about books.' It wasn't poetry. Definitely not Austen. But it stuck, like his foam moustache.

We didn't stop at coffee. One outing led to another—the movies, mini golf and a bookstore wander where I pretended not to judge his taste.

Then the first kiss.

Well, almost. Books promised rain, thunder and a kiss written in destiny, but instead, one lazy afternoon, Tony and I were sprawled on a tartan picnic blanket, reading side by side. Close enough to feel his warmth, I sensed his gaze on me. My cinematic moment had arrived. I faced him and he leaned in slowly. Heart hammering, I closed my eyes and waited … and waited … and waited … before opening them to find him holding a stubborn twig he'd been trying to pluck from my hair. It was a betrayal of expectation and I was mortified. I almost had my first kiss with his thumb.

For some reason, even after the twig incident, Tony kept wanting to see me. Day by day, we found a rhythm. I began to see the kind of person he truly was—soft, thoughtful and undeniably patient.

One ordinary afternoon, cuddled on his couch, books scattered around us, he asked quietly, 'So … what do you think about moving in together?'

His words hit like a stone. Familiar anxieties tightened in my chest—the same ones that sent me fleeing into upside-down worlds as a child. I realised he was asking me to lower every wall I'd ever built.

And that terrified me.

Reading about love was one thing but experiencing it was another. Books made vulnerability safe; real life did not. This kind of love with Tony asked for all of me, even the parts I hated most. Books never did. They only asked for my imagination, my attention. The more Tony asked about me, the more I recoiled. Deep down, I'd already learned that love could crack, that home wasn't forever, that people could walk away. Books never did. They stayed.

When it got too close, too real, I did what I did best. I slipped back into their safe arms, retreating to the stories that never demanded more than I was ready to give, burying myself back in marked-up pages, comforting arcs, and familiar spines.

Keeping my distance from Tony required careful maneuvers—delayed replies softened with emojis, flimsy excuses about errands, even changing my usual bookstore hours as if shifting routines could shift my feelings.

Just as I was ready to vanish between the chapters, Tony did something that startled me.

When I returned home late from the bookstore, I tripped over something hard and tumbled face-first into the door like a fool. The culprit? *Pride and Prejudice* was sitting innocently on the mat, unconcerned about my dignity. It was my copy, but no longer mine alone. Tony's handwriting had filled the margins, tabs on lines we'd loved and little sketches that made me laugh. It was a quiet gesture that spoke louder than any grand confession ever could.

And at that moment, I knew I was ready.

Ready to leave the comfort of pages behind. Ready to let him see the hidden parts of me tucked between the book covers. Ready to step off the page and into something real, messy and entirely alive.

Real love didn't look like what the pages promised. In my case, real love was dodging elbows in bookstores, laughing over foam moustaches, mistaking a near-first kiss, and yes, even face-planting into doors. But it also sat with you in silence. It grew not in grand gestures but in listening, in showing up repeatedly, not because it's written to, but because it chooses to.

And so, as I stand here, I don't say goodbye. I say thank you. Thank you for being here since childhood, through all the lonely corners of my world, and introducing me to a kind of love I once thought was impossible.

Thank you for being my first love.

No, I'm not abandoning books, God forbid. They'll always be there, lined neatly on my shelf, dog-eared and waiting; a quiet reminder of where love began.